COMPLICATED HEARTS

BOOK ONE

ASHLEY JADE

TRIGGER WARNING

This story is strange and unconventional. It's everything you hate. That's the only warning I can offer you.

COMPLICATED HEARTS

"Could have been easier on you.
I couldn't change though I wanted to.
Should have been easier by three.
Our old friend fear and you and me."
—Glycerine, Bush

*For Jamie: For being the very first person to believe in this story.
And Tanya: For trusting me to take her outside her box.
This wouldn't be possible without the both of you.*

CHAPTER 1

LANDON

Three years earlier...

I t was going to happen.

The moment I've been waiting for since the day I knew what *it* was.

I was going to have sex for the first time.

My only regret was that I'd waited so long...but it wasn't like it was by choice.

Being labeled the class *nerd* since middle school didn't boast a whole lot of sex appeal with the females.

The only time they sought me out was when they needed help studying for finals or someone to do their homework for them.

Too bad I never had the balls to suggest the cheerleading squad ought to exchange something for my services...but I wasn't a dick. Instead, I helped whoever needed it and never uttered a harsh word to anyone.

It kept the school's sports teams—or as I dubbed them—the *douchebags on roids* from making me a target of their bullying and provided me with enough fake friends that I wasn't a social outcast.

Just a nice nerd.

A nerd who had yet to get laid.

But now? Now my moment had finally arrived and I won't be going to Woodside University a lowly virgin after all.

A soft moan fills the air and the long legs that are wrapped around my head begin shaking. "Jesus, Landon. Oh god, I'm gonna come," she purrs and I continue to lap at her.

Like I always say...studying really pays off.

I suck her clit at a steady pace and continue finger fucking her to the point of oblivion...a moment later I get a mouthful of her orgasm.

Damn, pussy tastes good. I could have it for breakfast, lunch, and dinner.

I wipe my mouth with the back of my hand and stare down at her as she fights to catch her breath. I try like hell not to smile from ear to ear.

Amber Alpine—captain of the dance squad is currently spread eagle in my bed. I *never* thought I'd see the day. Hoped like hell for it, but never thought my wish would actually become reality.

Her blonde hair is splayed out over my pillow and her peach colored nipples are standing at full attention — just begging to be sucked on.

I crawl up her body and proceed to pull them into my mouth, lavishing them with my tongue. Giving each one the attention it deserves. My cock is so hard, I feel like I'm about to come before I even get a chance to accomplish what it is we came up here to do.

I reach into the nightstand and roll on a condom. With a grin, I prop her legs on my shoulders and press my hips forward.

Jesus Christ...this is the best feeling in the world. So warm and wet.

So *mine.*

There's no way this moment can get any better.

That is, not until she utters her next statement, "Fuck me doggie style, it's my favorite. I want it rough and hard," she pants, looking like an addict waiting for her next hit.

With a growl, I quickly flip her over and proceed to do exactly that.

The next four years are going to be the best four years of my life.

Of that I am goddamn certain.

CHAPTER 2

BRESLIN

Three years earlier...

My heart is beating so rapidly I can feel it in my rib cage. I force myself to take a deep breath and try and steady my breathing as the lights around me spin and slow music fills the air.

Right when I think I have it under control...I look up.

Smoldering blue eyes meet mine—and just like that—I'm right back where I started.

His full, sensual lips turn up and he gives me that cocky, panty-melting grin of his. Like he knows exactly what kind of effect he has on my body.

After three years together...Asher Holden can still manage to make my heart beat faster and slower at the same time. And I only want him more with every day that passes.

He twirls me around on the dance floor one last time as the song comes to an end. His eyes hold mine and his thumb softly brushes my cheek. "You look so damn beautiful tonight, Breslin," he whispers as the sound of clapping fills the air.

"Alright, let's hear it one more time for Truesdale High's very own, Prom King and Queen!" the announcer shouts.

The words echo throughout my head and I want to laugh at how odd it all sounds. I never in my life thought I'd be that girl. I never thought I would have this perfect life.

I was a nobody—a loser—before Asher came to town.

I was just a poor girl from the wrong side of the tracks, living in a trailer with an almost-always drunk father and a mother who took off shortly after I was born.

Asher changed all that. He made me someone special. He made me feel loved.

And then the bastard ruined me.

The second he collided right into me, knocking both me and my books down on the first day of 10th grade was the day my life changed.

I remember glaring up at him and sucking in a breath at the sight of his gorgeous face and huge, muscular frame.

He had to be a senior, I thought. What was he doing down the sophomore hallway?

Before I had a chance to ponder that further—the snickers started.

Kyle Sinclair had been the bane of my existence ever since I could remember. He always found a way to make fun of me and he never seemed to let up. Of course, he would be there witnessing me fall right on my butt, books scattered all over.

"You better pick those up, Bre," Kyle taunted. "Might as well get used to what your dirt poor, trailer trash ass will be doing for the rest of your life."

Shame crawled its way up my spine and I looked down at the

floor. Fighting back tears, I prepared to collect my books off the ground...until the sound of something hard hitting the lockers caused my head to snap up.

My mouth dropped open at the sight of what I would later come to know to be Asher pinning Kyle against a locker. "Apologize to her, now," he gritted through his teeth.

I tried to ignore how deep and deadly his voice was...judging by his jersey, he was an angry jock.

I tried to ignore his appearance...because I knew that sometimes the most beautiful faces hid the ugliest of souls.

I tried to ignore his overwhelming presence...because I knew that even the biggest people sometimes had the smallest of hearts.

I tried to ignore everything about Asher...but my sweaty palms and racing heart wouldn't let me.

Whatever underlying awful trait I tried to convince myself he might have...I didn't care. Because I wanted him.

Even though I knew all too well that I was the type of girl who could only admire someone like him from afar, it didn't matter to me.

I finally understood at that moment why people called it a crush.

Because it's that glimmer of hope that crushes you in the end.

Hope that when someone like *him* does something nice for someone like *me*...maybe it wouldn't be the last time.

Hope that maybe you're worth more than you were ever made to feel.

Hope that maybe he wouldn't turn out to be like all the others.

Kyle tried to get out of his grasp and run, but Asher slammed him against the locker for a second time.

"Sorry," Kyle murmured in my direction.

But that half-hearted apology wasn't good enough for Asher.

His eyes narrowed and the vein in his neck began to bulge. For a moment, I felt like I should protect Kyle, but then I remembered what a monumental asshole he'd always been to me.

Kyle must have realized how serious Asher was at that moment too, because less than a second later he looked at me and said, "I really am sorry, Bre."

And this time he actually sounded sincere.

Asher finally released him, but not before looking at me for approval to let him go.

When I gave him a nod he looked at Kyle again. "Pick her books up. *Now.*"

I watched in shock as Kyle begrudgingly proceeded to pick up both my books and my purse and hand them to me, right before he hightailed it down the hallway.

I didn't know who this guy was, but somehow in the span of two seconds, he'd managed to help me out more than most people in my lifetime.

People didn't collect trash...they *discarded* it. It was something I'd grown accustomed to.

My heart pounded in my ears when he knelt down beside me. "I'm Asher...and I'm also sorry about knocking you down." His eyes landed on mine and my stomach fluttered. "I should have been paying better attention to where I was walking."

I licked my suddenly dry lips. Heat crept up my cheeks when his gaze stopped and lingered on my mouth.

"So, what's your name, beautiful?" Asher then asked and I swear my eyes practically popped out of my head.

No one ever called me beautiful.

Smart? *Sure.* Shy? *Usually.* Weird? *Occasionally.*   Artsy? *Always.*

But never beautiful.

Girls who lived in trailer parks and wore hand me downs from thrift stores didn't get called beautiful.

Girls like me were hardly noticed at all.

This was an absolute first for me.

That glimmer of hope sparked again inside my stupid teenage heart.

I sat there, too stunned to move. Too afraid I would wake up and this would all just be a dream.

A minute later, Asher reached for my hand and hauled me to my feet.

His eyebrow slanted up, like he was waiting for an answer to something.

Oh, right. My name.

"Breslin," I all but squeaked out. "But, um. Well, usually, everyone just calls me Bre," I sputtered, like the world's biggest idiot.

His face broke out into a grin, showcasing his deep dimples.

Good lord, I wanted to live in those dimples of his. "Well, it was nice to meet you, Breslin."

I nodded my head, too afraid to stutter and make a fool out of myself again and he began walking down the hallway.

That is until exactly five steps later when he stopped abruptly and looked over his shoulder. "I'll be seeing you around."

*Thump, thump, thump...*went my stupid teenage heart and I went right along with it.

I soon found out that Asher was not only the new kid at school, but he came from an extremely wealthy family. And even though we were only in 10th grade, he almost overnight became a football God—thanks in part to his father owning a huge NFL team.

He had everything that people in my small town ate up like candy.

Money, glory, and a reputation for greatness.

Asher was going places. He was already a someone in a world full of no ones.

We were from completely separate worlds. I never thought I'd speak to him again...until he showed up on my doorstep a few nights later.

I couldn't believe my eyes when I opened the front door and saw him standing there...with flowers. "Told you I'd be seeing you around, Breslin," he said, his dimples proudly on display.

And that was it. I was hooked...line, and sinker.

I just didn't realize the sinker would turn around and eventually drown me.

From that moment on...we were inseparable.

Asher Holden took my entire heart and never gave it back.

My thoughts are soon interrupted and the clapping becomes louder when Asher grabs my hand and plants a soft kiss along my knuckles.

I hear a few whistles from our friends on the football team and I can't help but blush when he pulls me into an embrace and his lips collide with mine.

Frantic need far too potent for an 18-year-old tears through my body when his tongue strokes mine. My arms automatically find their way to his neck, pulling him closer to me.

The kiss becomes more intense and I'm running out of air again, but I don't care. There's nothing in the world I want more than to be right here with him, touching him, kissing him.

Well, except for...

Yeah, tonight is the night. Or at least, it damn well better be.

He groans against my mouth before pulling away and sliding his hand down my lower back. Since my prom dress is backless, his touch causes goosebumps to erupt over my skin.

I bring him down for another kiss but he presses his lips against my temple instead. I feel dissed, until his warm breath flutters against my ear and he whispers, "You really need to stop, baby. You're making me want to take you in front of the entire student body right here, right now."

To prove his point, he tilts his hips and I feel his hard-on against my lower stomach. I moan and purposely arch into him. "So do it then, Asher," I prompt. "I can't wait anymore. I want you."

I drop my voice to a whisper when I notice a few people eavesdropping on our conversation. "I love you, please don't make me wait any longer."

I'm two seconds away from full on begging at this point. I've been ready since the middle of 11th grade...but Asher wanted to wait. Seeing as his parents are not only influential in our town, but religious, I completely understood and agreed to wait until marriage.

But by the beginning of this year, it was becoming excruciating. Of course, we routinely fooled around and did other stuff—well, everything besides oral and actual sex.

And while that helped to ease the ache initially, and Asher surprisingly knew how to get me off with his fingers, it only made this insatiable want I have for him that much stronger.

I grind myself against him again and he groans. His lips brush my neck before I feel his tongue along the shell of my ear. "Okay, let's get out of here."

I can't help but do a double take. *Was this really happening? Finally?*

Before I have time to confirm, he grabs my hand and we begin making our way toward the exit.

"Yoooo. Where are you two lovebirds running off to? Prom isn't over yet."

I roll my eyes at the sound of Kyle Sinclair's voice. Even though we're technically friends now...and even though he'd never uttered a bad word about me since that day...the *last* thing I want to hear is him right now.

Asher releases a sigh and turns us around to face him. "We're heading out."

His tone is clipped, angry even.

I make a mental note to ask him later what happened.

I make another mental note to ask him sooner rather than later when I see Kyle's nostrils flare. "What about the after party?"

Asher squeezes my hand tighter—a gesture he does when he's nervous about something. "Not going. We're going to a hotel for the weekend."

I ignore the hint of defiance in his tone now because I can't help but concentrate on his statement.

A hotel? For the weekend? That must mean he had this planned all along. He wanted it to be special for us.

My heart soars and I'm elated...until Kyle takes a step forward and lifts his chin. "Yeah? It's like that?"

Asher's grip on my hand is now becoming painful. He leans down and plants another kiss on my temple. "Yeah," he says. "Yeah, man...it is." There's another squeeze of my hand.

Kyle takes a step back and his jaw ticks. "Whatever. Have fun," he says gruffly before walking away.

I look up at Asher because I honestly can't make any sense out of the last three minutes. "What was that about?"

He takes a deep breath as we walk out the exit doors and then to the parking lot. "Nothing, Breslin. Everything's fine. Don't let him ruin our night."

"Okay," I whisper and he holds the door to his pickup truck open for me.

A slow country song is playing in the background and his hand slides up my thigh—part comforting, part reassuring as he shifts the truck into drive.

After driving through a few towns, we finally end up at the hotel.

My heart begins its rapid flutter when we enter the room and I take in the rose petals on the bed and the candles flickering in the dark. "Asher, this is incredible," I breathe, beside myself.

His thumb strokes my cheek. "I wanted you to know how much you mean to me." His expression turns serious. "I love you, Breslin. I need you to know that."

I close my eyes and lean into his touch. I've never felt loved in my whole entire life...never knew I was worthy of it.

Until him. Until these last few years. The best years of my life.

And I know, it's probably unhealthy to rely on one person for all your emotional needs. But he's the only one who ever cared enough to fulfill them.

I know I'm probably—correction—I *am* borderline codependent on Asher...but it's only because I love him so much.

It took me years to get to this place with him...to trust him and give him every part of me.

But now that I'm finally here...there's no way I'll ever go back.

In my world— Asher is a supernova. He's the one who burns bright.

I'm merely the catastrophic explosion that dissolves into nothing.

I tear him down...but he builds me up. Far beyond my wildest dreams.

He's the sun...and I orbit around him.

It's impossible not to. Because no matter where you are...you can't help but feel his pull.

You can't help but watch him because he illuminates an entire room.

He sits down on the bed and begins undoing his bow tie. I reach for the zipper on my dress. "I love you, Asher," I finally say back to him. "I love you big."

There's a light in his eyes and I know he's recalling the very first time I ever told him I loved him in my sputtering, clumsy, mess of a declaration.

I meant to just tell him I had feelings for him. That he meant more to me than anything or anyone.

But in typical Breslin fashion, everything came out all jumbled and I couldn't find the right words to express myself.

The more I tried to explain my feelings for him, the worse it got. The only words that made any sense were when I told him that I *loved him big*.

The whole entire world stopped when he grinned and said he *loved me bigger*.

Swallowing hard, I unzip my dress and let it fall to the floor. I let any and all insecurities fall along with it.

Because the way Asher's looking at me now? Tells me I'm the most beautiful thing he's ever seen.

Something tells me he'll always look at me this way. Because he always has.

He smiles and sucks in a breath as his eyes scan over my body.

I silently thank my lucky stars that I saved half my pay check on a *Victoria's Secret* trip.

He reaches for me and gently pulls me down on the bed beside him.

I'm expecting a gentle kiss, but as soon as my head hits the pillow —he ravages me. Planting a line of sensual kisses from my throat all the way down to my stomach. I inhale sharply when he undoes my bra and pulls the straps down, putting me on display for him.

"Gorgeous," he murmurs before his tongue lands on my nipple.

I reach up and begin undoing the buttons on his crisp white dress shirt. Not wanting to slow down, I hastily toss it to the floor and all but lunge for his belt buckle and undo his pants.

Asher's body is akin to that of a Greek God.

Actually, that's wrong, I'm pretty sure no Greek God had ever looked half as good without clothes on as he does.

He loves working out, loves pushing his body to the limits...and it shows. Every single rippling muscle is crafted to perfection. He's beautifully built, his muscles are well-defined and tight and toned, but not oddly so or excessive like some guys.

I look down and remind myself to breathe. There's only a thin scrap of material between the both of us now. I notice his erection peeking out through his dark boxer shorts and my mouth waters.

I slide my hand below the elastic waistband and pull him out.

Both my heart and hormones are blasting into overdrive.

I swear, his cock is just as perfect and impressive as the rest of him. I begin slowly stroking his thick length the way I know he likes.

He closes his eyes and moans. "That feels good, baby. Real good." I maneuver myself until I'm hovering over his lap. "I can't wait to taste you."

I get off the bed and prepare to kneel in front of him but he hauls me back up on the bed. "No."

Is he freaking kidding me?

"Come on, Asher. Let me do it."

I purposely pout my lips out and crawl across the bed. "Let me suck that big, fat, cock of yours." His eyes open wide and he looks taken back. I have no idea where all these dirty thoughts are coming from, but I'll be damned if I'm going to stop now.

I dip my head and kiss the tip of him. "I know you've never had this done and I've never done it, but I'll make it good for you. Just tell me what feels good and I'll keep doing it. Tell me what you like and I won't stop until you come."

His mouth parts and he exhales. "Jesus."

In one fell swoop he pins both my hands above my head with one of his.

His other hand reaches inside my underwear.

"Why won't you let me do it to you?" I pant out through shaky breaths. Something flashes in his eyes but it's gone a moment later. "Because if you do, this will be over a lot quicker than either of us want it to."

He lets go of my wrists and moves down my body until his lips skim my navel. "But." His tongue traces the edge of my panties. "If you want." He plants a kiss over the now wet lace of the crotch. "I'll taste you," he whispers as he hooks his fingers onto the sides and slips them down.

Need like I've never experienced before shoots through me like a cannon. "No. I want you now, Asher."

"Are you sure, Breslin?" His eyebrows crash together. "Are you sure this is really what you want because once we do this, there's no going back."

I open my mouth to protest, but he continues, "It's just with us going away to different schools. I don't want you to regret this."

"I've never been more certain about anything in my entire life. I could never regret this." I run my hand along his jaw and his dark blond stubble that I love so much. "I could never regret you, Asher. No matter what the future holds."

He nods softly and digs his wallet out of his pants.

He puts on the condom and I lie back and part my thighs for him. "I love you." He leans his forehead against mine. "I love you bigger, Breslin." He kisses my lips. "You're my best friend."

Tears prickle my eyes. "You're mine."

He reaches down, entwines our fingers together and pulls them up over my head.

"I don't ever want to lose you." His expression is so pained it pulls on my heart.

I cradle his face in my hands. I kiss the scar above his eyebrow—the one he doesn't remember how he got. The only feature on his perfect face that isn't perfect, and his eyes squeeze shut.

"You won't. I'm yours forever. As long as you want me."

When his eyes open, they're determined and full of love. "I'll always want you." The tip of him starts to enter me and he entwines our fingers again. "I'll *always* love you."

Slowly, he begins pushing his way inside me, never breaking eye contact or our connection.

I want to put this moment in a treasure chest and keep it forever. When he's a little more than half-way in I feel some pressure but I take a deep breath.

"Are you okay?" He stills himself. "Want me to stop?"

I shake my head. "Never."

He pushes forward again and I wince.

I know it would probably be better to tell him to thrust hard and get it over with, kind of like pulling off a band aid—but that's not how I want this moment to be, despite the pain. "Just go slow...for now. Until I get used to it."

His hand leaves mine and I feel the loss immediately.

And then I gasp when the pad of his thumb begins circling my clit, touching me the way he knows I like to be touched. "Fuck, Asher."

I feel his cock twitch and I expect him to push the rest of the way in and start, but he doesn't.

Instead, he keeps slowly bringing me to the edge, giving me pleasure. "I want you to feel good, Breslin. I want to make this good for you."

My body begins to shake as the first stirrings of my orgasm break through. "I swear, I never want to hurt you, Breslin," he whispers as he pushes himself the rest of the way inside me. On some level, I register a bit of pain, but a big portion of it is shadowed by the fact that I'm in the middle of a mind-blowing orgasm.

He slowly begins thrusting inside me and his eyelids fall shut.

His expression is one I can't read and I hate that he's no longer looking at me.

"The pain is gone," I say, hoping my stupid body didn't ruin this moment for us. "You didn't hurt me."

I expect him to open his eyes then, but instead, he leans down and buries his nose in my neck. His breathing is staggered and his thrusting begins to pick up. It hurts, but I don't care. I want Asher to enjoy this moment instead of looking like he's in turmoil.

His entire body tenses over me and I know he's close. "I love you," I whisper.

His entire body shudders with his climax and I feel wetness drip down my neck and onto my shoulder.

Then I hear a muffled sob from deep in his throat. "I'm so sorry," he whispers, his voice strained. "So fucking sorry, Breslin."

His entire body begins shaking again...but this time, I know it's not from anything good.

My stomach sinks and I immediately bolt up, alarmed. "What's wrong? What is it?"

I grab his face in my hands. "What happened?"

I don't know much about sex...but maybe I hurt him somehow? Did something I wasn't supposed to?

He wipes away the few tears that are falling down his face. The fact that not only is he *not* answering me, but I've never in all our years together seen him even close to tears sends me into a tailspin.

I know I'm responsible for his state somehow. I just don't know what I did to cause it.

My heart leaps to my throat. "Did I hurt you, Asher? Did I do something wrong?" He kisses my cheek. "No. God, no. You were perfect, Breslin."

"I don't understand—"

"I have to tell you something."

He looks down at the floor but I force him to look at me. "You can tell me anything."

Another tear falls down his face and it's like a punch right to the gut.

I swear I feel his pain in my own soul. Whatever he's going through must be excruciating.

He runs one hand through his hair and the other clenches mine for dear life.

His gaze ping pongs around the room, like he wants to look anywhere but at me. "Breslin...there's no easy way to say this...but I think...I'm not sure. But I think I might...have feelings that I'm not supposed to."

I have absolutely no idea what to make of that statement.

"Can you be a little bit more specific? What kinds of feelings?"

"The kind I can't tell anyone about. The kind I don't know how to deal with, because I don't know what they mean." His face falls. "The kind that might make me lose you."

I shake my head, still baffled. "Unless you're about to tell me you're a serial killer I'm pretty sure we can deal with whatever it is you're going through together. So please, before I have a heart attack, tell me what's going on."

"I think I might—" He looks away. "I sort of think I might be gay."

I laugh. I laugh so hard I swear I almost fall off the bed. Asher's always trying to get me to laugh during serious moments and he's always pulling pranks to ease the tension in a room.

I roll my eyes and push him playfully. "Yeah, right. Nice one, especially given we just had sex for the first time. Now quit playing and tell me what's actually wrong."

He looks me right in the eyes. "I just did."

All the air gets sucked out of the room. My chest constricts and I place my hand over it because I swear the damn organ in it is shattering into a million tiny fragments in one single fucking moment.

How could this be? He has to be lying. Oh god...was I that horrible in bed that he'll say anything in order not to have sex with me again?

He'll say anything just to get rid of me?

I don't realize I've said these things out loud—not until Asher reaches for my hand again.

I snatch it away from him...I don't want someone who's trying to rip my heart out to touch me.

"No," he says quickly. "That's not it. I swear, that's not it at all. You are amazing and sexy. You're perfect, Breslin."

I pull the sheet around me, feeling vulnerable and exposed.

I thought I knew everything about Asher. How did something like this slip past my radar? How didn't I know?

Our connection has always been so strong...so potent. How is this happening right now?

I don't even realize there are tears streaming down my face until he's wiping them.

I turn away. I don't want him trying to fix what he just broke because I'm almost positive he can't. "Don't touch me, Asher."

I clutch the sheet tighter to myself.

"I never wanted to hurt you," he says and I tell my stupid heart not to believe him. "You're my best friend and I love you. I love you so much. Hell, I'm still *in love* with you. You're the only person I've ever loved."

I stand up and shake my head. His words don't make sense. *None* of this makes any sense.

Not unless...

"How long have you known you were gay?" I ask. "How long did you use me? How long was I your cover up?"

His jaw tics and he looks shocked. "You were never my cover up. Every single thing I felt for you was *real.*"

I jab my finger into his chest. "Bullshit. You just told me you were gay."

He drags a hand over his face. "I said...I *think* I'm gay."

I start getting dressed. Because thanks to him, I no longer have the heart to continue hearing him talk around in circles. "Obviously this didn't just occur to you all of a sudden. How long have you had these feelings? How long have you been stringing me along?"

"I've had these feelings for a few months," he whispers, looking disgusted. "But I didn't know. I mean, I never knew for sure because I was so into *you*, Breslin. I never even thought I could be gay until—"

I clutch my stomach. "Until you had sex with me," I finish for him.

He opens his mouth to say something but I cut him off. "But you
—" I swallow my pride and try again. "You *finished*."

I may not know all the ins and outs when it comes to sex yet, but
I'm pretty sure you have to be attracted to the person in order to
orgasm.

He closes his eyes and I feel sick...because I realize maybe that's
not exactly true after all. "You kept your eyes closed for most of it.
You weren't thinking about me, were you?"

"Of course—"

I don't give him a chance to finish whatever statement he was
about to make because anger explodes into my broken heart. "You
brought me here as some sort of experiment, didn't you? All while
knowing you've had these feelings for *months* and you kept it from
me. All while knowing how much I love you."

I glare at him. I didn't think it was possible for love to turn to hate
so quickly, but this moment right here is living proof it can. "I can't
believe you took my virginity as some kind of sexuality test."

The smoke screen clears and the rose-colored glasses come off.
And finally, I see the real Asher Holden for what he is.
An asshole.

An asshole who everyone thinks walks on water just because of
his looks and status.

But the real Asher? The real Asher is poison.

"No." He blows out a breath. "I brought you here because I
wanted you to be *my* first. I wanted to have this moment with you. I
wanted to tell you the truth about these feelings I've been having. I
wanted—"

What about what I wanted?

I grab my purse off the nightstand and dig around for my cell
phone so I can call a cab. "You wanted what, Asher? Did you
honestly think that this wouldn't destroy me? I'm in *love* with you."

I'm in love with someone who can never love me back. Someone
who used me and hurt me.

I gave my heart to someone who jumped on it like it was his personal trampoline.

I shrug my shoulders, a razor's edge from breaking into sobs. "Were you hoping I would turn into your little sidekick and we could eat ice cream and gossip about cute boys...like you didn't just wreck my heart?"

The poor girl from the trailer park who put him up on a pedestal for all these years was all just a ruse. Because that's what people like him do. That's what they've always done. People like him...use people like me. It's the way it's always been.

My stupid heart should have known better.

"No, I didn't want you to be my sidekick. I wanted..." His words drift off.

"What?" I snort. "What did the great Asher Holden, star quarterback, prom king, and popular rich boy want? What else does he want from me after I already gave him every single fucking piece of me and he stomped on it!"

He stalks toward me and gets in my face. "I wanted *you*, Breslin! I wanted you to be there while I sort my head out." His voice drops to a whisper. "I *want* you to wait for me while I figure out what the fuck is going on with me. It's scary and confusing...and I know it's hard for you to hear, but I need you. I don't think I can do this alone."

For a second, I almost give into him. I almost tell him that I'll wait for him...that I'll hold his hand every step of the way. Because my heart is an idiot...and it's so easy to fall for Asher. It's so easy to get sucked in by him.

But then I realize...

If I'm one of the choices...it means someone else will be as well.

And unfortunately, I still love him so much I'm certain I can't bring myself to share him with another.

A sickening feeling snakes up my spine. *What if there's already someone else?*

I practically choke trying to get the words out. "Did you cheat on me?"

When he doesn't answer, I swear I don't know whether to punch him or go ballistic. "You owe me the truth, Asher. You already broke my heart...at least do the decent thing and give me the courtesy of letting me know you broke my trust too. Don't lie to me again."

He visibly swallows and I feel like I'm going to vomit cheap spiked prom punch all over the expensive hotel carpet. "How many times?" I hold up my hand because I don't want to know all the details after all. Just *one*.

"With who?

He takes a deep breath. "It's not what you think. I never, ever wanted to hurt you. I swear to God, I *never* meant to hurt you."

It's a little too late for that.

I shake my head in disgust and head for the door.

I take one final look back at him. "Who?"

He opens his mouth to answer but intuition fires through me and I feel it in my damn bones.

I already know the answer...everything from earlier makes sense now. "Kyle Sinclair."

The guy who bullied me, made me cry myself to sleep so many times I lost count, said horrible things about me and my family...and generally treated me like I was worse than trash for most of my life.

And Asher knew all of this.

It's not a question anymore, but he gives me a small nod.

"I never want to see you again."

I slam the door and take every single shred of my bludgeoned, tattered heart with me.

CHAPTER 3

ASHER

Three years earlier...

"You look so damn beautiful tonight, Breslin," I whisper as I brush my thumb along her cheek.

I mean it. She always looks incredible, but tonight? She's like something right out of a fantasy.

Too bad I feel like I'm trapped in a nightmare.

When she finds out the truth about me...she's going to hate me.

Hell, *I* hate me—so I can't really say I'd blame her.

The crowd around us cheers and I pull her against me tighter. I hear a few whistles and I tip my chin and nod in the direction of my teammates.

I'm feeling on top of the world, tonight has been amazing so far. I know Breslin's loving every second of it, and that's really all I care about.

People haven't been kind to my girl in the past. In fact, most were downright mean. Including her own father. Lazy drunk bastard that he is.

But then again, people like to throw rocks at things that shine.

People ridicule the unusual and unique. People mock what they don't understand...what they'll never be.

People fear girls like Breslin Rae.

Breslin's a hidden gem amongst a sea of dull pebbles.

I just hope my gem still wants me when she finds out the truth. I hope she gives me a chance to explain something I'm not so sure that I can.

Breslin nuzzles her cheek against my chest and I continue swaying us to the music.

I look around the room again and aim my smile for the chick holding a camera, giving her the perfect shot for the yearbook.

There's another round of whistles from my buddies on the football team which is soon followed by shouts of, "Number 3! Number 3!"

I feel Breslin's heart beat out of sync and her body goes stiff in my arms for half a second. She'll never say it, but I know how uncomfortable all this attention makes her.

About as uncomfortable as the pedestal she's had me on from the moment our eyes first locked makes me.

I never wanted Breslin to watch the show that is *Asher Holden* like everyone else in the world. I wanted her to see what was behind the curtain.

I know how to work a crowd. I know how to give people what they want. And I most certainly know how to walk the walk and talk the talk.

I know how to capture everyone's attention and force them to take notice.

All that glitters *is* actually gold when you're a Holden.

Because we're forced to learn how to play the game at an early age.

I never played the game with Breslin...but she fell for me anyway.

I fell for her harder.

I spin her around the dance floor and there's more oohs and ahhs from the crowd.

Then, my eyes lock with his.

And I'm reminded of everything I am on the inside. I'm reminded of the ugly truth.

I'm a disappointment. I'm a cheater. I'm a liar.

And... *worst* of all...I'm...

Gay?

Or at least...I might be.

The only thing I know for sure right now is I'm *fucked.*

I close my eyes and think back to that day a little over four months ago.

The day my life went to complete and utter shit and I ended up in this position.

The day Kyle Sinclair threatened, blackmailed, and ultimately ruined my life.

O ne minute.... I'm cruising through life. I have the most beautiful girl by my side, great friends, an awesome football team that I'm the quarterback of—I'm without a care in the world.

The next?

I'm waking up in the middle of the night to a warm mouth around my dick.

Then I'm fisting their hair right before I come so hard down their throat the entire bed shakes underneath me.

Freaked the fuck out, I opened my eyes and cursed.

Because I was staring right into the red light of a video camera. One that just caught my unwanted first blow job on tape.

My reaction was automatic, I kneed Kyle in the face so hard I heard his nose break and pushed him off my bed. "What the fuck?"

Kyle's hands flew to his face, attempting to control the blood pouring out of his nose.

"Don't act like you didn't like it." He picked up his shirt off the floor and brought it to his nose. "The mouthful of your jizz I just got tells me you enjoyed yourself."

I never in my life thought I'd be capable of murder before that moment.

But right then? I wanted to grab the nearest weapon I could find and slice the fucker's throat.

I knew Kyle had issues—hell most genuine assholes and bullies do. But thanks to his father and mine not only being business associates, but actual friends; I had no choice but to befriend him myself.

Something I wish I fought my father harder on at that moment.

Kyle routinely slept over on occasion after non-stop hours of grueling football practice. I knew how much of a hard ass his own father was and I felt bad.

Him crashing on my bedroom floor a few nights a week was nothing new.

But this? This was definitely *new*.

I kicked the camera off the stand and took a bat to it.

"Won't work," Kyle informed me after I smashed it to smithereens. "I had it set to go straight to my own computer at home and save. There's also someone else it was sent to just in case you try to hurt me."

I didn't believe that for a second. It was his reputation on the line as well as mine if he was stupid enough to show that tape to anyone. He was just talking shit to scare me.

I held the bat above his head. His eyes went wide and he looked about ready to shit a brick.

He knew he didn't stand a chance in hell against me *without* a bat, so he was right to be afraid.

Kyle wasn't exactly what you would call sports material... let alone football material.

Not only was he one dumb and clumsy motherfucker— he was about 3 inches too short and 40 lbs. too light to make anything other than second string. The coach only kept him in first because he didn't want to deal with any shit.

Which is why at the root of it, his own father, a successful sports agent; hated his only son.

Kyle couldn't play the game to save his life.

I knew his dad was trying to pull some serious strings to get him on a college football team, on a scholarship no less, but no one wanted him.

Despite being a jock and almost failing out of every English class I'd taken...I wasn't dumb.

I registered pretty high on the IQ test.

High enough to know Kyle just set me up with a video camera and a blow job because he wanted something.

Right before I was about to take out both his legs he shouted, "I swear to God, I'm not going to do anything with the tape. I need your help, Asher. I'm desperate."

It wasn't his words, but the way his voice cracked and the pitiful look on his face that caused me to pause mid swing. "You have 30 seconds to explain or you'll be eating from a feeding tube for the rest of your life."

He swallowed and nodded. "My father's not giving me my inheritance when I turn 18, not if I don't make it onto a sports team. He's gonna kick me out and I'll be living on the street without a dime to my name."

"And you thought sucking my dick while I was sleeping and taping it would somehow help you with your problem?"

He started blubbering like a little bitch and it took everything in me not to pummel him. "Asher without my family's money, I'm nothing. I don't have the grades to apply for regular scholarships and we both know I definitely don't have the talent to make my dad proud. I'm fucked, Asher. I'm completely screwed."

I glared at him. "Not my problem."

"It is if I go public with that tape. One that's been edited to the last 5 seconds where there's no mistaking your enjoyment and participation."

I dropped the bat and clenched my fists, because not only could he be more *wrong*, he forgot something. "You're on that tape too, dumb ass."

He shrugged helplessly and laughed. "I've got nothing to lose anymore, Asher. It's either this or I take a gun to my damn head and end the torture." He ran a hand down his face. "Look, I'm sorry about the way this is going down. I wish there was another way, but I'm literally in so deep right now, there's no limit to what I would do to crawl out of this hole."

When he pulled something out of his pocket and showed it to me a moment later, I knew he was right.

Because I was staring at a candid picture of a very naked and wet Breslin in a locker room—appearing to be looking for both a towel and her clothes.

She was clearly set up, but that's not what people would see or care about if it went public. They wouldn't care about Breslin's humiliation or embarrassment. They wouldn't care about her honor roll status or possibly putting her scholarship at Falcon University in jeopardy. The one she worked her ass off for.

They wouldn't care about possibly ruining her life.

My blood boiled and I seethed. Kyle could ruin my life all he wanted. I'd fight him tooth and motherfucking nail the entire time.

But Breslin?

He had me right where he wanted me.

There were so many questions I had for him. Questions like— who set her up? Who's helping him?

But Kyle wasn't going to answer any of them. Just like Breslin never told me when anyone picked on her or gave her any trouble. She always wanted to handle her own battles and never wanted to be a bother. Despite all the times I'd told her she was anything but.

"Fine, asshole. What exactly is it that you want from me?" I gritted through my teeth. "What will it take to make sure that picture and video never get out?"

I was prepared for the next words out of his mouth to be about my own inheritance that I'd be getting when I turned 18, but to my surprise; it was something different entirely.

"Secure me a spot at Duke's Heart for the next four years."

I'd almost rather he'd asked for my inheritance. It'd be a hell of a lot easier.

Kyle knew my top pick was Duke's Heart. I was still being scouted and going over my options—but thanks in part to my father owning a very successful NFL team—my options and offers were damn near limitless.

My father also happened to be an Alma mater at Duke's—before a tragic knee injury took out his career and he had no choice but to turn to his second love—business.

Me going to Duke's was damn near in the bag...but my father told me to make them sweat it out a little. This way they'd up the ante.

It was exactly what I'd been doing.

So far, they'd offered me a free full ride—despite my grades, and a brand new shiny car—under the radar of course.

Telling them to give Kyle a spot on the team though? Yeah, I was sure that wasn't something they'd be willing to do. Duke's football team had a great season, they were nearly undefeated.

I knew they were expecting me to uphold that. My father being who he is might give me the upper hand, but it's my talent that took it the rest of the way.

That aside, they wouldn't be dumb enough to sign a disaster like Kyle.

"Kyle," I said, attempting to reason with the moron. "You and I both know that's not going to happen." He opened his mouth to argue, but I cut him off. "However, I'll be willing to help you out after I get my inheritance. Maybe work out a monthly payment or some shit in exchange for both the picture and video."

The shithead laughed. "A few thousand dollars a month isn't worth the shit that I have on you right now. Besides, who's to say if I agreed that you would still hold up your end of the deal? I'm not dumb, Asher. There's no negotiating. Secure me a spot, and everything between us will be just fine for the next four years."

That's when I opened *my* mouth but he cut me off. "Four long years, bro. That's how long I'll be holding on to this." He narrowed his eyes. "Maybe longer depending on what kind of contract the NFL deals you when you go pro." He winked. "You're a great investment, Asher." His eyes dropped down and an uncomfortable feeling churned in the pit of my stomach. "Worth every penny."

Anger barreled into me but it was pointless.

Because whether I liked it or not...I was officially Kyle Sinclair's bitch.

T he next four months were hell on earth.

Kyle permeated my every thought, my every move.

Lurking, waiting for me to uphold my end of this fucked up arrangement...letting me know he had my balls and my destiny in a vise.

He was like a slow seeping poison that festered and grew until it was all consuming.

He made me paranoid, utterly crazy. Every time he looked at me I could hear the proverbial ticking of the clock.

I could physically feel my life falling apart whenever he was near.

Everything I worked my ass off for was in the hands of a manipulative snake.

Not only was he enjoying the power he held over me, he also became too close for comfort. So close, it was hard to decipher if he was blackmailing me for personal or professional gain anymore.

I countered by making sure I was never alone with him again.

Our former forced friendship was a thing of the past...he was the enemy.

An enemy I couldn't tell anyone about. Not my parents, not my younger brother Preston, and for obvious reasons, definitely not Breslin.

How do you explain to the only girl you ever loved that some guy —a guy she used to *hate*—blew you without your permission and you ejaculating down his throat was caught on tape for the world to see?

How would I even begin to explain to her that if she ever saw that tape with her own eyes—the supposed *edited* version—because according to Kyle it was the only version that existed now, that it wasn't what it seemed?

How would I explain to her that after that night...unwanted dreams plagued me? Dreams that straight teenage guys who were football Gods with beautiful girlfriends were *not* supposed to have.

Seemingly overnight, Kyle and this fucked up situation became the catalyst for something I was too afraid to let hit the surface of my thoughts.

So, I stuffed it down. Because what I had with Breslin was better than anything I'd ever have in this lifetime.

I didn't need to explore my thoughts or subconscious desires. They didn't matter.

Breslin was my touchdown from the 50-yard line with only seconds to spare.

But if she saw that tape? There would always be doubt between us. Assuming she'd even believe my side of the story in the first place.

Because no matter what, that tape would live between us and be a part of every single private moment we would ever share.

That tape would destroy us. *Everything* about this situation would destroy us if I wasn't careful.

And that didn't even include the naked picture of her that Kyle had locked up. The one I was fighting to make sure didn't get out.

The one I was ultimately responsible for—because Kyle wouldn't have set her up if it wasn't for me.

Bottom line?

If Breslin knew *any* of this, she would either A—freak out and go public with what Kyle was doing, which would only cause him to retaliate. Or B—leave me.

Neither of those options were a possibility for me.

Falling for her was like stumbling into quicksand.

It didn't happen gradually. The exact opposite.

It happened so fast I never had a moment to think about it.

All it took was one haphazard step and I was done for. Too far under to be pulled out.

The shy and unsure redhead with the bright green eyes was my teenage kryptonite.

Breslin never asked me for a future, but I wanted to give her one anyway.

Even with the new storm that swirled around in my head...the calm was and always will be *Breslin*.

Unfortunately, with the shit happening under the surface, Breslin and I became distant...only she didn't realize it.

Or if she did, she never called me on it.

Because for the very first time?

I played the game with Breslin.

I turned on the infamous *Holden mask* and fought my inner demons all on my own. Because Breslin was worth fighting them for.

I let them eat at me every day.

Let them change me.

And eventually...let them win.

Two weeks before Prom...

I slammed my head against the tiles and swallowed back tears.

If there was ever a moment where I'd come close to suicide.

It was this one.

The moment where I had no choice but to let Kyle go down on me in a locker room.

He got what he wanted.

Seemingly last minute Duke's Heart caved and agreed to let Kyle come along for the ride as a courtesy to me. One they didn't dig too deep into, thankfully. They most likely chalked it up to me wanting to bring my childhood best friend and fellow team member with me. They couldn't have been further from the truth.

But still, they caved. And that was all that mattered.

Of course, it was only after they heard through the grapevine that I chose another school and scheduled a meeting to make it official with them.

Even my father was nervous about how far I was taking it.

But he didn't know just how serious the real circumstances were.

And Duke's severely underestimated just how stubborn a teenager who was under duress could be.

Kyle decided to celebrate the news with another round of blackmail.

Or whatever the fuck it was at this point.

It was clear he was either attracted to guys, me, or both—in addition to getting off on the power and control he wielded over me.

It was going to be four long years.

I had no doubt they would be the worst four years of my life.

Trapped with Kyle. Trapped without my Breslin.

Trapped in a nightmare.

Trapped not knowing who I really was.

I didn't recognize my own skin anymore, it felt foreign.

Was I attracted to guys?

I knew I was attracted to Breslin. Hell, I was attracted to her in an almost unhealthy way, but was she an anomaly?

Or was Kyle the anomaly.

No, Kyle was definitely the anomaly.

In fact, it wasn't even him that I was attracted to. I hated him.

But there was something there.

Not with him, but something...something I didn't understand.

Something that had me watching gay porn as an experiment one night and sporting a hard on that scared the living shit out of me.

Something that made me close my tear soaked eyes and groan when Kyle took me deeper into his mouth.

I tried to rationalize that it was most likely because it was a blow job.

A warm mouth around a dick would always feel good on some level, I reasoned.

But then I realized that I enjoyed the sensation of him kissing his way down my body right before he worked me over with his tongue.

My life as I knew it...flipped right on its axis.

Because Kyle or no Kyle...I enjoyed the feeling of another dude's lips and mouth on me.

It was only after a good five minutes of him going to town on my dick that the reality that I was now *cheating* on Breslin hit me.

She sure as fuck didn't deserve to have that done to her. Regret and remorse filled my chest with the awareness that I was cheating on a girl I loved more than life itself.

The circumstances didn't matter.

I shoved Kyle off me and he released my erection with a loud pop. "What the hell?" he sputtered, trying to get close to me again. "Come on, I know you're enjoying yourself. It's pretty fucking obvious."

I reached for a towel and slung it around my hips. "This is a mistake."

I scrambled out of the showers...until a force yanked me back and shoved me against a wall. "I've wanted you since sophomore year, Asher."

"Never knew you were gay," I exclaimed, because it was the best I could come up with.

He still had the ultimate leverage over me. I had no choice but to tread lightly.

He gave me a smirk and leaned into my body. When his hand disappeared under my towel and he grazed my balls, my cock twitched.

Traitorous bastard. My erection was at full force again.

"I guess I hid it about as well as you did then," he whispered before he began kissing my neck.

I closed my eyes and moaned when his hand wrapped around me.

This was wrong. My body might not realize it, but I didn't want this. I could fight it. I was stronger than whatever the hell this was.

I quickly opened my eyes, because Kyle's last statement reverberated throughout my skull.

He thought I was gay.

My brain swirled and neurons fired on all cylinders.

Was I?

It was the first time I ever let the statement hit the surface and actually thought about it. *Really thought about it.*

Up until Kyle's blackmail...I assumed I was straight from the day I was born.

Not to mention...there was Breslin.

I loved being with her. I loved kissing her. I loved feeling her tits, loved playing with them and driving her crazy.

I loved *her*...all of her. She was my best friend and the love of my life all wrapped up in one.

How could I really be *gay* if I felt that way about *her?* It just didn't make any sense.

But then again...nothing about *any* of this made sense.

I'd just turned 18 and officially became a man, but I didn't know who I *was*. And it was honest to God, the scariest thing I'd ever encountered in my life.

Without warning, Kyle pressed into me again and my cock throbbed.

I didn't stop him when he went down on his knees again. In fact, I practically whimpered when he licked and sucked my tip.

Nothing had ever felt so amazing before.

Well, except for being around Breslin.

Breslin.

What the hell was I doing?

I couldn't do this to her. I wouldn't. I needed to find a way to make Kyle understand.

He got what he wanted, and I wanted to keep what I wanted.

"Stop," I shouted. When he ignored me, I forcefully pulled him off of me. My dick turned flaccid with my new-found determination.

I ran out of the shower room and back to the lockers, Kyle stayed right on my heels the whole time.

"What's the problem?" he asked.

I pulled my jeans on in a hurry, desperate to get some clothes on. Desperate to get away from *him*. "I have a girlfriend, asshole. An amazing girlfriend who I'm in love with."

It was the truth. Although somehow between deception and extortion...the wiring in my brain got screwed up—but my feelings for Breslin were still very much there.

He tipped his head back and laughed and I debated knocking

him out. "Oh please, Asher. Considering what just happened between us—it's clear she's just a coverup." He smiled and my anger grew. "Even I have to admit she's the perfect one. I mean, everyone at school knows *little miss innocent* won't put out."

I steeled my jaw and fixed him with a glare.

He was wrong.

The only reason we weren't having sex yet...

Was because of me.

Shit.

The furthest we'd gone so far was some over the bra and under-wear action during a long make out session. My parents—or rather, my father; mostly shoved football and the importance of not getting a girl pregnant in high school down me and my brother Preston's throats.

He said it would ruin our lives, ruin football. That he'd seen plenty of talented men taken down by a money hungry girl with stars and dollar signs in her eyes and high school was where they were bred and born.

My brother Preston didn't give a shit—football wasn't his thing. My father's second love—*business* was. Preston didn't play sports and had no desire to. Even though he was two years younger than me, he was smart as a whip and already on his way to becoming one hell of a businessman.

My father didn't put nearly as much focus on him, which was something I was grateful for when shit became unbearable at home.

It was me who was destined to fulfill the shoes my father never had a chance to.

Lucky for me, I loved football. It was in my blood. In my soul.

And lucky for my father...me playing football hid all his handiwork.

Every time I was on that field, I knew it was my calling. It was my home.

It was my escape.

Despite the attention I always had from the opposite sex, I never really gave them any of mine. My mind was too focused on the field.

Sure, I jerked off to porn and had my share of crushes throughout the years, but my hormones never ran rampant like so many of my peers.

My father taught me to be disciplined. Sometimes the lessons involved words...most of the time, though—it involved his fists.

Either way, I didn't act like the rest of my friends when it came to the opposite sex.

Not until Breslin at least.

The first time we went past first base was like lighting a match.

But I had to contain that fire. Because if I didn't and something ended up happening—something like an unplanned pregnancy?

I'd drop the game in a heartbeat.

It was something my father knew. Breslin was the most important thing in my life. Even more important than my future...because as far as I was concerned, she was my future.

It's why he was biding his time until I went away to college. According to him, Breslin would be a thing of the past and my future would be set in stone.   He didn't care that I didn't want a future that didn't include her.

Or maybe he did...because I knew deep down that my relationship and my feelings for Breslin petrified him.

So while he handed out condoms to my brother like candy...it was me he gave the sermons and threats to.

He constantly warned me that I would ruin not only my life but hers if she were to get pregnant. Said if I really cared about her, I'd wait until after high school, or better yet, marriage; to have sex. Told me to hold out, because if I gave in now—I'd never be able to stop. And if I knocked her up, sooner or later I'd end up hating her and my child for destroying my dreams.

Hell, he even threatened my inheritance at one point in addition to the   continuous beatings he doled out since I was a small child.

Maybe if Breslin didn't live in a trailer park and have a drunk as a father, it would have been different. Maybe if she'd come from a wealthy and prestigious family, he wouldn't have felt the need to drill those things into my head every damn day and screw with me.

But that wasn't the case.

Therefore, I never pushed the sex issue with Breslin.

Maybe subconsciously I knew my father was right. Once we started, I'd never be able to stop and an accident was bound to occur sooner or later. Maybe my brain realized that one taste of her wouldn't be enough. Maybe I feared the downward spiral and it was my way of self-preservation.

I didn't want to lose my dream and I didn't want to lose her, either. There would be plenty of time for sex once I secured our future together, I reasoned.

It was only over the past summer going into our senior year that she seemed to want to take things further...but I was reluctant.

I figured it was because of everything my father ingrained in me.

But what if that wasn't the truth after all?

What if it was because of the other truth.

The one hiding deep below the surface the whole entire time?

I threw my jersey over my head. "You don't know what the fuck you're talking about, Kyle. First of all, my sex life is none of your business. Secondly, I'm not gay. I love her and what we have *is* real. No amount of threats or blackmail will ever change the way I feel about her."

It was true. I *knew* with every fiber of my being that my feelings for her were genuine.

He rolled his eyes. "The only thing that's real is the massive erection I gave you. Face it, Asher, you're gay."

I punched the locker beside his head and looked at him. "I have no idea what you're talking about. As far as me and my dick are concerned...*nothing* happened between us. Nothing I wanted to have happen anyway."

I felt something inside me snap and I grabbed his neck. "But I swear on all that is holy—if you go back on your little fucked up arrangement and it causes me to lose Breslin...I will fucking *destroy* you."

He visibly swallowed against my palm and I damn near grinned at the shift in control between us. Until his next statement.

"You're a pussy, Asher. You want *me,* not her. You enjoyed it."

I squeezed his neck until he started choking. "Fucking try me, Kyle. I dare you. Say one fucking word. *Hurt* her and see what I do to you. See what I'm really capable of."

I moved close to his ear, never letting up on the pressure around his throat. "You're nothing to me, faggot. Nothing but a lying, manipulating, little fudge packer who has to ride my coattails because you suck at life. Everything you did to me *without* my permission, only served to prove how into *her* I am." I snorted. "Enjoy the next few years, Kyle, because they won't be what you had in mind. I'm done being manipulated. Next time your mouth or anything else of yours comes close to my dick...I'll have my father's lawyers slap you with a lawsuit so thick you and your little faggot mouth will choke on it. Got it?"

When he started gasping for air, I finally eased my hold on him. "That's not the way this works," he croaked. "Assault me again and *I'll* be the one pressing charges. I'll sue your parents for every dime they have and go public with our little video and locker room hookup. He narrowed his eyes. "I'll post Breslin's naked picture everywhere I can think of, along with her name and address. Whatever you do to me...she'll suffer the consequences. So I suggest you shut the hell up and do what I want for the next four years, Asher. Don't fucking test me."

I grabbed my jacket and advanced toward the door. I was at a loss for words, because no matter what Kyle had me where he wanted me.

The look on his face told me he knew it. "You may think you're not into what's happening between us... but the next time her hands and mouth are on you...you'll be wishing it was me the whole time." He snapped his fingers and laughed. "Oh, that's right. You won't, because it's not like you fool around with her. Gee, I wonder *why.*"

I didn't answer him. Kyle was not only obsessed, he was down-right delusional.

And unfortunately, I was nothing but a puppet to my sick and demented puppeteer.

I had to figure a way out of this. There was no way I could survive this shit for the next few years or longer.

I slammed the door behind me and sprinted down the hallway.

"Hey, babe. Your workout ran a little late today, huh?"

I inwardly flinched at the sound of her sweet voice. A voice that was usually pure music to my ears.

I knew it would hurt to look at her, knowing what had occurred only moments prior. Part of me just wanted to break down and tell her the truth.

Instead, I forced myself to turn around and meet her big green eyes. Beautiful, kind eyes. Eyes that I damn near drowned in every time I stared into them.

Eyes that I had to look into while I lied.

Breslin wore a smile on her full lips that was brighter than the sun. Her long dark auburn hair was pulled into a messy bun and she had the faintest smudge of charcoal on her cute little nose. Judging by her own appearance, I knew that she had stayed after school herself; working on her designs in the art studio.

I cleared my throat, remembering that she had asked me a question. "Yeah. I mean, no. Kyle and I stayed after throwing the ball around for a little while."

My stomach recoiled and I almost threw up.

She nodded and smiled.

One would never tell from her expression that Kyle had mercilessly bullied her since the first grade. Well, up until two years ago when I put a stop to it.

Once we became an item, she decided to extend the olive branch to Kyle. Not only was he my teammate, she knew my father and his father were friends, and in typical Breslin fashion, she didn't want to cause any waves. Even though she didn't do a damn thing wrong in the scenario. Surprisingly, Kyle apologized for what he did to her in the past and things were fine between them soon after.

Of course, it's not like he really had a choice in the matter. I would have made his life a living hell if he hadn't.

She accepted his friendship with a bright smile and an open heart. There wasn't even any lingering resentment when it came to him. That's just how Breslin is, though. Pure and kind. Not a bad bone in that gorgeous curvy body of hers.

Bile ascended my throat and I swallowed hard. I really didn't deserve her.

She studied my face for a moment too long. "You feeling okay?"

I averted my gaze. "I'm fine. Nothing a warm soak won't fix."

She brushed my hair out of my eyes. Her nose crinkled just like it always did when her fingertips grazed the scar above my eyebrow.

The scar caused by my father repeatedly ramming my head face first into the corner of a coffee table when I was nine and told him I was too tired to go to practice.

The impact almost took out my eye, but Preston who was only seven at the time, moved the table away in the middle of my beating; or rather he tried to. Still...ten stitches were better than not having my vision.

"You should probably go home and rest." The corners of her lips turned up. "Ease those big, strong, tired muscles of yours."

She bounced up on her tiptoes and her soft lips brushed against mine. I kissed her back...until thoughts of Kyle flashed through my head. Thoughts of how the *hell I* could ever cheat on this amazing girl.

Kyle was right after all. I was thinking about him, just not for the reasons he thought and hoped I would be.

I could tell she only meant to give me a quick peck. But just when she was about to pull away, I spun her around until her back was against the wall.

Then I claimed her mouth. I could feel her chest rising and falling against me as I pried her lips open and demanded access. I groaned when she complied and turned to putty in my arms. Her fingers wound through my hair sending shock waves up my spine as she nibbled my bottom lip in such a seductive way, my brain muddled.

There was no doubt I wanted Breslin, she damn near drove me insane I wanted her so bad.

Maybe it was time I finally took what I wanted.

My lips worked down her neck, sucking the spot where her pulse was beating rapidly.

"Jesus, Asher," she breathed and her skin flushed. "That feels so good."

I moved her shirt down, exposing her shoulder and ran my lips over the adorable patch of freckles sprinkled there. "It's about to feel even better."

"Is that so?"

My hands dropped to her waist before they ventured lower and I slipped my thumbs inside the waistband of her jeans. "You tell me?" I caressed the delicate skin right above her panties until her head fell back and her eyes closed.

"I thought you were going home?" she questioned and I grinned.

She couldn't hide the lust in her tone if she tried, and fuck if that didn't make me want her even more.

I pushed her shirt up and teased the edge of her bra with my fingers. "*You* said I should go home," I reminded her. "I'd much rather stay here with you." I gave her a smirk as I tugged her bra down. My mouth watered at the sight of her nipples through her white t-shirt. "And do this."

I bent down and sucked one of her nipples through the material, my cock strained so hard against my zipper it was almost painful.

"Asher." I sucked harder as she moaned and gripped my hair. "We're in *public*."

I pulled back slightly and she blushed, her cheeks turning an adorable shade of pink, almost matching the perfect color of her nipples which were at full attention now.

She looked around nervously. "I mean, we're still at school."

"Are you saying you don't want this?"

She opened her mouth and I licked and sucked her tits again, which were damn near see through thanks to the thin fabric of her shirt.

"That's definitely not what I'm saying." Her breathing became shaky. "It's just—" She looked down where my head was buried and the blush spread to her ears. "Anyone could see us."

She had a point. Doing what I had in mind in the middle of a hallway where anyone could find us would be just as bad as that picture of her being leaked.

I grabbed her hand and led her down the end of the hallway to an abandoned classroom.

When I locked the door behind us she gave me a questioning look. "Here? Really?"

I nodded and lifted her into my arms. "Almost everyone's gone home. The only people around now are the janitors."

A slow grin spread across her face. "You have a point. Even if they did catch us, I don't think we'd get in too much trouble for making out."

She let out a soft squeal when I set her on top of the teacher's desk and reached for the hem of her shirt. "That's where you're wrong, because I want to do much more than make out with you right now."

She stared at me wide-eyed when I motioned for her to lift her arms for me.

Less than a second later, her t-shirt was on the classroom floor.

She didn't have to say she was nervous for me to know she was. I didn't want her to be nervous with me, though. I'd never hurt her...not *intentionally* anyway.

"Relax," I whispered as I lowered the straps of her bra. "I wouldn't fuck you for the first time in some abandoned classroom. I would make it special."

I undid the clasp and groaned when those hot as hell tits of hers spilled into my hands. Tits that I was officially seeing for the first time in all their glory. Not hidden behind a lacy bra like in the past. Tits that I had every intention of coming all over before we left this classroom.

"Because you are special to me, Breslin." I cupped her breasts and lifted them into my mouth. "So special."

There was no way in hell I was gay. Not when I'd never been more turned on in my whole life—thanks to a half-naked, sexy as fuck Breslin at my mercy.

She moaned and leaned back, giving me even better access to her boobs.

Goddamn, they were perfect.

Even playmates didn't have tits as nice or as natural as Breslin's. Hers were more like ripe, sweet cantaloupes rather than oversized watermelons. Either way, they were perfectly proportioned to her curvy little body. Not to mention, perky as hell.

I continued kneading her breasts with my hands, pulling them into my mouth, sucking on them like they were the best things on earth, because as far as I was concerned right now they most definitely were.

Breslin's   little moans became more frantic and when I glanced up, I saw that her eyes were hooded and her mouth was parted slightly. My cock stirred and it was all I could do to not rip off those jeans and take her.

"So perfect," I mumbled as I lavished her nipple with my tongue. "You have no idea how much I want to fuck these perfect tits of yours, Breslin." I thrust into her hard and she gasped.

For the first time, I was giving in to my urges. I didn't give a shit about anything else. Not my father, not Kyle, not the blackmail looming over my head.

The only thing I cared about was Breslin and all the things I wanted to do to her.

"Do it," she said, sounding impatient. "Please." She looked into my eyes. "I want you. I want this." I didn't miss the way her voice shook for a moment before she found her resolve. "I'm a little nervous...but I know I'm ready for this. You're the only person I want this with. It wouldn't feel right with anyone else, Asher." Her voice dropped to a whisper. "I know we're going our separate ways after we graduate." She ran her hand along my jaw. "But it needs to be you. Don't let me lose it to someone who doesn't love me."

I closed my eyes and anger coursed through me. It killed me that she thought I was going to leave her and that us going to different colleges would be the end of us. No matter how many times I tried to tell her that I wanted her...in the forever kind of way, she never believed me. She never trusted me.

And I just broke the trust she never gave me today.

I had to tell her. I had to tell her about Kyle, the blackmail, and these weird feelings that were scaring the shit out of me.

But I couldn't.

"I love you," I said, my voice sounding strained even though I meant every word of it.   I started to pull away, the guilt wrapped around me so tightly it was hard to breathe.

That's when Breslin snaked her hand around my neck and kissed me. And this time, she kissed me with even more fervor and passion than she ever had in the past. I became breathless for a different reason entirely.

That spark between us. *God, that fucking spark.* I swore, it was enough to light the whole world on fire.

I was certain nothing could diminish it. So certain I debated taking my chances and spilling the truth again.

That is until she reached down and stroked me through my jeans.

Fuck.

Hormones, attraction, lust, want, and need hung in the air between us. All the things that made people forget anything and everything, including right and wrong, pummeled into me like a 300 lb. linebacker.

I broke the kiss and popped the button on her jeans open. "Take these off and lay back on the desk," I instructed her while silently instructing my dick not to come just yet.

I helped her out of her jeans and she leaned all the way back, stopping only to give me a wink before she let her head hang off the side of the desk.

Holy hell. She looked better than any centerfold in any magazine ever could or would.

Breslin was the kind of beautiful that could bring a person to their knees. Not because she was perfect, but because of her imperfections.

Those imperfections consisting of the random patches of freckles on her pale skin. The way her green eyes were almost too big for her small nose. The fact that she didn't have an athletic bone in her body and wasn't a size two like the cheerleaders, but a size eight. Something I only knew because I caught her crying in the girl's bathroom on the first day of our junior year after Marcy Bush—the bitchy head cheerleader, and her bitches in training cronies—called her fat and filled her locker with diet pills and cow manure.

I was so pissed, I refused to play in our first game if Marcy wasn't off the squad permanently. Of course, my father gave me shit, but I didn't give a shit. I needed everyone at school to realize that if they hurt Breslin...they hurt me.

And I'd hurt them back.

How anyone in their right mind could ever call Breslin anything less than beautiful anyway was beyond me.

My gaze landed between her legs. She still had her underwear on, but those would soon be a thing of the past. "Spread your legs for me, baby."

I heard her sharp intake of breath as she proceeded to do what I asked.

I zeroed in on the damp fabric sticking to what I knew was uncharted territory. "Take off your panties. I need to see you."

She hesitated for the briefest of moments before she slowly slipped them off.

She was so smooth, so wet, so damn perfect, I had to bite my knuckle to stop myself from coming.

People always called me an asshole behind my back, and for the first time I fully understood why that was.

Apart from Breslin, I always took whatever it was that I wanted. I never once gave a fuck about the consequences, because there never were any. I was a Holden. Consequences didn't exist for us.

And I knew at that moment—the moment where a naked Breslin was spread out on a desk for me—this time would be no different.

I wasn't going to waste the opportunity. I'd wanted Breslin since the moment I saw her...it was time to finally do something about it.

I wasn't going to completely defile her in a classroom, but fuck me if I wasn't going to dirty my innocent Breslin up a little today.

I stood directly behind her and she swallowed hard, no doubt wondering just how far I was going to take this.

I leaned over her and skimmed my hand down her stomach. "Gorgeous," I whispered, and any trace of doubt left her face when she looked up at me.

That's when my hand wandered further and she gasped.

The sound of my finger entering her wet pussy for the first time was almost obscenely loud in the quiet room.

There was a small part of me that was nervous, for a few reasons. One—the obvious...it was my first time fingering a girl and I was worried I wouldn't be any good at it. The second reason—was much more frightening and the ultimate game changer.

What if I didn't like it? What if it turned me off?

I prayed to whatever God I wasn't so sure I believed in anymore that wouldn't be the case.

Even if my dick didn't like women...I *needed* it to like Breslin.

Panic gripped me and I was about to crumble.

Until I looked down at her.

A potent rush of calm followed by arousal hit me as I slid my finger deeper inside her and my cock twitched.

I didn't have a damn thing to worry about.

Her eyes searched mine and her breath hitched. She looked at me with so much love, lust, and adoration I swear my heart stopped beating entirely.

I paused for a moment, unsure of what she liked, but then her hand landed on top of mine and she moved my finger upwards.

"Touch me here," she whispered and I eagerly complied. "Keep rubbing my clit."

She let out a low moan a moment later and I was right there with her. I'd always dreamed of what touching Breslin would feel like, but it was nothing compared to the real thing.

Or the fact that I was the one doing this to her. That it was me eliciting those hips of hers to buck against the hard wood of the desk and the soft moans to leave those full lips.

I looked down and relief barreled into me.

I was harder than a fucking rock.

I was an idiot for ever doubting my attraction to her in the first place. Not only was our connection out of this world, but my dick was clearly a major fan of Breslin. My body was enjoying everything about the way her body responded to mine.

"Asher—" Her words fell and she looked up at me. I knew she was close. Or at least, I hoped she was.

"Don't stop," she panted. "Please don't stop what you're doing. It feels so good."

I wouldn't stop if someone paid me.

Her nails dug into the desk. "Oh, God."

"That's it, Breslin. You're almost there, baby. You're so close to coming all over my fingers, aren't you?"

She blushed ten different shades of red and nodded. I didn't miss the gleam in her eyes, though; and I really didn't miss how she grew wetter for me after those words.

My girl liked dirty talk.

Before I could whisper any more of it, her body squirmed. "Don't stop, Asher. I'm coming."

All I could do was stare at her. I was utterly transfixed as she screamed my name and a rush of wetness hit my fingers a second later.

Breslin coming apart in front of me was like watching a meteor shower.

Completely hypnotizing...and as soon as it was over I wanted to watch it all over again.

My own arousal zapped me, the force stronger than ever before.

Without wasting any time, I unzipped my jeans.

"What the hell?"

I looked down at my dick bobbing in front of her mouth. I was about to change positions, maybe to one where my balls weren't dangling right in front of her face, but she wrapped her arms around my thighs. "No, don't move. That's not why I said that."

I opened my mouth to ask what the problem was but then she laughed and said, "At the risk of sounding like a staged chick in a porno...your cock is *massive.*"

I couldn't help but grin and she rolled her eyes. "Cocky bastard."

I reached over and pushed her tits together with my palms. "I believe that's *massive* cocky bastard."

I was a second away from fucking her tits when she pulled my boxers all the way down and her warm breath hit my balls. Before I could stop her, her tongue dragged across my sac and I cursed.

It's not that I didn't want Breslin's tongue there, of course I did...I just didn't want it there now.

Not after what Kyle did.

I groaned and my body jerked when she repeated the movement. My cock throbbed and that little devil on my shoulder said to hell with it, but both my conscience and stomach recoiled.

I slammed the desk with my fist when her tongue darted out again, this time, circling one of my balls.

Fuck me. This was my personal hell and I knew right then and there that I had to tell her...and soon. "Don't."

Her face scrunched. "Why? Did I do something wrong?"

"No, you didn't." *I did.*

"Asher what's going—"

I had no choice but to cover up my fumble somehow. If I didn't...she would know something was up. Teenage guys didn't stop in the middle of a hookup...not unless they got caught or came.

Then again, most teenage guys weren't blackmailed via the tail end of an unwanted blow job caught on video camera and a naked picture of their girl.

My life was a mess.

Guilt snagged me again, only this time, I reassured myself that I was going to tell her the truth. There was no other option at this point. I couldn't have this shit hanging between us any longer.

The world could think whatever they wanted about me. Breslin's thoughts about me were all that mattered. I'd let her decide what we should do about Kyle, the tape, her picture and we'd take it from there...together.

After prom.

Breslin wouldn't admit it, but I knew she was excited about it.

As much as she tried to pretend she didn't care about being prom queen or any of *that crap* as she called it—the way her eyes lit up and the fact that she worked non-stop doubles at her job on the weekends for the last three months saving up for a dress, told me all I needed to know.

My girl wanted the night to be special. Therefore, I was going to do everything in my power to make sure it was.

Breslin was going to have the time of her life, because at the very least, she deserved that before I pulled the rug out from underneath her.

I walked around to the other side of the desk. "I don't want your mouth right now," I lied, because there wasn't a part of Breslin I didn't want. "I want these."

I held her tits and slid my dick between her cleavage.

I was an asshole and I was certain I'd earned my seat in hell for this, but I didn't care.

My balls tingled and I groaned. I'd been a razor's edge away from coming since the moment my finger slipped inside that sweet pussy of hers. There was no way I could hold back any longer. "Fuck, Breslin. I'm gonna come all over these tits."

It wasn't a request, it was a warning.

She pulled her bottom lip between her teeth and gave me a devilish grin. "So do it."

And that's all it took. My cum jetted out all over those perfect tits of hers and for a moment, I felt every part of my body relax.

Until the door opened and in walked Mr. McGinty.

The senile, albeit harmless; science teacher the school desperately wanted to get rid of but the students fought to keep every year because he let so much shit slide due to his mental incompetence.

"Holden, what in the Sam Hill are you doing over there?"

And here I thought it was obvious.

"Oh my God," Breslin whispered, loud enough for only me to hear. I bent over and tried to shield her with my own body as much as I could.

McGinty cleared his throat. "Turn around, Holden. And for Christ's sake pull up your pants. That lily-white ass of yours is damn near blinding."

Breslin's lips pulled into a smile and she snorted. I fought like hell to hold back my own laughter. This was probably one of the worst-case scenarios after a hookup—but as usual with Breslin— nothing was ever as bad as it could have been.

She had a way of turning the worst things into the best things.

"Um—" I paused. I was pretty sure he hadn't even seen her underneath me yet. Maybe there was still a way out of this.

"Are you hard of hearing, boy? I said pull up your pants and turn around."

Or not.

I smiled down at Breslin—we were toast and she knew it. "Afraid I can't do that, Mr. McGinty."

"Why the hell not!"

"We're gonna get in so much trouble," Breslin whispered before she started laughing again.

I took a deep breath, covered her tits with my hands, and straightened myself. "Because I have the world's most gorgeous girl underneath me. And I gotta be honest with you, McGinty. There's no way in hell I'm letting you see her fantastic tits. They're for my eyes only."

Breslin slapped my shoulder. "Smooth, Asher. Real smooth."

"Thank God," he said, the relief apparent in his tone. "For a minute, I thought you were urinating on Mrs. Henley's plant. That woman's a goddamned whack job. She would have demanded you be benched for next week's game."

Breslin raised a brow and I bit back another round of laughter. Not only was football season over, this wasn't Mrs. Henley's classroom.

He banged on the door. "Now get dressed, Holden." His footsteps stopped. "The both of you."

When he shut the door behind him we both burst into an uncontrollable fit of laughter.

I leaned my forehead against hers and kissed the tip of her nose. "I love you."

She looked down. "I bet you say that to all the girls covered in your cum."

I stood up and wiped her chest with my jersey. "Shit, I'm sorry."

She sat up and proceeded to get dressed. "Don't be." She wiggled her eyebrows. "I had a lot of fun."

Just when we were about to walk out the door, she reached for my hand and squeezed it. "We're okay, right?"

My stomach dropped. "Of course. Why wouldn't we be?"

Her brows pinched together. "It's just—" She fidgeted with her hands. "I haven't said anything because I didn't want you to think I was being one of *those* girls...but something's been kind of off with us for a few months."

I opened my mouth but she continued, "I know it's probably my fault. I keep saying that us going to different colleges will be the end of us."

"It doesn't have to be—"

She reached for my hand again. "I know. I don't want it to be." She blew out a breath. "I don't want to break up."

A tear slipped from her eye and I brushed it away. "I have faith in us. I think we'll make it. Or at least I think we owe it to one another to try."

I wasn't sure how it was possible for a single statement to break your heart and put it together at the same time.

"And just so you know," she added. "I love you, too." Another tear fell. "I love you big."

I pulled her hand to my lips, warmth spreading through me, and

for the first time in my life that didn't involve me being on the football field...I said a prayer.

Please, God...fix me. Fix me so I don't have to lose her.

Three hours before Prom...

"T hanks, Mrs. Callahan. Breslin's going to love it."
 She beams at me and fixes her hair. "You look very hand-
some, Asher."

I hold back my laugh. I'm an asshole, but even I had my limits.
Laughing at an 80-year-old woman who was sweet as sugar was one
of them.

Instead I smile and swipe my credit card. "Thanks—"

I stop mid-sentence when I catch *his* reflection in the security
camera of the flower shop.

Mrs. Callahan hands me the receipt and I straighten my spine.
I'm getting ready to walk out the door, but Kyle grabs my shoulder.
"We need to talk."

"No, we don't." I glance at my watch. "I'm running late."

"Prom isn't for another three hours. Give me five minutes out in
the parking lot." He drops his voice to a whisper. "Please, Asher."

I push past him. "Fine."

I can hear his footsteps behind me as I make my way out to my
truck.

I silently debate murdering him and paying off any potential
witnesses.

Especially when I spin around and he crushes his mouth against
mine.

I shove him off me. "What the fuck!"   I pull my arm back,

intending to sail it straight into his face but the shithead says, "I'm in love with you, Asher." Before he breaks out into a fit of sobs.

I open the door to my truck. "You're out of your mind, Kyle." I place Breslin's corsage on the passenger seat. "Real shit? I honestly think you need help, man."

I turn back around to face him. "I'm telling Breslin about you...about what you did."

He wipes his eyes and they turn hard. "I think that's a bad move."

I snort and cross my arms. Of course, he would think that, he's the fucker trying to blackmail me.

He holds up a hand. "Forget the arrangement between us and forget that I'm in love with you." He gestures between us. "I'm talking about the elephant in the room that you won't acknowledge."

"I have no idea what you're talking about."

"The longer you keep denying it, the worse it will get. Take it from me. You're going to snap one day and sooner or later, it's all going to come to a head."

He takes a step forward. "Would you rather break it to Breslin now? Or seven years from now when she's pushing out your first kid and you're paying for blow jobs on the down low from the men seeking men section of Craigslist?"

I lift my chin and glare at him. "I love her—"

"I know you do." His expression turns serious. "But you're going to hurt her, it's inevitable. There's something that you need...something she can never give you."

"You don't know what you're talking about, I'm not gay." I pause. "And even if I was into that shit...I'm into Breslin more."

"That's not the way it works. You're still at the beginning stages, Asher. Or as the rest of us who have already been there like to refer to it—the denial and confused stage. But sooner or later, you'll realize the truth. And then you'll realize there will always be a piece of yourself that you can't share with her. A piece she won't ever be capable of understanding."

He stuffs his hands in his pockets. "And not for nothing...but don't you think you owe it to yourself to explore the side of you that you're so afraid of? Don't you think you owe it to yourself to *be* yourself?"

I narrow my eyes and he takes another step forward. "I'm sorry about blackmailing you. I wish it didn't have to be this way, but trust me when I tell you that I have no other choice."

He looks down. "But that doesn't mean we can't make the best out of the situation. I can give you the things she can't...and she deserves to know the truth. Hate me all you want, but you know I'm right."

I open my mouth but he cuts me off. "You have until tomorrow morning to make your final decision."

To say I'm confused would be an understatement. Hell, I'm practically getting whiplash from how often Kyle's changing the stakes. "Decision? What decision?"

He starts backing away. "The next four years with me. Or the rest of your life without football, your family's money...and most of all, yourself. The *real* you." He snickers. "But hey...you'll have Breslin, right?"

He throws open his car door. "Depending on what kind of truth you decide to give her." His gaze softens. "But if you decide to come clean for real—I'll still be here when she smashes your heart into a thousand pieces...because she's going to. She'll never accept you."

He runs a hand through his hair. "Like I said before, I'm sorry about blackmailing you. But I'm not sorry about giving you an ultimatum, because no matter which road you choose to go down tonight...you'll end up with me."

I hop in my truck and rev the engine.

That's what he thinks...but he doesn't know Breslin.

He doesn't understand what we have. I have no doubt that things will be complicated after I tell her the truth...but they won't be broken.

Two hours after Prom...

"It's not what you think. I never, ever wanted to hurt you. I swear to God, I *never* meant to hurt you."

Please, Breslin. Don't do this.

She shakes her head and walks to the door.

When she stops and looks at me, my stomach free falls, because I know the next question out of her mouth before she even utters it. "Who?"

I can feel the color drain from my face. I don't know how to even begin to explain the Kyle situation and I'm almost positive she doesn't give a fuck.

But still, I have to try. I swallow hard and open my mouth, preparing to tell her everything.

Until she shoots me such a venomous look and says, "Kyle Sinclair."

I give her a small nod, because the look in her eyes tells me what a piece of shit I am.

The look in her eyes tells me that even if she knew the truth—that I didn't want what Kyle did, and that it really fucked me up. And that even if she knew just how scared and confused I am and how much I need her—none of it would make a bit of difference to her now.

I fucked up. I lost her.

He was right.

"I never want to see you again."

Her words feel like a boulder on my chest and I can actually feel my heart crack when she slams the door behind her.

I brace myself against the wall of the hotel hallway and take another swig of my drink.

It burns like hell going down but it's nothing compared to the other feeling barreling into me.

She's gone.

And not just in the she broke up with me sense. More like the— her father said she left town for good sense.

Of course, I didn't believe the drunk asshole when he told me— but when I pushed past him and ran into her bedroom, everything was missing.

That's when he offered me a beer.

And one beer turned into five more.

Until I left in search of something stronger to cope with the pain.

My phone vibrates and I have to concentrate to see the text.

Kyle: *I'm inside the room. Got the key from the front desk.*

Yeah, I should have seen that one coming.

Asher: *Did you bring it?*
Kyle: *Sure did.*

He better not be lying because I'm not in the right state to listen to my conscience at the moment.

There's only one thing, correction two things I want from Kyle right now, but I'll settle for one.

I'll sell my soul for the other.

I finish off the bottle of whiskey and stagger to the hotel room. I'm so drunk I barely manage to get the card in the door, but I start to sober when I remember the mission I'm on.

Get Breslin's picture.

I find him sitting on the bed when I walk in and he snickers. "Well aren't you a sight for sore eyes."

"Get up."

Apprehension flashes in his eyes for a beat before he walks over to me. "I'm not giving you the video, Asher."

"Then I'm not giving you my dick." When he opens his mouth, I cut him off, "That's what you really want, right?"

"The video's mine until we graduate college."

I figured as much. Lucky for him there's something even more important that I want. "I want Breslin's picture."

When he looks like he's going to object, I make my move.

He's so stunned he almost trips over the small table when I back him into the wall behind him.

The groan that erupts from him when I press my mouth to his makes me sick.

Not because it's a guy...but because of the manipulating asshole attached to the lips I'm kissing.

He reaches for my zipper but I'm already three steps ahead of him.

"Jesus," he sputters when I spin him around and press him against the wall.

I feel his entire body shake underneath me when I bring his hand over my dick. "You want this?"

"You know I do."

"Then give me Breslin's picture and leave her out of this little arrangement permanently. She's gone, Kyle. Whatever your reason for pulling this shit is, it has nothing to do with her. She doesn't deserve this."

When he looks like he's still not going to cave, I trail my tongue along his neck and nip at his skin. "You want me to fuck you right now?"

"Yes." He closes his eyes. "Please."

I thrust my cock against his ass. "You want this dick for the next four years?"

"God, yes," he whimpers.

I drag my teeth along the shell of his ear. "Then drop your fucking pants and give me the picture."

He mutters a curse and reaches inside his pocket. I snatch the picture and rip it to shreds.

I motion for him to give me the USB and the disk next and he does. "This all of it?"

When he nods, I pin him with a stare. "It better be."

I walk over to the nightstand and smash both the USB and disk with an ashtray.

Then I walk back over to him and grab his neck. "Bend over."

He looks nervous and my dick twitches.

His pants barely hit the floor when I'm entering him in a flash and he cries out in pain. "You didn't use lube."

I squeeze his throat and pump into his ass again, harder this time. "You weren't gentle when you fucked me, Kyle. I'm just returning the favor."

CHAPTER 4

LANDON

Three years later...

I lift my eyes from my laptop and stare at her. I don't know how she does it, but I swear she only gets prettier with every day that passes.

The customer she's taking the coffee order from is annoying at best, but she gives him a bright smile as he continues rattling off his 50-item coffee order, taking it all in stride.

When he finally stops for air, her eyes catch mine and she gives me the cutest wink I've ever seen before turning her attention to her customer again.

That is until her gaze snags on the container of sugar I'm holding and she frowns. Those piercing green eyes of hers glare daggers at me. I put it down and pick up the sugar substitute instead.

I look up to the ceiling and snort. Breslin Rae is going to be the death of me.

My eyes roam over her long red hair, full perky tits, gorgeous curvy body and I smile.

But what a lovely way to go.

We haven't been dating for long—or whatever it is that we are because she refuses to put a label on it and make it official—but it's been the best summer of my life.

We'd been attending the same college for the last three years, but it was only two months ago that we met by chance when she rented out the apartment next to me for the summer break.

Meeting Breslin was one of the best things that ever happened to me, and I'm not looking forward to when she goes back to her dorm at the end of August.

Maybe she doesn't have to.

I push that thought to the back of my mind before it can take root. The girl won't even agree to be my girlfriend, there's no way she's going to agree to move in with me.

On the bright side, I've got another full year before we graduate to convince her to take the leap.

Stirring my coffee now laden with god awful sugar substitute instead of the good stuff, I put my headphones back on and focus on my music.

That is until my phone vibrates and I inwardly groan. I'm not in the mood to tutor one of my pimply faced, summer school, dipshit students tonight.

I'd much rather spend the night with her.

But, I need all the extra credit and cash I can get since I'm technically a double major and my second major—*music*—is according to my family—doomed to fail.

It's why teaching is my backup plan.

I'm about to reply to my new text but then I see Breslin's face fall when she brings her own phone up to her ear and excuses herself to go in the back.

My eyes lock with her coworker, roommate, and friend—*Kit,* who gives her head a shake, silently telling me not to follow her.

I know Breslin has her secrets. I know she doesn't open up to just anyone and I get it...I just wish she'd let me in more.

Not that I'm not appreciative of all the ways she does let me in—like the holy grail between her legs—but lately I want more than just to stick my dick in her all the time.

I want her...all of her. I want those secrets she keeps, the past she refuses to talk about, and the future she's too scared to give me.

I want the place inside her no one else can reach.

CHAPTER 5

BRESLIN

I clutch the phone in my hand and close my eyes.

I hate it when he calls me.

I have ten guesses what it is he's calling me for but I only need one.

To say he was pissed about me not coming home for the summer would be an understatement. His little cash cow finally did something selfish and left him stranded.

Guilt slams into me and for a moment, I hate myself. *I left him just like my mother did.* No wonder he's such a mess.

Swallowing back my tears I manage to utter, "Hello?"

"Breslin," he snaps and I steel myself, preparing for the battle that hasn't even started yet.

"Hi, Dad," I say cheerfully, mostly because I know it will piss him off.

I love my father. Or rather, it's not so much *love*...it's pity.

Once upon a time he wasn't such an incorrigible and bitter drunk, but my mother leaving took a toll on us, most of all him.

But I'm the one who lives with the side-effects of her departure.

"I'm late on the rent again and that dang electric company is threatening to shut my power off if I don't pay them soon."

Well, at least he got straight into it this time instead of placating me by asking how my classes were going...and then cutting me off mid-sentence when I started to tell him.

My stomach knots. I have a little money saved, but it's mostly for after I graduate. As it is, I try to send him half my check every pay day, but of course I didn't send him any money from my last two checks.

Because I quit my second job.

Because I didn't want Landon to find out about my second job.

Because I think I might be falling for him.

I press my forehead against the dingy wall of the supply room and force myself to breathe. "How much do you need?"

"A little over a grand." His tone is clipped, aggravated even and it takes everything in me not to yell at him and say things I can't take back.

Things like—maybe if he got off his lazy, drunk ass and got a job of his own, he wouldn't be in this predicament. And that his 21-year-old daughter who's busting her ass in college shouldn't be responsible for putting the roof over a grown man's head. And maybe if he got help for his 15 beer a day habit, the money I send him would go further.

I've forked over my paychecks to him ever since I started working at the age of 14, and for once; I'd love to only have to worry about myself.

But I don't say any of that, instead I mentally calculate the numbers and cringe because sending him a grand is going to put a huge dent in my meager savings account.

I open my mouth to tell him that I'll write the check and send it out in the morning, but he clears his throat and says, "Listen, Bres. I've been thinking."

I hold my breath because lord knows no good comes when my father starts to *think*.

"It's still not too late for you to come home this summer. I talked to Johnny over at the *Tease and Please* and he said he's got an opening for you."

Anger burrows deep in my gut. My father has said some really fucked up things to me in the past, but this is without a doubt, in the top five. "You want me to work as a stripper?"

I fight back the shame that slams into me when thoughts of taking off my top and serving drinks for high class businessmen at my former job swirl through my head.

"Stripper is such a harsh word, sweetheart. Johnny says the term they use 'round there is exotic dancer. You used to like to dance, remember?"

No, that was my mother. I hate dancing and don't have rhythm to save my life.

It's on the tip of my tongue to ask him just how much he's had to drink today, but to my dismay he continues, "Granted, you'll have to lose about 10 or so pounds to fit in and really make a killing there, but we can get you some diet pills or something. You've got your mother's looks and it's time you used it to your advantage. You won't be young forever you know." I'm too flabbergasted to speak as he rambles on. "Come back home and work for Johnny, Bres. Then you can put this college bullshit on hold and—"

Prove everyone in that God forsaken town right about me? Not a chance in hell. "I'll put the check in the mail tomorrow."

I hang up the phone before he can protest or continue this shitty conversation.

My eyes sting with tears and I hate that I'm letting him get to me. I have to remind myself that I'm not the shy and weak girl that I used to be...but right now?

Right now, I feel like her.

I feel someone's presence behind me and I already know who it is before I turn around.

Kit doesn't say a word, because she doesn't have to. Instead she rests her head on my shoulder and squeezes my hand.

"I swear sometimes I hate him," I whisper, a second away from losing it.

"And I hate him even when you don't." She wipes the tears from my eyes and cups my face. "What did the asshole want this time?"

"He's late on the rent and electric. Says he needs a grand."

"Wow he's a real piece of—"

"He also offered me a once in a lifetime job opportunity at the *Tease and Please*. Says his friend will hire me and make all my dreams come true."

Her mouth drops open and I laugh. "All I have to do is drop out of college and drop 10 lbs."

"Jesus," she mutters, then she glares at me. "Please tell me you're not going to send that piece of shit a dime."

I shrug and start organizing some supplies on a shelf. "He's my father, Kit." She puts a hand on her hip and I don't have to look at her to know she's scowling. "He wasn't always this bad."

I draw in a shaky breath. "He really loved her. But that love ended up destroying him in the end."

Because that's what love does. I know that fun fact first hand.

It's why I should be putting an end to things with Landon...not letting myself fall further down the rabbit hole.

"B," she starts and I know the next words out of her mouth before she says them.

Kit's the only person I ever confided in about Asher. Or rather, the truth about what happened.

We met when the powers that be at Woodside University decided to pair us up as roommates.

I counted my lucky stars and knew the moment we met that making the rash decision to attend Woodside University instead of

Falcon University like I had originally planned, was the right call in the end.

Kit is crazy, unpredictable, and her hair color changes with her mood.

But she's one of the kindest, coolest, and best people in the world and I honestly don't think I would have made it through the last three years without her by my side.

"He didn't deserve you," she continues, jabbing her finger in the air.

I start dusting the shelves, not wanting to hear the same words I've heard from her too many times to count.

She lets out a frustrated sigh. "B, you need to stop wasting your golden years on the ghost of assholes' past."

When I stop what I'm doing and give her a look she adds, "You have a good thing going with Landon. He actually realizes what's right in front of him. Don't pull away from him and make him pay for that dickhead's mistakes."

When I stay silent, she stomps her foot and exclaims, "Asher Holden is 6'4 inches and 234 lbs. of pure Douche Canoe."

Here we go. The one-woman *Asher Holden is an asshole* brigade has officially started.

I ignore the way my heart does a double take at the sound of his name...because Kit's right. He is an asshole.

I'm more than grateful that we managed to avoid one another in town during our breaks for the past three years.

Of course, I'm basically a hermit whenever I step foot in that town so it really wasn't all that hard.

Plus, I tend to use any excuse not to stay with my father in the trailer and rent a motel a few towns over, blaming my lack of a visit on having found a job at the motel.

But hey, as long as my father had a steady flow of cash in his pocket for his 24-pack, it didn't matter to him where his daughter spent her nights.

She cocks her head to the side, grips her now platinum blonde hair with bright pink tips, and groans.

Her eyes—which are only a shade off from my green ones—narrow into tiny slits and she takes a step forward. "As far as I'm concerned, anyone who could cheat on you and hurt you shouldn't be breathing." Her expression turns serious and her voice cracks. "I don't care what his reasons were. I'm always going to want to rip off his balls and put them in a blender."

My heart pulls, because again, she's right. I remember back when I told her what happened, I automatically thought she was going to side with Asher seeing as she herself is gay.

Hell, part of my heart even secretly *wanted* her to side with him —the weak part of my heart where Asher still resides wanted an excuse to forgive him for the unforgivable. Because I once loved him so much.

But that wasn't the case—complete opposite. Kit was outraged for me and she picked me up when I fell apart.

And she keeps picking me up whenever I fall apart.

Not many people understand what it does to your soul when you've been cheated on...by the one person you gave everything to.

The one person you trusted.

And the fact that it was a guy—a guy I hated? Causes a swell of self-doubt of epic proportions to come crashing to the surface constantly.

It doesn't just make it hard to trust men...it makes it damn near impossible.

Asher Holden emotionally disfigured me with his betrayal, and even after three years; I'm still not sure how to move on.

There's a place deep inside me, underneath all the hurt and pain — a place that just can't manage to cut the cord that desperately needs to be cut.

Asher wasn't the one who got away...he was the one who left a grisly scar on my heart for the entire world to see.

He's my own aching and constant reminder of the cold, hard truth—*real love can hurt like hell and it's just not worth the risk.*

"Say it," she prompts, her face breaking out into a grin.

When I shake my head, she stomps her foot again. Kit's all of 5'2 to my 5'4 but the girl is a tiny tyrant. One who's pretty much broken every boys heart on campus because she plays for the same team they do. It also doesn't help that she usually ends up going home with the hottest girl in a room at parties.

When she doesn't look like she's going to relent, I do. "It was his loss," I grit through my teeth. "Because I'm beautiful and smart—"

She crosses her arms when my words drift off. "And?"

"And I have a really nice ass."

"Fuck yeah you do."

She wraps her arms around me and I take a deep breath. I hate these little mantras that she swears by, but sometimes...sometimes they're not so bad.

She grabs me by my shoulders. "Now you're going to go out there and spend some time with that hot as fuck genius who can't keep his eyes off you, okay?"

"I can't I'm at work—" I shove her back, panic now rippling through me. "Kit, there's no one at the counter."

She says something but I'm too busy running back out to the front.

Where I find Landon manning the station, much to the confusion and annoyance of the ten or so grumpy customers in line.

"I want a double mocha venti, steamed skim milk, 3 ½ pumps of vanilla syrup, light whipped cream, extra hot, no foam, and a dash of chocolate and cinnamon sprinkled on top," the man on the other side of the counter barks to him.

I roll up my sleeves, preparing to jump into action, but Landon pushes his black rimmed glasses up his nose and makes a face. "Yeah, you can have coffee and milk. Take it or leave it, guy."

The man looks ready to argue, but I'm used to this customer's order since he's a regular. "Coming right up, Mr. Finnegan. Just give me a second."

"Sorry, Landon. You can sit, I've got this." He starts to protest but I turn my head and shout, "Any time today, Kit."

She slinks back out, cradling her cell phone between her cheek and shoulder, talking a mile a minute to who I'm sure is Becca, her new girlfriend.

When three more customers take a spot in line, I hand Mr. Finnegan his order and snap my fingers. "We're *working*, Kit."

She waves me away and continues jabbering on her cell phone.

I love her, I really, really do...but her work ethic truly sucks. But then again, her family is as rich as the day is long so money isn't exactly a problem for her.

She thinks having a job is akin to that of an accessory.

Landon gives me a wink before he takes the next customers order, which lucky for us both isn't anywhere near as complex as Mr. Finnegan's.

Ten minutes later, all the customers have their drinks and Kit finally gets off the phone. "Do you mind if I take my break?"

Landon takes off his apron and throws it on the counter. "You just had one."

"Careful, Landon," she tells him, picking up the apron. "I'm rooting for you."

Landon rolls his eyes before focusing them on me. "You alright?"

I nod, stuffing down the ball of pain working its way through my chest. "Yeah." I look at Kit, silently begging her not to bring up my father or the phone call. "Nothing I can't handle."

He takes a few strides, until he's standing directly in front of me. My mouth goes dry and my heart flutters when his thumb grazes my cheekbone. "Will I be seeing you tonight?"

"Yes—" I pause, because the lack of funds in my bank account and the check I need to write my father is something I can't ignore.

I don't really have a choice other than to beg for my old job back for the time being. I disregard the look Kit's shooting me and I'm thankful Landon can't see it.

Kit might be the worst coworker in the world, but she's a great friend. Therefore, Landon has no idea where it is that I used to work up until four weeks ago.

"I can't. I totally forgot I have this thing that I need to take care of and I won't be done until 2 am."

Kit makes a slitting motion across her throat, but I don't have time to deal with her little temper tantrum about me going back to work at the topless bar.

The disappointment is more than evident on Landon's face. And when his chocolate brown eyes turn sad, my heart aches.

I seriously don't deserve someone like Landon.

As per usual, Landon knows something's a bit off with my statement, but he squeezes my hand and kisses my cheek before he whispers, "Okay, no problem. You have my key, let yourself in whenever you're ready."

His lips touch my forehead and I close my eyes and breathe in his addicting scent. I want to fight my attraction to him, but it's like telling my heart not to beat.

"I'll have tacos waiting for you," he murmurs against my skin and I giggle.

"Jesus, Landon. Even my pussy wants to turn straight and crawl into bed with you now," Kit mutters, much to the horror of the customer who's now standing at the counter.

"Eyes on the menu, lady," she snaps, gesturing to us. "This is an A and B conversation. So I suggest you C your way out before D meaning *me*, jumps over this counter and F's you up!"

"Well I never," the lady gasps, putting her hand over her heart.

"Yeah I bet you haven't." She makes the peace sign and sticks her tongue between her fingers. "Trust me, it shows."

"Kit," I growl, pushing Landon away so I can apologize.

"I'm sorry, Mrs. Carter. She's new."

"She's here almost every day."

I start preparing her order and give her a smile. "I'm working on making her more civil, I promise."

Kit bristles and I hand Mrs. Carter her tea. "The world needs more do-gooders like you, dear," she says before leaving.

I turn to face Kit. "Are you seriously trying to get me fired?"

She looks offended. "Of course not, B. It's not my fault Mrs. Carter is a frigid bitch."

I rub my temples and Landon squeezes my shoulder. "I have to run, Bre. I have a tutoring session starting in 20 minutes."

"Well if you were serious about those tacos, I guess I'll be seeing you later."

He grins before pulling me in for a kiss. My toes curl and I melt into his lips. But the second my lips part and his tongue meets mine, he pulls back. "If you want more of that in addition to the tacos...make sure you stop by."

I bite my lip as I watch him walk over to one of the tables, grab his laptop bag, and walk out the door.

"You're not showing your tits to a bunch of pedophiles at a bar again," Kit says behind me.

Of course, it's when Mr. McGillicutty and his two grandchildren are standing at the counter now. His face pales when one of his granddaughters asks him what a *pedophile* is.

I shoot Kit a death glare and quickly pour two hot chocolates and a cup of black coffee. Then I toss three glazed doughnuts in a bag and hand it to him. "This one's on the house. Sorry about that."

He huffs and gives me a curt nod before leaving.

I don't have the energy to yell at her anymore, so I start wiping down the counters and sweeping the floor.

She hoists herself up, sitting on one of the counter tops I just cleaned. "B, please look at me." Her tone is pleading for me to hear her out and I stop mid sweep, gripping the broom handle.

"Look, I'm like the least judgmental person in the world."

When I make a face she sighs. "Okay, that's not exactly true," she amends. "Point is—I hated when you worked there. I was so damn proud of you for walking out of that hell hole and never looking back."

She nods in the direction of the door. "Landon is good for you, B. And I know you don't want to admit it right now, but I can tell you care about him. And Lord knows, he cares about you. Don't do that to him."

I go back to sweeping. "I'm not doing *anything* to him. But I'm not putting my father out on the street, either."

She jumps off the counter. "But why—"

"Because he's all I have left, Kit." I pick up the pan and bring it to the garbage can. "My father isn't exactly father of the year, but he was there when she wasn't. He was there when she walked out." I go over to the sink and wash my hands. "He could have given me up after she left, but he didn't." I look at her. "I know you don't understand—"

"You're right. I don't."

She reaches underneath the counter and takes out her purse. Before I can stop her, she's writing a check and handing it to me.

I back away. "I'm not taking that."

"Then I'm mailing it to him."

"Kit, it's not your responsibility."

"It's not yours, either.   And I'm hoping one day you finally realize that, but until you do; I have no problem taking care of the issue for you."

"Kit—"

"I love you and I have more money than I know what to do with. I'm not taking no for an answer. You want to do something nice for me? Then don't go back to that fucking bar. Don't do things that you don't really want to do in order to make ends meet for *him*. Don't let another man take another piece of you that he doesn't deserve." She smiles. "Go curl up in bed and eat tacos tonight with the guy who does."

"I can't—"

"You can and you will...because it's non-negotiable."

I open my mouth to argue again but my phone rings. This time, it's the college calling, which causes my stomach to somersault.

With shaky hands, I bring the phone to my ear. "Hello?"

"Is this Breslin Rae?"

"It is." I look at Kit who shoos away the next few customers in line and puts the closed sign on the counter top.

I don't have time to yell at her because my stomach is in knots. I say a silent prayer my scholarship isn't in jeopardy. "Is everything okay?"

"Absolutely," the lady on the other line assures me and I can practically hear my lungs sing when I start breathing again. "I was calling because someone had to drop out of the European Architectural study tour last minute and you're listed as the next alternate student."

I clutch the side of the counter because my head is spinning. I was so disappointed when I wasn't one of the students originally chosen. I had even saved up money working triple shifts through the holidays in preparation last year because I was so certain I would be chosen.

Money.

Most of my savings consists of what I had saved for this trip, and now I have no choice but to hand it over to my father.

"I—" A piece of my heart cracks and I blink back tears. "I'm sorry, I can't—"

I don't get to finish that statement because Kit snatches the phone and says, "Hello, this is her personal assistant speaking. Of course, she'll be going, just tell me where to send the money."

I start shaking my head but Kit runs to the back with my phone and I have no choice but to follow her.

"The tour is for three weeks. Got it." She starts jotting things down on her notepad. "And she leaves when?" There's a pause and then. "Shit."

There's murmuring on the other line and her eyes widen. "Nope. That won't be a problem at all. I'll make sure she has everything she needs and is ready to go in two days."

Two days?

Kit rattles off what I'm sure is a credit card number off the top of her head and I plop down on an empty crate because I'm suddenly lightheaded.

"There's no way I can go on that trip," I tell her when she hangs up the phone and hands it back to me.

"Why not?"

"First off—I no longer have the money. Secondly—I didn't take the time off work. And finally—there's no way I can pack to go to freaking Europe for three whole weeks in two days."

She brushes me off. "One—you do have the money because I've already taken care of it. Two—you've worked here since freshmen year and have never even once called in sick. I'm sure the—" She snaps her fingers. "What's that guy's name? He comes around sometimes. Wears really cheap suits and reeks of gross cologne."

"Larry...otherwise known as our boss."

"Yeah, him. Anyway, I'm sure it won't be an issue. In fact, didn't he cut our hours last week because we're overstaffed this summer?"

When I nod, she continues. "And of course you can pack for Europe in two days. It's called a shopping trip." When I start to protest she says, "And you're not digging into your bank account, it's my treat."

"Kit—"

"And finally," she says, ignoring my objections. "You have to go because I'm going."

"You can't go, Kit. You have to be selected to study abroad. You're not even an architect major, you're a business major—"

She looks like she smelled sour milk. "I'm not going there to study. Hell no, this trip would be strictly for my pleasure." She waggles her eyebrows. "Actually for Becca's pleasure. I want to show her the sights...amongst other things."

I place my head in my hands. "I can't let you pay—"

"It's happening," she says, and the look in her eyes tells me there's no point in arguing anymore.

CHAPTER 6

LANDON

My fingers glide over the ivory keys and my eyes fall shut, getting lost in the waves of sound that permeate my small makeshift home studio.

About an hour ago I recorded the guitar and drums section, but the piano is what will make it really shine; and I can't wait to merge all of it together.

I haven't written lyrics to the piece I'm working on yet, but I'm thinking it might not even need any after all.

It's powerful all on its own. Just like her.

The hand on the far left of the piano hits those deep keys I love so much, giving the song a much darker tone, which is a beautiful contrast to the lighter keys my right hand is delicately strumming over.

It reminds me of Breslin in so many ways, because just like her; the song starts off light—and then when you least expect it, there's a depth that sneaks up on you. One you can't quite grasp because it's just out of your reach.

Even still, the complex rhythm is addicting and one you can't ignore.

The only thing I'm stuck on right now is the melody, because neither my fingers nor my mind can seem to settle on a single tone— therefore the rhythm keeps changing, making the piece particularly complicated for me. Without the right melody to carry the song and make it whole, it won't ever actually *be* a song.

My left hand starts to shake, signaling low blood sugar. I know I should check my level and eat something, but I wave it off because I'm so lost in the music.

That is until I feel her presence enter the room and I open my eyes and look into her green ones. I'm about to stop but she gestures for me to keep going, so I do.

I play Breslin's rhythm without the melody because it's beautiful and strong even without one.

I play my soul out for her and hope with every beat of my heart that she finally lets me inside hers.

I'm falling for this girl standing in front of me. The rational part of my brain knows I shouldn't—not only is she too guarded, it's clear she doesn't want to make this a serious thing.

I'm not the kind of man to hold someone when they want to go. But Breslin's different. I know she cares about me. I know she has feelings for me.

She's just too scared to take the leap because she doesn't think I'll catch her when she does.

So, I'll wait and bide my time. I'll wait for that heart of hers to open up to me.

Because it will be worth it when it happens.

Breslin Rae has her hooks sunk so deep into me I can't see straight when she's around...and I hope she never pulls them out.

I peel my eyes from hers and focus on the music again, my fingers striking all the notes and chords. All the things I'm unable to say to her with words.

When I'm finished playing, she sits and gestures for me to play something else. I know my girl loves the guitar and has a fondness for the stripped and acoustic versions of songs, so I stand up and grab it.

I want to ask her what happened tonight because she's here earlier than she said she would be, but I love that half amazed, half aroused expression on her face and the way she can't seem to take her eyes off me.

I've played in front of large audiences before, I even have a semi-steady gig once a month at a small venue...but it's nothing compared to the energy in the room between us now.

Breslin might want the stable job of an architect, but she'll never be happy unless they're her own designs. The girl is a creator and a visionary if there ever was one, and when I watch her in her element; it's spellbinding.

Therefore, she understands my creative side like no one else ever has, and instead of trying to dim it like my family always does, she pulls it out of me.

I make the split-second decision to reach over and press a few keys on my laptop, letting the piano version I recorded for her a few weeks ago play in the background so she can have the full effect.

She smiles from ear to ear when I start strumming the guitar and tapping my foot. Her smile grows even wider when I open my mouth and start to sing for her, something I've always been self-conscious about, no matter how many times I've heard how great my voice is.

I was born with only partial hearing in my right ear so I constantly second guess myself. The only time I don't is when I'm performing straight from the heart.

And right now, that's exactly where this performance is coming from.

She's damn near glowing as I continue singing her favorite song— Colorblind by the Counting Crows. The irony, given she's an artist and all isn't lost on me.

The song is completely stripped, raw, and exposed. The music and lyrics are both simple and profound at the same time...reminding me of Breslin.

When the song ends she has tears in her eyes, and that's when I make a risky decision.

I switch gears completely, and start to perform a song from a band she says she hates.

I keep telling her to give them a chance, and that she just hasn't found the right song to begin her love affair with my favorite band yet.

I'm hoping this song will be the one. Besides, I can't think of a single person who doesn't like the song *Glycerine* by Bush.

It isn't until she closes her eyes in turmoil and looks like she's fighting back tears—and not the good kind this time—that I realize I've made a horrible mistake.

I guess there's a reason she doesn't like the band after all.

Way to go Landon.

I don't know the asshole responsible for Breslin's pain, and I'm not quite sure what he did to her exactly, but if I ever came face to face with the fucker I swear I'll make him pay for hurting her so much.

I drop the guitar and walk over to her. "I'm sorry. I knew you didn't like the band. I shouldn't have—"

"I actually love the band." She laughs but the tears only fall faster down her cheeks. "It's just...I had my first kiss on my 16th birthday while this song was playing." Her brows draw together and she shakes her head as if shaking off the memory. "Outside in the pouring rain."

"That sounds like a pretty epic first kiss," I say, completely confused now, but not wanting to push her. "Mine was with some chick I never met before during a game of spin the bottle in 8th grade." I lift a shoulder in a shrug. "I never even knew her name and to this day all I remember about her was that her breath smelled like tuna."

Breslin makes a face before she bursts into laughter. "How do you always do that?"

"Do what?"

"Find a way to make me smile through all the pain?" She tucks a strand of hair behind her ear. "You make everything better, Landon. Every single thing."

She looks at me and the air between us shifts. I suck in a breath, because the only thing better than Breslin looking at me like I hung the moon while I'm performing for her? Is the way she's looking at me now.

Like she has some kind of preeminent appetite that only I can satisfy.

She leans forward, her lips ghosting over mine and I don't waste the opportunity to suck that plump bottom lip of hers before I claim her with my mouth entirely.

She reaches for the hem of my t-shirt and yanks it over my head before going for my belt buckle.

Surprise crosses over her features briefly when I lift her up and place her on the piano.

I slowly undo the buttons on her shirt, savoring every inch of smooth, creamy skin that I uncover.

My cock twitches when I pause and laser in on those pink nipples puckering through the turquoise lace of her bra.

I make quick work of removing her jeans and undoing my own.

"Landon, your hands are shaking. When was the last time you ate?"

I give her a smug smile and trail my fingers along the sides of her panties. "Funny you should mention that, because I'm about to have one hell of a meal right now."

I shred the flimsy fabric down the middle and she gasps when I dive head first between her legs.

"Landon," she screams, slapping at my back. "You need to eat."

My response is to suck on her clit right before I roll my tongue and start fucking her with my mouth.

Her hips buck and she pounds the surface of the piano with her palms. A moment later, some part rock, part orchestral song fills the room and I laugh to myself.

Breslin's always told me she wanted to be able to experience music like I do. She like so many others think you listen to music, but that couldn't be further from the truth...because you *feel* it.

The timbre of the guitar is dark and sonorous and I deepen the strokes of my tongue to reflect that. Breslin's reaction is damn near instantaneous, she pulls my hair and grinds her pelvis into my face.

A second later the music switches up and I focus on the violin, which is light and mellow compared to the guitar. Breslin mewls and whimpers, begging me for more, but I don't give it to her...not until I choose my next instrument to focus on.

The drums.

I flick her clit, keeping in perfect time to the beats. She raises her hips and meets every stroke of my tongue, losing herself just like I want her to.

"More drums, Landon. Fuck, I need more drums—" She cuts herself off with a long moan when I decide to focus on the lyrics and start humming along with the singer.

She gyrates those hips of hers into my face again and I finally focus on my favorite instrument...*the piano.*

In my world the piano brings the perfect balance to any song, something Breslin realizes when I slip two fingers inside her and latch onto her clit.

She pulses and vibrates around my tongue, gripping my hair so tightly my scalp stings. "I need you to fuck me, Landon. Right now."

"We're not up to the crescendo yet," I say between long, languid, teasing licks and her head rolls back.

"This song is over twenty minutes," she whines, before the drums pick up again and I proceed to fuck her harder with my fingers.

Her eyes lock with mine as she clenches around them, playing her own little game now. One that's working because the music seems to fade into the background and becomes louder all at the same time.

"God, I need to come so bad," she moans. "Please make me come with that thick cock of yours deep inside me."

I groan and have to give my cock a jerk because there's nothing hotter than hearing my innocent angel with filthy wings talk dirty to me.

Fuck the crescendo.

Silently thanking the fact that she's on birth control because my body can't wait another second, I hitch one of her legs around my waist and enter her a moment later.

I hear all the instruments thrum together and I know she's close. I keep my thrusts in time to the music, every single sound now becoming one big whirl as the world's most perfect symphony plays inside my head because Breslin's the conductor.

My movements become rougher, just the way I know she likes it and her eyes roll back. "I'm so close," she rasps. "So fucking close."

I know she is, and if she grips my cock any tighter I'm gonna get off before she does.

I reach between us and start strumming her clit. There's no way I'm going to last with her naked and writhing underneath me the way she is now. My only choice is to speed things along.

I pull her nipple into my mouth and suck, rubbing her clit between my two fingers as I continue driving into her.

Her chest rises and falls and she screams my name right before she spasms and a rush of wetness surrounds my cock.

Two pumps later I'm collapsing on top of her and the room is spinning.

Something's not quite right and my body feels off, despite just having been on cloud nine.

My head is fuzzy, and I know it's my blood sugar dropping. The problem is, I'm so out of it, I can't bring myself to move.

"Bre." Her name on my lips is a whisper. I hate being so weak around her but I'm a moment away from passing out.

She moves out from underneath me and what feels like a second later something sweet is hitting my lips.

I guzzle the container of orange juice, suddenly thankful for the care packages my mother seems to send me every week.

Breslin doesn't say a word, she just holds the juice and brushes my hair out of my eyes, something I'm grateful for; because there's nothing worse than being nagged when you feel like absolute shit.

I've struggled with diabetes since I was 12, and I know I should do a better job with my health. It's just not so easy when you're 21, a musician, and a double major in college.

I don't tell many people about my illness for two reasons. One—I don't need or want their sympathy. And two—I don't need or want their unsolicited advice. Everyone seems to know someone who has diabetes and with that comes a slew of information that I either already know or don't care to know.

Both my illness and my hearing are impairments, but I refuse to focus on those aspects of my life.

I want to live in the here and now.

And right now? I have a gorgeous girl staring down at me with so much adoration in her eyes, I find myself feeling dizzy for a whole different reason.

"Landon," she whispers, running her hand along my jaw. She doesn't say it, because she doesn't have to.

I know I fucked up. I know I probably scared her.

I know it wasn't the first time I've done that to her.

I sit up. "I'm okay. I'm fine."

"I feel like it was my fault. I knew you were shaking before and I—"

"You didn't do anything wrong."

She nuzzles against my chest and I wrap my arms around her. "Are you okay?"

"I'm still a little out of it," I tell her honestly. "But I'll be fine." I tip her chin up. "Thanks to you running and getting me juice."

"Landon, I don't want to sound like a pain and I know you hate talking about this but you can't constantly ignore your body." She rubs her temples. "I mean what if I wasn't here? What are you going to do when I'm in Europe for the next three weeks?"

Europe...for three weeks? Just how out of it was I?

The questions I have must be written all over my face because she looks down at the ground and mutters, "Shit." Before she squeezes her eyes shut. "This is not how I planned to tell you."

I stroke her cheek and she leans into my touch. "Babe, you're going to Europe for three weeks, not jail." I hop off the piano and throw my jeans back on. "When do you leave?"

"Two days," she says, failing to hide the gleam in her eyes. "There was a spot that opened up last minute for the Architectural study tour and they called me."

Her face breaks out into the biggest smile I've ever seen, and I'm honestly thrilled for her. There's no way I would do anything to damper her happiness, even if I am a little sad about our time together being cut short.

Besides, going to Europe for the rest of the summer sounds like an amazing opportunity and she'd be dumb not to take it.

I lift her into my arms and she wraps her legs around me. "I was so afraid you were going to tell me not to go." I can hear her voice breaking with emotion and my chest stings.

"I would never stunt your dreams, Bre. I would never try to tame you."

I just want to love you.

I put her down and cradle her face in my hands. I can't think of a better time than right now to tell her how I feel. "Breslin, I'm in love with you."

It's not the most poetic or profound way to tell a girl how you feel, but hell, it's my first time ever uttering the words to another person.

Her mouth parts in surprise, her body tenses, and her face falls.

In other words, the exact opposite reaction I was hoping for.

She picks her clothes up off the floor and begins getting dressed, almost like she can't get out of here fast enough.

If it wasn't for the tears clogging her eyes, I'd think she didn't care about me at all right now.

The silence between us is deafening and since I know she's not going to break it, it's up to me.

I open my mouth, but just then she whispers, "This was never supposed to be anything serious."

My hands clench at my sides and a bolt of anger shoots through me. As usual, this is Breslin's standard response whenever I bring up anything long-term.

I glare at her. "Maybe for you it wasn't."

Another tear rolls down her face, and it only makes me angrier. She wouldn't be all choked up right now if she didn't have feelings for me. I don't understand why it's so hard for her to just take the leap. Why it's so hard to trust me.

"I'm not him," I grind out.

She sits down and puts her head in her hands. "I never said you were. I know you're not him."

"Then let me in. For months you've been skating around this issue. You keep saying you don't want anything serious, but the way you look at me and the way you act around me says otherwise."

I kneel in front of her and reach for her hands. "I know I sprung this on you, and I don't expect you to say it back; and I don't want you to if you're not there yet, but I need you to trust me and jump."

"It's not that easy."

"Why?"

"Because he cheated on me," she yells. "I loved him so much and he cheated on me with the enemy."

I knew what her ex did to her was bad, but this is even worse than I thought. "Shit—"

"He broke my heart into a thousand pieces along with every ounce of trust I gave him. All on the same night I gave him my virginity."

She laughs bitterly. "I loved him. I loved him *so* damn much. It was a hit I never saw coming, I was completely blindsided that night."

She wipes her tears with the back of her hand. "I'm trying to get to the same place you are, Landon. Because you're right, I do have feelings for you. Real feelings. And I'm trying so hard to demolish the space in my heart that he still takes up in order to let you claim it all, because I want you to. But I'm just not ready yet."

She stands up. "I just...I need—"

"Time?" I offer, standing next to her now.

She nods. "Just a little more." Her hand goes to the back of my neck and she looks me right in the eyes. "I'm into you, Landon. I'm so into you." Her lips skim over mine and I can feel her heart beating erratically. "You give me butterflies."

I close the short distance between our lips. I pour every single ounce of passion I have for her into a single kiss and her body melts against me.

"I'll wait for you," I say before I take her mouth again, because I can't help myself.

"Don't." Her voice is broken and fragile, defeated. "I don't want you to wait for me"

I let out a frustrated sigh. Round and round we go again. "Why?"

"I don't want any obligations or commitments. Not while I'm in Europe."

"Bre—"

"No." She backs away. "We'll check in when I get home, see

where we both stand then. But you're free to do what you want. It's just the way it has to be."

"What I want is you." I take a step forward but she takes another one away from me. My chest tightens with every step she takes because it feels like she's walking out of my life for good.

She pauses right before she walks out the door. "Take care of yourself."

Her voice cracks on the last word before she slams the door behind her.

And I'm left hating the man who ruined the future we'll never have.

CHAPTER 7

ASHER

A pair of eyes appraise me up and down and I smile.

Another pair of eyes burn a hole into my back when I turn around and I grin. *Tonight's going to be fun.*

The grin wipes clean off my face when I glance at the clock on the wall. There's still another five hours left in my shift and I'm the only one here tonight, which means I have to wait to get off until after I get off.

Muttering a curse, I grab a towel to wipe down the bar. My phone vibrates and I don't even have to look at it to know it's a text from my brother Preston, most likely telling me he and his new girl-friend Becca are on their way.

He hasn't been dating her long and she goes to a different univer-sity than he does, but from what I can tell; he's completely head over heels for her.

I haven't met her yet, but I hope she's not like the ditzy twats he's usually so fond of.

Not that I'm one to talk, since I've been enjoying them myself this summer; but I want more for my brother than I do for me.

Preston's going places and he doesn't need some gold digger taking advantage of him.

My entire body freezes and my breath stutters in my chest.

Christ, I sound just like him.

I haven't spoken to my father in months, not since Kyle leaked the tape and ruined my future.

Needless to say, my father didn't take watching his son get blown by another dude so well.

Neither did my coaches or my teammates. Of course, Duke's didn't kick me out for *that* reason, though. They blamed it on my poor school performance and low grades in the end.

Grades that I'd maintained for three years straight without so much as a warning.

But one leaked video from high school was all it took to make everything I'd spent my life working my ass off for vanish.

I guess karma really does exist after all. I just wish it would have taken Kyle out first.

If it wasn't for my brother Preston, who knows where I'd be right now.

After my father cut off my inheritance and the university kicked me out, I had nowhere to go. Nowhere to live.

Thankfully, Preston gave me some of his inheritance money under the radar and I was able to get a small studio apartment and find a job at some hole in the wall bar a few towns over from his university.

I hate mooching off my younger brother, but I intend to pay him back for every dime—with interest.

As soon as I figure out what the hell I'm supposed to do with my life...again.

Football was my everything.

And all because of my stalker, forced roommate, and undercover blackmail lover catching me fucking both my hot tutor and her even hotter boyfriend at the same time, my dreams were stolen.

I'd severely underestimated Kyle's jealousy and his obsession with me.

But most of all? I had enough of being blackmailed by him and being forced into a fucked up relationship I didn't want to be in.

I needed my freedom back.

I had an itch I was dying to scratch since freshman year and I didn't care about the consequences at that moment.

So I fucked her...and him.

I have no regrets. It was a damn good time.

That is until he barged in our dorm and started screaming that I was cheating on him and they both grabbed their clothes and bounced.

Things only got worse when I reminded an irate Kyle that I never actually *wanted* to be with him in the first place and that as far as I was concerned he was never my boyfriend.

Because there's only one person in the world who still has my heart.

And that will never change.

However, I refuse to let myself think about her. Because the weight that crushes my chest and the remorse that slams into my heart is downright unbearable when I do.

The fucked up thing is that part of me actually hopes she heard about the scandal that went down at Duke's through the grapevine.

Not that I think I'll ever get Breslin back, but hell; maybe she'll put two and two together and somehow realize that it was blackmail.

But knowing her, she's most likely working her ass off at Falcon University and is enjoying her life like she's supposed to.

Like I want her to.

I've wanted to reach out to her so many times over the years, but I couldn't.

Because there's not a damn thing I could ever say to make up for the way things went down between us.

I've done a lot of growing up the past three years, but that doesn't excuse my past transgressions.

And while I didn't cheat on her because I wanted to, I took something from her for my own selfish reasons.

I hurt her. God only knows how much.

And for that, I'll never forgive myself, no matter how many times Preston says I need to.

I scan the bar, I can still feel the two sets of eyes appraising me from head to toe.

I grin at him first and he bites his bottom lip before my gaze drifts to her and she bats her eyelashes and licks her lips.

With the way their stare is fixated on me, one would never guess they're engaged to be married at the end of the month.

Preston told me not to get involved with them...but I told him to mind his business.

It's not like it was my relationship on the line, and I'm more than happy to provide my services to the both of them. They're a young, attractive, and successful couple. Neither of them have a problem turning any heads.

And it's kind of reassuring how open their relationship is.

And it's definitely a turn on watching her get all hot and bothered by her man sucking my dick.

And yeah, the money they throw my way isn't bad either.

The way I see it, I'm helping to make their fantasy a reality.

And they're helping me put food in the fridge and pay a few bills. No one gets hurt with our little arrangement, and after it's done they go home, cuddle, and watch reruns of *Friends* in their million-dollar home located in the suburbs.

I walk over and my smile grows bigger, purposely putting my dimples on display for them.

"What can I get you two?" I throw the towel over my shoulder and Gwen's gaze drops to my belt buckle and stays there.

"You?" Her voice sounds out of breath and my mind conjures up images of what her soon to be husband's hand is doing underneath her skirt.

I laugh and give her a wink. "My shift isn't over for a few hours."

She pouts and I turn to look at Tom. Believe it or not, he's the shyer of the two; which turns me on even more because I love having all the control when we're together. And call me crazy, but I think that's what really gets him off. He owns a private stockbroker firm and I think the high stress job really wears him down and he enjoys being told what to do and giving up the control to me in the bedroom. Or wherever it is that we end up during our little rendezvous.

"And what can I get for *you*?"

He loosens his tie and looks around the bar, checking to see if anyone is listening before he says, "I'll have what she's having."

That only makes Gwen moan and I venture to where—sure as fuck— his hand has disappeared under that short skirt of hers.

I press myself against the bar, attempting to hide the giant hard on I now have. I'm two seconds away from calling my boss up and telling him I came down with a bad case of food poisoning in order to have my way with the both of them, but just then the door opens and in walks Preston and some blonde chick whose tits—nice, albeit fake ones—are spilling out of her blouse with every bouncy step she takes.

I try not to roll my eyes, this is exactly what or rather, *who* I was afraid Preston would end up with.

Another trophy wife just like our mother. A mother who never cared about the way her husband acted with her first born as long as the neighbors never overheard the arguing and she had access to all the credit cards.

I swallow my anger down, because one look at Preston and I know he's happy with her. After all he's done for me, the least I can do for him is give the woman he loves some respect.

After the scandal broke out at Duke's and I was at my lowest—I ended up breaking down and telling Preston there was something wrong with my dick because it was attracted to dudes' and that I needed to be fixed because I was obviously gay.

His response was to give me a big hug and tell me that gay or not, there was nothing wrong with me and no matter how our father would react to the video—it would never change the fact that I was his brother.

He also pointed out that my dick wasn't gay or straight...it was what he called...*greedy.*

He was there for me during the second worst day of my life. Therefore, I could be nice to his future Barbie trophy wife for him.

I open my mouth to greet them but I'm cut off when some shrill voice exclaims, "Oh my God, babyface. You didn't tell me you had a twin."

I raise a brow and look at my brother. One for the obvious reason —that's a shit nickname. And two—we're not twins.

I mean, we do have a resemblance to one another given we're brothers, but we're certainly not identical. He's 6'3 to my 6'4 and his body is leaner and has less muscle due to hitting the gym and not a sports field. His eyes are also grayish blue instead of clear blue like mine, and his hair is dark brown as opposed to my dark blond.

We do have those deep Holden dimples that make people lose their shit, though.

And unlike me who's clad in jeans and a t-shirt most of the time, he's wearing one of his suits because he most likely just got off from one of his summer internships.

The fact that he even made it all the way down to my job in the middle of a work week means his visit is important.

My brother is ridiculously smart. Smart enough he attends *Yale* and is at the top of his class. How he met his latest girlfriend is anyone's guess, because she doesn't seem like she travels in the same circle as he does.

I motion for them to take a seat and I try my hardest not to look at her tits which are now resting on top of the damn bar. I feel bad for her poor excuse for a shirt, it's barely containing those puppies, something everyone around us stops and takes notice of.

This has to be a test of some sort—because who meets someone's family member for the first time when they're a sneeze away from showing some nip?

I see my brother smirk and everything becomes crystal clear.

This is nothing more than a physical thing between them...clearly.

Or at least that would have been my guess until I see the way he looks at her. And unlike the rest of us, he's looking at her eyes.

"Can I get you something to drink?"

"Do you have any Cristal?"

I smile, because if I don't I'm going to say something that will end with her leaving in tears and my brother disowning me.

I gesture around the bar. "Sorry, sweetheart, we're all out. Snoop Dogg and his buddy Jay-Z ran through here just a moment ago and ordered everything we had in stock."

"Oh my god, *really*?" She mopes and Preston puts an arm around her, giving me the stink eye.

I decide to ignore Barbie for now, because he's the person I want to interact with.

I reach in my back pocket and whip out my wallet. I haven't saved much over the summer, but it's something.

He holds up a hand. "I'm not here for that."

Barbie puckers her lips and a crease forms between her eyebrows when he refuses the money I'm offering him for a second time.

I glare at her and she straightens her spine.

"So what brings you down here?"

Barbie tries to interject but he shakes his head, points to the Jukebox, and hands her a few bills. "Look, babe, they have music. Go dance."

I look around at the 60-year-old drunk regulars who's eyes suddenly light up like Christmas trees and I stifle a laugh.

"You sure that's a good idea?"

He gives me a look. A look I haven't seen since we were kids and he accidentally broke one of our father's prized trophies and my stomach sinks.

Preston's in deep shit.

I force myself to breathe, because just like back then, whatever he managed to get himself into now, I know I'll take the rap for.

Barbie twirls her hair. "Um, I don't know how to work that."

I pinch the bridge of my nose because she's reaching the end of my short fuse. "It's like a D.J without arms. You just press a few buttons. It's not all that hard to figure out unless you have zero brain cells instead of five."

She stares at me wide-eyed before she hops off the bar stool and skedaddles.

"You didn't have to be so mean to her," Preston snaps. "You actually have a lot more in common than you think."

I watch her fumble with the Jukebox and I snort. It isn't until a few men walk over to her and one of them press a button that music starts playing.

"Yeah? Like what?"

"She's into sports. Believe it or not, she attends Woodside University and is majoring in Sports Medicine."

I cross my arms, because there's no way in hell that's true. Then again Woodside is a shit University, they'll let just about anyone in.

"What's her favorite sport?" I ask, because I'm truly curious now. "And is she planning on opening her own practice after she graduates or traveling with a team?"

He averts his gaze, looking sheepish. "Yoga. Her dream is to open her own yoga studio."

Yeah, I should have seen that coming.

I start howling with laughter and have to brace myself against the bar.

"Jesus, you're such an asshole," he mutters. "I almost forgot what a judgmental prick you can be sometimes."

He narrows his eyes and I know the words on the tip of his tongue.

The words he won't say.

I'm just like him.

My laughter comes to a halt. "Sorry, brother. You obviously came here to talk about something important. What's up?"

Maybe yoga Barbie wasn't too far off with her assessment of us being twins after all, because when he gives me another look—I know exactly what kind of trouble he's in.

He made a bet with the wrong bookie and they're going to collect soon.

"Fuck, Preston, I thought you were done with that shit for good?"

He had an issue with gambling a few years ago, one that almost ended up with him in the hospital, but luckily, I was able to work out a deal and things were fine.

I get that Preston likes to roll the dice and take his chances in life. And I know his brain is like a computer when it comes to numbers and odds and he's going to make a killing when he opens his slew of businesses after he graduates because he's hands down one of the smartest motherfuckers around—but playing with fire like this is going to get him burned, or worse, *killed* one day if he's not careful.

"How long?" My voice comes out low and deadly, because not only am I disappointed, I'm pissed.

"A few months." He rubs the back of his neck. "It's not the same people as before. In fact, one of them, the head guy; is an assistant college football coach."

His gaze drifts back to yoga Barbie who's currently dancing those tits out of her shirt across the room. "And Becca's uncle."

I may not be the smartest guy in most rooms, but even I can connect the dots of this fucked up situation now. "So you're not actually dating her because you want to, she's basically keeping tabs on you because she's his goddamn lackey."

"I wouldn't go that far, I mean she has her good points." He wiggles his eyebrows and I seriously fight the urge to punch him because this shit is not amusing at all. "She's a sweet girl, Asher. It's not exactly a hardship dating her."

"It will be when this messed up *coach* and his undercover gambling team take out your kneecaps before they put a bullet in your chest."

I want him to tell me I'm over exaggerating and that it's not that serious. I want him to tell me that he settled for a fee and that he has a plan to weasel it out of our father. I want him to tell me there's a way I can fight this asshole and win like I did the last time he got into this mess and whatever debt he owes will go away.

"How powerful are they?" It's the question I should have started out with.

He pales. "They have ties to the mob."

"How much do you owe?"

"More than I can pay."

"How much," I repeat, my tone sharper than before.

"Six."

"Thousand?"

"Figures."

"How the fuck does that even happen?"

He runs a hand down his face. "I lost the last two bets, which has never happened before, and instead of paying what I owed, I got cocky and tripled each bet."

"You know they were playing you, right? Giving you the wrong info or some shit so you would make the wrong bet. There's no way you'd lose twice."

"Yeah, I realize that now, big brother. Thanks." He takes a sip of his water. "The cuts were nice at first, I kept winning for months, thought they were reputable."

"Bookies are never reputable, dumbass."

He stands up and tosses money on the bar. "It was great seeing you, brother. Take care of yourself."

"Preston," I grind out as he walks to the door. "Don't leave. You came here because you needed me. Whatever it is you know I'm going to do it. Just tell me what's up."

His shoulders tense and then relax before he spins back around. "It will only be for a year. Everything including room and board—Hell, even tutoring—will be taken care of for you as long as you take them to the playoffs and then the championship this year."

My head starts spinning. "What—"

I'm cut off when yoga Barbie bounces her and her tits back over and smiles from ear to ear. "So, did you tell him the big news?"

"I was working up to it," Preston mutters before she claps her hands and says, "My uncle is so excited that you're going to be the new starting quarterback at Woodside University!"

"You have the best arm out there," Preston says, looking at me earnestly. "Blackmail video or not, you deserve to be out on that field."

"I can't guarantee a championship for a team that hasn't seen one since the 70s, Preston," I shout, recalling their horrendous statistics in my head. "A football team is more than just a good quarterback."

"They'll kill me, Asher."

"Oh yeah," Yoga Barbie chimes in. "They totes will if you don't take the offer."

"When—"

"You're going to need to move within the next two days. Classes won't start for another three weeks, but the Dean had a look at your academic record and won't grant you a scholarship until you agree to tutoring for English. You have to maintain a C+ or better in all your classes, in addition to the side table agreement from the assistant coach."

I choke on my saliva. There's no way I'll be able to do that. On my absolute best day I'm lucky to get a D in English.

He rubs his forehead. "I'd tutor you but—"

"You can't because you're gearing up for your second year at Yale."

He nods. "I'm sorry, Asher. But I heard the tutor is good. And if worse comes to worst you can probably pay him off and work out a deal with him."

He stands up. "But if you can't, you're smart, Asher, I know you'll be fine." He smiles. "Think of this opportunity as your second chance. You love football and if anyone can bring a crappy team back from the brink of death it's you."

I ignore the way my chest flutters at the thought of being out on the field again. "Preston."

Yoga Barbie looks at her watch. "Can we go? I told you I need to go shopping before I leave for Europe."

When I give Preston a questioning look he says, "She's going to Europe with some friends for the next three weeks." He hands her his keys. "Go wait in the car, I'll be there soon."

She stands up on her tiptoes and pulls him into a kiss. One that's far too inappropriate for a trashy, run down bar—and that's saying something—before she bolts out the door.

I walk over to him. "Preston—"

He cuts me off with a hug. "Thank you. No one looks out for me the way you do. I don't know how I'm ever going to repay you."

"I could fail at this and get us both killed."

"You won't," he says. "Put it this way—if I had to make a sure bet on anything in my life. It would be on you."

I stuff my hands in my pockets. "I guess I really don't have much of a choice in the matter."

"Thank you."

I nod my head in the direction of the door. "Does this mean you and yoga are done now?"

"No." He grins. "Believe it or not I'm into her. She's really open and free spirited, it's kind of hot."

I roll my eyes as I watch him walk out the door.

I feel those two sets of eyes burning a hole into my back again, and it's my turn to grin; because I've never needed to get off more than I do right now.

CHAPTER 8

BRESLIN

I look out the plane window and groan as Kit continues to tell me all about how wrong it was for me to end things with Landon before I left.

I seriously regret being nice and letting Becca borrow my only pair of headphones now. I glance over at her bopping her head along to the music while Kit rambles on and on about how I keep letting Asher Holden ruin everything good in my life and how I need to take the control back.

She even went as far as to make a pro and con list. Well, her version of one anyway because all the pros were on Landon's side and the cons were on Asher's.

It was a futile attempt though, because I already know better than anyone what a virus Asher is—one that contaminates and surrounds my heart like a force field, restricting anything good from entering and preventing any of the bad from dissipating.

And Landon...he's everything Asher's not. He's safe, sensible, and sweet. Not wild, reckless, and an overall asshole like Asher.

Landon gave me back the butterflies I once thought were dead.

He was like a jump start straight to my heart, awakening things within me I thought were long gone.

Landon is good for me, *healthy* even.

And I know, it *was* stupid of me to let him go, but I had to. Because until I find a way to let Asher and all of our memories go for good...he's going to continue dominating my every waking thought.

And Landon deserves more than that.

He deserves a girl who doesn't need a safety net with love like I do. A girl who could go all in, no holds barred because she isn't still nursing all her painful wounds from the past.

He deserves a whole heart...not half.

Because try as I might to forget him...that other half will always belong to someone else. Someone who doesn't even deserve it.

I wasn't just in love with Asher...I was obsessed with him. He'd walk in a room—and while people around me would reek of envy because of who he was—every nerve in my body orbited into a different dimension. My heart and brain would fizzle and I'd hold my breath with every step he'd take toward me. I was so in love with him, he made me downright certifiable.

He was my fixation, my neurosis...and ultimately, my demise.

Because there's no recovery from a love like that.

Or a heartbreak.

You'd think my infatuation with him would have let me see all the signs. The crash that was bound to be my undoing.

And no matter how many times I go over it in my head, it never gives me the clarity that I'm seeking. It only makes the overwhelming self-doubt and this feeling that I'm not good enough slink into my innermost thoughts until I'm drowning in it.

And yet...no matter how many times I try to convince myself that what we had wasn't real...some part deep inside me swears that it *was*.

And that right there is what tethers me to him after all these years. That and this violent need I have to make him *pay* for hurting me so much.

"I can't believe I'm about to say this," Kit says, digging around for something in her purse. "But maybe you should reach out to him. Get some kind of closure for once and all so you can finally move on."

My stomach flips just as the wheels on the plane touch the runway. The captain makes an announcement over the loudspeaker but I don't hear a word of it.

"No," I say sharper than I intended and Kit makes a face.

There's no way in hell I could ever see what Asher was up to...because once I lit that match and gave in?

There would be a fire. An irrational, obsessed fire that couldn't be contained. It's why I avoided social media altogether and avoided googling him like the plague for all these years.

I don't need to see where he ended up and trek down that bleak tunnel of doom with no light at the end.

The captain makes another announcement and I switch my phone off airplane mode. Something I almost regret doing when I see two texts from Landon pop up on my screen. One wishing me a safe flight and the other telling me to call him so we can talk.

Sadness crawls up my spine until it stomps on my heart. I want nothing more than to respond to Landon...take back ending things with him.

But there's no way I can give him those things until I can figure out what the first step toward giving him what I so badly want to is.

I clutch my carry on to my chest and take a deep breath.

Because...maybe...just maybe the first step starts here. In a different country, far away from my past and my present.

My heart is going to let go of Asher for good and give Landon every damn part of me that he deserves before my three weeks are up, I decide.

No more of this downward spiral. I'm going to force my heart to choose a final destination by the time my feet land on Woodside's soil again.

I walk over to the luggage terminal where the rest of my class-mates are already gathered and I smile the biggest of smiles.

Something big is going to happen during these three weeks.

I can feel it.

CHAPTER 9

ASHER

"Asher Holden."

The man—Luis Crane—otherwise known as my new head coach says my name like he still can't believe I'm here in the flesh.

I steal a glance at the man standing beside him—the assistant coach—Vincent Dragoni. In other words, the fucker who put me in this position. His eyes narrow, reminding me of what will happen to both me and Preston if I tell the head coach my real reason for wanting to come play at Woodside University.

Dragoni already cornered me no less than one hour after I first stepped foot on campus and said this little arrangement was off and so was Preston's head if I squealed to Coach Crane about anything going on under the radar.

Apparently, the head coach thinks I reached out to Dragoni and I'm here on my own accord. Coach Crane was so thrilled at the prospect of *Asher Holden* coming here, he pulled some massive strings to make it happen, including getting the Dean at Woodside to grant me a scholarship, despite my poor English grades.

I'm beyond pissed at Preston for putting us both in this position, but every time I think of being back on the field, my entire body damn near sings with euphoria and possibilities.

Maybe Preston was right. Maybe this is my second chance. Not only am I back on the field where I belong, but now I can finally have the college experience like I've always wanted without Kyle being a constant anchor dragging me down.

Hell, maybe if I work hard enough a scout will still take a chance and sign me after all is said and done. They'll have no choice but to stop and take notice if I manage to bring one of the worst college football teams back on top again.

Coach Crane looks at Dragoni. "Give us a few minutes."

Dragoni makes his way to the door, but not before giving my shoulder a sharp squeeze and saying, "Welcome to the team, Asher. I'm sure you'll do just fine this year...as long as you follow our *guidance.*"

I don't miss the real meaning behind his words. I give him a curt nod before he leaves.

On paper, Crane seems like he should be a fairly decent coach. I haven't done a lot of research on him, but a quick google search told me he used to be a quarterback in the NFL back in the day, but it was short lived due to a shoulder injury. But that's not what makes me question his ability as a coach. It's the fact that Woodside hasn't had a championship in decades and he's been here for the last eight years.

I stuff my hands in my pockets and look up to the ceiling. This conversation hasn't even started and already it's awkward as fuck.

Not only am I *not* looking forward to being the starting quarterback for a horrible team like the Woodside Wolverines—I know he knows about the scandal at Duke's...he just hasn't brought it up yet.

He leans back in his chair, assessing me. I feel like I'm under a microscope and right when I'm about to ask if I can leave, he says, "Just so we're clear, I don't give a shit who you stick your pecker in."

I don't know whether to laugh or to deny what he's not even accusing me of.

"The only thing I care about," he continues. "Is how you play out on that field and that you give it everything you've got." His expression turns serious. "I know you have your doubts about me and this team." He leans forward and his kind eyes turn hard. "Just like I know you don't really want to be here."

I open my mouth to tell him he's wrong, but he holds up a finger. "Don't start off what will be the most important relationship of your life for the next year with a lie, Asher."

I nod in agreement and he smiles to himself. "It's funny how things work out."

I have no idea what he means by that statement, but I don't have time to question him because he shoves a piece of paper in my hand.

"I've taken the liberty of talking with the Dean and coming up with a schedule for you this semester."

I scan it, seeing the usual core classes, English included. "Thanks —" My sentence drops when I see what electives he's chosen for me. "Ethics? Painting? What the hell?"

I'm expecting him to tell me it's some kind of mistake but he shrugs. "Those are going to help shape you into a better quarterback, trust me."

I take a step forward. "Ethics I can maybe wrap my head around but Painting?"

A smile touches the corner of his lips and my annoyance grows. "You're going to be the big man on campus here, Holden. Something that from my understanding, you've had a lot of experience with in the past." He folds his arms across his chest and meets my eyes. "Taking an art class will force you to think creatively...something every great quarterback should be able to do. It will also challenge you and make you see things differently, and ultimately; pull you out of your comfort zone and allow you to observe the world around you, a world that's much bigger than you."

Great, my coach is apparently some kind of fucking Yoda in his spare time.

I turn to walk out but he slams his hand on the desk. "I didn't dismiss you, *Holden*. We're not done talking."

"What else needs to be said, *Coach*."

I'm aggravated and annoyed. Not only do I not want to be here, I really don't want to take these shitty classes. I'm a fucking liberal arts major for Christ's sake and the quarterback at this god-awful university. My schedule should be a walk in the park.

"That entitled attitude won't get you far with me. Great arm or not, I'll send your ass packing quicker than you can say 'has been'." He gestures to the chair across from his desk. "Now take a goddamn seat."

I begrudgingly sit...might as well get this over with.

"I've pulled some strings with the head of the student center and was able to get you a tutor."

When I don't say a word, because I already know about the tutor, he hands me another piece of paper. "Landon Parker is one of the best tutors on campus. He's also the TA in the Ethics and English courses you'll be taking. I've spoken to him personally about how important it is for you to keep your grades up and he's promised that he will do everything he can to help you this year."

A personal tutor for an entire year? The last thing I want is a desperate nerd following me around campus like some kind of puppy dog.

"That seems a bit excessive," I argue. "It's mostly just English class that I have issues with. I've always done fine with the rest of my classes."

"I know," he says. "It's part of the reason why the Dean agreed to the scholarship. With the exception of English, your grades are good."

I can see the confusion on his face now. It's the same look I've had from every guidance counselor and tutor in the past. How can I do well in things like Math and History and royally suck when it comes to English?

Easy—English is boring as fuck and not enough to keep me interested. And the books they insist on forcing us to read and write papers about are better used as coasters.

Math and History come down to nothing more than memorizing a series of rules and facts. And as long as you do that...you can't possibly fail. Hell, the answers are already given to you.

When it comes down to it, I prefer things that are logical. It's the so-called creative shit that grinds my gears.

Breslin flashes across my mind briefly, because she was always so good at the creative shit. It was just another thing about her that I admired and loved. Remorse fills my chest but I stuff those memories down and focus on the conversation again, because there's no doubt in my mind that it will be the most important one I'll have this year.

I shift in my seat as I listen to him ramble on and on about what is expected of me. I quickly come to the frightening realization that arguing with my new coach won't work. Because both me and my brother's fate is in my hands, literally. So even if this man decides he wants me to wake up at 4 am and scrub toilets in order to remain on the team...I'll have to do it.

My stomach drops and I become lightheaded. I'm so tired of being in the fucking position of having to bend to everyone's will and never doing what I want.

I don't even realize that I've zoned out until he's reaching across the desk and handing me a bottle of water. "Take a deep breath, son. I know it's overwhelming but I'm not in the business of setting my players up to fail."

"Yeah, your track record really supports that," I bite back and I immediately regret it when I see pain flash in his eyes.

"You don't always have to win in order to win," he grumbles, adjusting the cap on his head.

"Then what's the point?" I look him right in the eyes, determination flowing through me like a river. "I don't play to lose."

He intertwines his fingers and pins me with a stare. "So why do you play?"

I tell him the most honest thing I've ever told another person. "Football saved my life."

It's more than just a sport to me, it's the thing that saved me from getting my ass beat even more by my father while growing up. It's the thing that saved me from taking my own life back when Kyle's blackmail forced me to confront the truth about myself.

It's what I look forward to every single morning when I wake up and what I think about every night before I close my eyes. And besides my relationship with Breslin back in high school, I've never found another thing that comes close to making me feel complete. "There is no option for me other than playing football. It's in my bloodstream. It's who I am."

"And that right there is why our record isn't the greatest."

I'm baffled by that statement, until he adds, "We haven't had a quarterback with this much raw passion for the sport since—" His eyes move to the framed picture of some guy in a uniform on his desk and it hits me.

"Since you?"

"Busted rotator cuff in my throwing arm during the first year I went pro," he says, answering the question I wanted to ask but didn't know how. "90% of athletes make a full recovery." His face falls and there's something even more profound than pain in his eyes now. *Sorrow.* "Unless the surgery wasn't successful and the surgeon ends up doing more harm than good to your arm."

"Jesus," I say, my heart in my throat because that's honest to God one of the worst things to happen to a quarterback.

"I know," he says solemnly. "My career was over before it started...but I knew I still needed football in my life and I needed to be part of the sport somehow."

"So you became a coach."

"So I became a coach." He rubs his forehead. "Well, after I spent the first 10 years or so being an asshole who wallowed in my own misery day in and day out."

"Can't say I blame you."

He snorts. "My wife would disagree with you on that. Poor woman was put through the wringer."

He shakes his head. "Anyway, I decided to start coaching. Unfortunately when I came to Woodside, the football team was already in bad shape. And as I'm sure you already know, this isn't the university that all the star athletes tend to flock to."

His jaw tics. "The former quarterbacks' treated being on the team like it was an elective class before they all moved on." He looks at me. "Now I can train and coach to the best of my ability...but I can't make a team bleed football without the right leader to back me up. Bottom line, we haven't had a quarterback like you in a long time. I'm hoping you're what we need to rise from the grave."

He sits up in his seat. "I haven't made an official announcement to the team about you, but a few of them have asked if the rumors that I'm bringing you on board are true." Something that looks a lot like nervousness crosses over his features. "Some of them aren't going to be so welcoming, Holden. They've heard the rumors and I'm sure they've googled the video. I'll step in when I can, but it's up to you to make them respect you. You have to make them listen to you so you can lead them. *You* have to make them see there's more to you than rumors and your daddy's connections and money."

"I know." I look at my watch and curse. "Sorry but I have a meeting with the Dean in 20 minutes. And from what I've heard he's a real hard ass so I don't want to be late."

His lips quirk up and he sticks out his hand. "Welcome to the team, Holden."

I stand and shake his hand. "Thanks—" My stomach rumbles, alerting us both to the fact that I haven't eaten breakfast or lunch.

"Classes won't start for another few weeks but since summer classes are still in session, the cafeteria's open. It's also on your way to the Dean's office."

I nod. I know where the cafeteria is, but moving was more expensive than I thought it would be and I no longer have a job thanks to my new schedule and the fact that the campus buses don't go out that way at night. I'm going to have to figure something out, though because although tuition, tutoring, and my dorm room is included with my scholarship, food isn't.

He studies me again and I shift uncomfortably. "I take it you and that father of yours aren't exactly on speaking terms right now."

"I haven't spoken to him since my last day at Duke's."

I decide to let him come to his own conclusions as to why that is.

He thinks about this for a moment and rubs his chin. "You know, I could use some help around here on the weekends. There were some budget cuts to the team recently, and we don't really have cleanup crews and equipment managers anymore. I was planning on taking care of it myself, but I would be willing to give those jobs to you if you want them. Of course, they won't pay a whole lot; but it's enough to keep you fed during the school year. As long as you keep your nose out of trouble and arrive on time."

"Thank you," I whisper, because I desperately need some kind of job, even though I'm sure people will talk when they see me on the field filling up water jugs before practice and cleaning the stands after games.

I glance at my watch again and curse. "I really have to go. Like I said, the Dean seems like an asshole and I don't want to piss him off and ruin my scholarship offer."

He chuckles and throws a protein bar at me. "Her."

I look down at my schedule in confusion. A *Stevie Crane* is listed under the Dean's name. Not only does that sound like a dude's name...she's apparently related to my new Coach. *Perfect.*

"*She's* my wife," he says with a laugh as he points to the door. "And you're right, you really don't want to piss her off."

I guess that would explain how he was able to pull all the strings he did.

I close the door behind me, but not before I hear him call out, "Don't forget you have your first meeting with the tutor tomorrow afternoon at the campus library. Don't be late, because he'll be reporting to me."

CHAPTER 10

LANDON

I hike my laptop bag up on one shoulder, my guitar case on the other, and balance my coffee and notebook in my hand as I sprint up the steps to the campus library. I have a tutoring session with one of my regulars at 12:15 and my next at 1:30.

I was hoping to get some music time in between tutoring sessions today, but since one of them is studying for their summer school final, and the other is an introductory meeting and I'm not sure just how much this new student will need, I know it probably won't happen.

The new student—some guy named Asher Holden—is a jock, and although I haven't had a chance to go over his academic record and see what classes he struggles with the most, it's been my experience that jocks' never want to put in the time and work it takes to succeed. They expect things to be handed to them all because they can throw a few balls around.

I groan because I'm going to have my hands full with yet another privileged ass who will expect me to do all the work for him.

I shouldn't even be taking on another student right now, especially since I'll be the TA in not one but two classes this semester, in addition to my own course load. But when the Dean called me into her office and all but begged me to take this *case* as she called it—I caved.

Dean Crane is someone I look up to and have the utmost respect for. Not only was she the one who suggested that I consider being a double major when I confided in her about what I really wanted to do—and my conundrum regarding my parents'—who outright refused to pay for any classes that didn't have to do with me earning my teaching degree. She also offered me a job tutoring at the student center. In addition to finding a way for me to obtain grant money to help pay for some of my music classes.

She's been a godsend to me and she's worked hard to get where she is. She's taken this university which was once in shambles, and turned it around. She truly wants each and every student on campus to succeed. And her husband, who happens to be the coach of the football team, is a good guy too. So when he tracked me down right after the meeting with her and told me how important it was to him personally for me to tutor his new quarterback—so important he's taking money out of the football budget in order for me to privately tutor him all year—I really couldn't turn it down.

I don't know what the big deal about this Asher guy is, but if he has both Cranes' going crazy, he must be something special.

I glance at my watch and curse. My regular student—Nina—usually shows up early for her sessions, so I know chances are she's already grabbed a table in the stacks and is waiting for me.

I open the door to the library and despite it still being summer, it's more packed than usual. The university offers summer classes to the local students around here and I know most of them are taking their finals this week.

I glance at my watch again and pause. I have another three minutes before the session starts. Maybe I should call her.

Not only did she end things with you, I remind myself. She won't even give you the courtesy of returning your texts or phone calls.

I hover over the button that highlights her name. It's not like she'll pick up when I call *again*. My heart tugs—because I'm coming to the realization that maybe it's just best that I let her go.

If she wanted me...she'd pick up her phone.

If she wanted me...she wouldn't have ended things.

If she wanted me...she wouldn't have...

"Jesus, shit!" I scream when some massive force plows into me, causing coffee to spill down my shirt.

"Damn, that sucks," some deep voice says, and I don't mistake the hint of amusement in his tone. "You should probably watch where you're going there, bud."

I should probably watch where I'm going? I wasn't even the one walking.

I look up and come face to face with some guy who's about two inches taller and 35 lbs. bigger than I am. He smirks as he continues to stare down at me from underneath some hipster beanie hat.

Seriously, who the fuck wears a beanie in the summer?

I open my mouth to tell him off, but he's gone in a flash. But not before I hear him call out, "Your glasses are on the ground if you're looking for them."

Son of a bitch. I bend down and pick up my glasses, which thankfully aren't broken.

After I clean up the best that I can in the bathroom, I make a beeline for our usual table. It's kind of hidden since it's near a non-popular section of books, therefore it's not frequented by many people. Nina has a hard time concentrating, so she likes to be away from people when she studies, which is fine by me. I prefer to be away from people too.

I look up at the clock on the wall when I reach our table but don't see her. I'm only a few minutes late for our session and she wouldn't leave the library without texting me first.

Setting my laptop and books on the table, I decide to shoot her a text while I sit and wait for her.

When another 10 minutes have passed, I send her another text. I know she's worried about her final, so I'm a little concerned as to why she's still not here.

I take out my notes for our session and lay them on the table in front of me...and *that's* when I hear it.

At first, I'm sure I must be mistaken. But when I hear frantic and muffled whispers followed by some low and deep groan...I know I'm not.

I don't consider myself a buzzkill, but I am a responsible human being.

And a curious one.

I drum my fingers on the table, debating my next move. My curiosity seems to get the best of me, because the next thing I know I'm on my feet and moving toward the muffled sounds which are no doubt coming from the back of the library.

The sounds become clearer with every bookshelf I pass.

I hear a female voice giggle and it's immediately followed by a slurping and sucking sound. It's such a *distinct* sound that not only is there no mistaking what's going on behind that last bookshelf...it sends a rush of blood straight to my own dick.

I swallow hard and remind myself that I'm well respected here on campus. Not only am I the head of the student center, I'm a freaking TA.

I instruct my cock to stop being such a pervert, and roll my shoulders back, getting ready to put my authoritative face on.

There's another low groan followed by, "That's it. Just like that." Which is soon accompanied by, "Oh, yeah. Take those titties out for me and play with them."

I pause briefly, caught between right and wrong. I don't want to ruin their *time* together, but they shouldn't be doing this in a library where people are working their asses off studying for finals.

It's distracting.

I stand behind the shelf that's one over from where they are and remove a few books, deciding to get a better look. I'm probably going to hell for this, but oh well. They only have themselves to blame for doing this in public where anyone can see.

An alarming thought hits me just then. I really have no idea who's hooking up and there's no way to tell until I do in fact *see* them for myself. For all I know it could be Mrs. Jones, the librarian and Mr. Brown, the mail guy on the other side. Everyone knows they make eyes at one another whenever they're in the same room.

I shudder—they're both in their 70's. I quickly put the books back, because I no longer have any desire to witness the show anymore.

"That's it, baby," the deep voice groans and I pause, listening intently. "Don't forget to share with your friend. She looks like she wants a taste too."

The sucking and slurping intensifies and two things hit me at that moment.

One—it's definitely not Mrs. Jones. And two—there's *three* people getting it on.

"Yeah, both of you keep doing that," the deep voice instructs. "Let's see which one of you will get the prize."

Prize? Really?

I roll my eyes. Does that shit actually work?

I can't believe a self-respecting woman—let alone *two* of them— like hearing stuff like that.

Your loser is showing, Landon. These girls are clearly enjoying themselves.

I back away from the bookshelf and take another step toward them, my feet moving of their own accord and my curiosity coming to a peak.

The guy groans again, much louder this time. Annoyance and maybe even bitterness—thanks to my own current dating situation— barrel into me.

Before I can stop myself, I'm rounding the corner.

And coming face to face with the asshole wearing the beanie from before.

I don't even have time to react, all I can do is take in the scene before me.

Two girls—one of them *Nina*—are on their knees before him, pleasuring him. Neither of them see me since their backs are to me and they're obviously very busy.

But that's not what snags my attention. It's the fact that Beanie guy is looking right at *me*.

The corners of his lips turn up and he smirks. "You want some of this?"

I open my mouth in shock—which in retrospect was probably a bad idea—and he bites his lip and grunts.

He grips the back of both their heads and thrusts his hips into one of their mouths. There's more slurping, hell even gagging, but I'm too transfixed to move, for two reasons.

One—if I look down I'll get an eyeful of his dick being passed between them.

And two—the confidence bordering on downright cockiness oozing from this guy has me envious.

Most people would be embarrassed at being discovered in this position. Or at the very least, fear the possible consequences of getting caught.

But not this guy. If anything, it's like me *watching* only seems to heighten things for him.

He swallows hard, his Adam's apple bobbing as he rests his head against the bookshelf. His eyes connect with mine again and his mouth parts, lost in a world of pleasure as his grip in their hair tightens.

And even though I'm not the one coming in Nina's mouth, it almost feels like it because his orgasm is so potent it damn near borders on compelling.

I clear my throat, feeling both uncomfortable for watching this, and pissed that he's here enjoying himself after being such a jerk to me.

I also can't help but feel incredibly *wrong* about this whole thing, given I'm a tutor and a TA. And even though this specific scenario isn't listed in the rules, I'm positive it's frowned upon and that I should be reprimanding them, at the very least.

"Landon," Nina all but screeches as she and her friend get up off the floor. "Oh my god. Please don't report me."

Beanie guy looks confused for a moment before he turns pale, yanks up his pants, and mutters, "Shit."

I guess the clarity of the situation just hit him. I could report them all, but I'm not going to. I might be uptight when it comes to certain things and more responsible than other people, but I'm not that stringent.

Nina starts blubbering and her friend, who I've only met a few times before, joins her.

And somehow, *I'm* the one feeling like the asshole in this equation now.

"Please," Nina says, sidling up to me. "I'll do anything you want, Landon. Just don't tell my parents."

At this, Beanie guy's eyes widen and his expression turns panicked. Guess he didn't realize these girls were still in high school.

Lucky for him, Nina at least, is legal. She just hasn't graduated yet due to her poor grades and the fact that she never attends class, hence why her parents hired me to tutor her this summer.

"You're still in *high school*?" He puts his hands on his hips and blows out a breath, the terror more than evident across his face.

Inside I'm smiling. Karma is a bitch and this guy deserves it.

"Well, yeah," Nina's friend says and he looks like he's a heartbeat away from passing out. Until she adds, "But don't worry, we're both 18."

He sucks in air and slowly the color finds his cheeks again.

Both girls turn to face me and I back away, letting them know I'm not interested in their offer. I'm already well acquainted with Nina's antics and propositions. I've never fallen for them in the past and I'm sure as hell not about to now.

"Go home. We'll reschedule for tomorrow morning, Nina." The girls all but run past me. "I want a thousand-word essay and pages 50-68 completed in your math textbook."

Nina pops a hand on her hip. "You've got to be kidding me."

I point to my face. "Do I look like I'm kidding?"

With a roll of her eyes and a flip of the bird, she walks away.

"I'd rather just suck his dick," her friend whispers behind me and I pinch the bridge of my nose.

The youth of America.

I don't realize I've said that last statement out loud until Beanie guy snorts. "Dude, you're like the youngest grandpa out there. What's your secret?"

I glare at him. "Not propositioning high school girls' for starters."

His eyes narrow. "Whoa, first off—I had no idea they were still in high school. And secondly—they propositioned *me*."

"Yeah, right," I scoff.

I'm secure with myself enough to admit that the guy is good looking—in the all American and conventional kind of way, dimples included. That said, girls don't just go around offering guys blow jobs for no good reason. No matter how troubled they might be.

His mouth tightens. "I'm telling you, they *offered,* man. We started talking and as soon as I told them—" His words drift off suddenly. He's the one who appears uncomfortable now.

"Told them what?"

He shuffles his feet and looks down at the ground. "I'm Asher Holden."

Fucking figures. "The new quarterback?"

He nods and looks back up at me. Then he raises an eyebrow, almost like he was expecting me to follow my last statement up with something else.

"Not a big sports fan I gather?" he questions after another minute goes by.

"Not particularly."

Something like relief flashes across his face. "Look, I'm sorry for —" He pauses, there's the slightest hint of a grin on his lips. "I don't know, getting my rocks off at your sacred library with two consenting 18-year-old's. But I'd appreciate you not making a bigger deal out of this than it has to be."

I lean against the bookshelf that's directly across from him. "Well when you put it like that, sure no problem."

If he can't detect the sarcasm in my tone, he's a bigger idiot than I give him credit for.

"Please don't tell my coach." He swallows thickly and for a moment, he drops the cocky facade and I see a glimpse of vulnerability. "I'm kind of trying to start over again and get my shit together. I can't afford to be thrown off the team. And while I don't think he'll make a big deal out of this, I'm not looking to give him a reason to doubt me so early on."

I feel myself cave. I had every intention of reporting *his* ass to the school, just to get back at him for earlier. But now I'm realizing this guy might not be such an asshole. Or rather, he deserves the chance to prove me wrong about him. Plus, I'm stuck tutoring him for the rest of the year. And all things aside, it *was* just a hookup.

"Fine. Your secret is safe with me."

He breathes a sigh of relief. "Thank you. For a minute, I thought I was going to have to offer you the same thing they did."

A laugh escapes my throat as I make my way back to the table and he follows me. "Wow, offering to suck another guy's dick?" I inwardly shudder. "Guess my silence really is important to you seeing as you'll resort to such drastic measures."

He laughs nervously and looks around. "Right. Look, uh—do you mind if I run to the bathroom before we start?"

I hike a thumb behind me. "After you reach the librarian's desk it's on your left-hand side."

"Thanks," he mumbles before he jets off.

I'm not sure why, but his demeanor completely changed during the last 30 seconds of our conversation. Almost like I personally offended him in some way.

I'm flipping through my notes when I recall his words from before. *"You want some of this?"*

I had thought he meant, 'Did I want to partake in the activity and whip my dick out.' But what if what he *really* meant was, 'Did I want to suck his—'

I shake my head, feeling like an idiot. There's no way he meant that, and what the hell does it say about *me* that I would even think that in the first place?

He's clearly into chicks'. He had not one, but two back there. And hell, even if he was into dude's—which I'm willing to bet almost anything isn't the case, it shouldn't weird me out. I'm all for equal rights and have a few gay friends.

Quite frankly, I'm more concerned about the past that this guy seems to be running from.

And if he's so serious about sports, and he must be, given how scared he was about possibly being kicked off the team—why in the world would he come to Woodside? We're not exactly known for our sports.

I pull out my laptop, hoping a quick google search might tell me where he transferred from and give me some background information.

A moment later, I'm finding out way more about him than I ever intended to.

CHAPTER 11

ASHER

My forehead hits the cold tile of the bathroom and I close my eyes. I've never had a panic attack before, but I'm pretty sure I'm having one of the worst ones in the history of panic attacks right now.

If they were handing out trophies for horrible first impressions today, that honor would sure as shit go to me.

I didn't mean to hook up with those two girls. Well, not exactly. I mean, of course I *wanted* to...once it was already in motion.

But it wasn't desire that was behind it originally.

It was determination and resolve.

It was *indignity*.

A mere 15 seconds after I entered my first public place on campus, and already a few people—mostly guys who were into sports—were starting to recognize me. I could hear the whispers and the murmurs behind my back. The *names* they were calling me.

I pulled a hat out of my gym bag and kept my head down, deciding to go to the library early. I figured no one there would recognize me. Least of all the two scantily clad girls talking and giggling by a bookshelf.

They eyed me up and down and I'd be lying if I said I didn't enjoy it. It felt good to be in my element again.

That is until the faintest trace of recognition lit up the brunette's face and she whispered to her friend. She wasn't that quiet, though, because I heard her tell her friend about the video that went viral.

"You know, you're really hot," One of them, because fuck if I can remember their names, purred. "Too bad that big dick of yours doesn't like girls, because we could really show you a good time...*together.*"

They giggled again and called me a homo before they dismissed me entirely—like I was the equivalent of a smashed bug on their expensive shoes—before they went back to their conversation.

Shame rose up my throat, threatening to strangle me.

I was tired of being treated like a second-class citizen because of the leaked video and my sexual preferences. I also wanted to shove my dick down their throats in order to make them both shut the hell up for good.

And so I decided to turn on the Holden charm. Less than a minute later, they were practically putty in my hands when I told them to meet me in the back of the library where I would take them up on their *offer.*

What I didn't expect was to come face to face with my tutor—who ended up being the clumsy guy I'd met only minutes before—when I was a second away from coming down their throats.

The strangest thing is? It wasn't either of those girls who got me off in the end.

It was looking at *him*. Him with his cute little glasses and open mouth, gaping at me in shock and hell, maybe even a bit of admiration.

And while it wasn't love at first sight or any of that bullshit—it was certainly attraction.

He looked so conservative and sheltered it had my cock and mouth dying to do things to him he'd never forget.

It had me dying to make him do things to *me* that he'd never forget.

Every cell in my body wanted to corrupt the hell out of him.

Well, at least until I found out that the adorable nerd...was my new tutor and TA.

It was like a record skipping. Everything came to an abrupt halt.

Especially when one of the girls begged him not to report us and I realized how much trouble I might get in.

I wasn't lying to him when I told him I was trying to get my shit together...and him reporting me would have possibly put me in a bad position with the coach. Something I couldn't afford to have happen.

Luckily, my new tutor wasn't that much of a monumental and uptight asshole. He seemed like he might even be cool...for a nerd.

And then I went and did the worst thing of all...I inadvertently propositioned him. Because not only was I attracted to him...but *that's* the type of shit I was used to, thanks to Kyle.

I'd encountered years upon years of doing things to him and for him, not out of attraction, but coercion...and I don't think I realized just how fucked up it made me until that moment.

The moment where Landon was looking at me like I was insane for offering to possibly suck him off if it meant him not telling a soul about what happened.

The moment where I felt judged, because tutor or not, blackmail or not— I was attracted to him on some level, and I wasn't sure what to do about that because I'd only ever pursued women before and I only had the Kyle situation to go by when it came to guys.

So *that* was my fucked up way of testing the waters. Because I didn't know any different.

The look on his face and the disgusted shudder he tried to suppress told me all I needed to know. And instantly, I was reminded of the thing deep inside me that I can't ignore.

I'll *never* be able to change who I am and the fact that I'm sexually attracted to both girls and guys.

Therefore, I'll always be talked about and made fun of. I'll never fit in anywhere.

And with the exception of the nights filled with the friction of hips and secret moans in the dark—I'm going to end up alone.

Women will always be uncomfortable because I like dick, and men will never trust me because I also like pussy.

And the one person I loved more than anything in this world— the person I miss so much that I swear I can actually *hear* all the shattered pieces clanking together with every fucked up beat of my heart...

I lost. *Forever.*

And I need her so badly right now.

I need my Breslin so fucking much, I'd do anything and give up everything just to have her again.

I need her to hold me and love me. I need her to look at me like I'm the most important thing in this world.

I need to feel her love and our connection, because it's the only time I've ever felt like someone actually gave a shit about the *real* me.

I need her to hold my hand just like she used to, because *she's* my calm and my shelter in the most fucked up of storms.

Tears threaten to spring to my eyes, and I'm a second away from going off the deep end and losing it completely—but I turn the faucet on, dip my head under the water, and force myself to get my goddamn shit together.

I'm not a pussy. No matter where I put my dick, I'm *still* a fucking Holden. Fuck what people say about my sexuality. Fuck if they don't understand.

I might not have anything real ever again, but I can have a life filled with dirty fantasies and getting off whenever I want.

And maybe if I work my ass off, I can still play football. I can still live my dream.

And hell, maybe this Landon guy isn't so bad after all. He didn't report me, and he didn't resort to bribery or give in to those girls, even though he could have.

Maybe Woodside can be a good thing for me, because Kyle and his blackmail can't get to me here. Not if I stay strong and never let anyone see me break.

Words and actions are only powerful if you let them penetrate you, if you let people see that they are getting to you.

As long as I never let these people at Woodside see me sweat, I'm indestructible.

These people will never destroy me. Because I won't let them.

At least, that's what I tell myself, until I walk back out to meet Landon...and see what he's watching on his laptop.

I see the contempt and judgment in his eyes as he sits there...watching the video.

I feel my armor start to crack before Kyle's tentacles wrap around my neck, squeezing.

Letting me know there's no escape for me.

CHAPTER 12

LANDON

I've always been too sensitive for my own good. I've never been the type of person who can stand there when another person is hurting and not do anything about it.

In fact, when I was a small boy, my mother used to cradle me on her lap when I would cry over all the injustices of the world. She used to call me her sensitive little elephant. When I asked her why an *elephant*—she told me that not only were they her favorite animal, but in her opinion, elephants are the most emotional and intelligent.

She told me not to be ashamed that I was sensitive, that in her eyes, it was a majestic quality to have.

But over the years, I learned that being sensitive was a hindrance.

Not only did it not impress girls, who seemed to only want alpha males and jocks, it left me open to ridicule.

And through careful observation, I quickly figured out that it was the people who seemingly felt nothing that always seemed to get everything in this world.

Because they just didn't give a shit.

Therefore, I no longer cried over my own or other people's injustices, no matter how much I felt them bubbling inside me like a cauldron ready to boil over—instead I bottled them up and poured it out through my love of music. Exposing every scar etched in my soul for the world via rhythm and melodies, finding the perfect harmony to soothe my heart, making it so I could go on another day without the anguish inside wearing me down with every breath I took.

But it doesn't mean I don't still feel every ounce of it. I care about others, even those I shouldn't.

And when Asher took off like a bolt of lightning after catching me watching his video, it gnawed at me all day.

I didn't mean to hurt him by watching it, but that's exactly what I did.

Because in that moment...I felt him.

I saw his scars...I felt his embarrassment. I felt his shame.

And I hated that I was the one who caused it. Even though he's just some dumb jock, an asshole who laughed when I spilled coffee on myself, and probably a womanizer and hell, maybe even a manizer.

I cared that he was hurting.

Which is why I lied to Coach Crane and told him the first session went fine and that it wouldn't be a problem to tutor him.

It's also why I find myself wandering up the steps of the co-ed dorm building. Even though it's the last place I should be right now.

He answers on the third knock, the final knock before I was going to give up and walk back down the stairs.

The scowl on his face tells me I'm the last person he wants to see. And the half empty beer in his hand, sweatpants he's adorning, and bare feet tell me I've probably interrupted his evening.

And now I feel like an even bigger idiot for coming here.

"Well if it isn't my favorite voyeur nerd," he greets me, stepping out and standing in front of the door.

I find myself grateful the co-ed floor is empty and the students haven't moved in yet.

I'm suddenly at a loss for words. I have no idea what to say to that...because in a way he's right. As much as I hate to admit it, it would make sense for him to think I'm some kind of voyeur after what happened earlier.

Not once, but twice in the span of 10 minutes he caught me watching *him* in a sexual act.

"Look," I start, finding my voice. "I'm sorry about—"

I swallow, because my mouth's unable to formulate words again. *How exactly does one apologize for coming off like a pervert?*

His eyes turn to steel. "For what?"

When I don't answer, he crosses his arms and takes a step forward, letting me know he's got the clear advantage over me due to his size.

I jut my chin out, push my shoulders back, and match his stare. I'm not one to be intimidated easily. I might be non-confrontational by nature, but it doesn't mean I allow myself to be walked on either.

This guy wants to elicit a reaction out of me because he's uncomfortable with what happened today. I get it. But I'm not going to play into whatever hand he's currently trying to deal me.

I simply came here to apologize and let him know that I don't give a shit what or who he likes to do in the privacy of his bedroom. The only thing I care about is that he shows up for our sessions on time and makes a genuine effort to do the work.

"I'm sorry for watching your video." I take a step back, intending to leave. "It's none of my business what you're into or what you do outside of our tutoring sessions."

His nostrils flare, and for a moment, I honestly think he's going to punch me. But then he closes his eyes and says, "It's not what you think. I—"

"Jesus, I don't care that you like guys!"

He shakes his head. "That's not what I was going to say. But thanks for being so concerned about where I stick my dick."

Before I can say another word, he walks back inside and slams the door behind him.

I take a breath. Not only should I not even be here, but I shouldn't give two shits about being nice to this guy.

I just...I feel bad for him. I know what it's like to be bullied and to have people make fun of you for being different every day. I also know he's going to catch a lot of flak from not only the students on campus...but his own teammates.

I knock on the door again and he yanks it open, appearing even angrier now. "Unless you're going to bend over or get on your knees for me, get the fuck away from my door."

I take another step back, appalled. Here I was trying to be a friend and this is the shit he spews?

"What—"

I don't have a chance to finish that statement because he shoves me against the wall. And then he gets in my face, intentionally invading every inch of my personal space.

My hand forms a fist, ready to defend myself.

He smirks and braces his arm on the wall beside my head. "You heard me, nerd."

He's so close, it's uncomfortable. When his lips are a centimeter from mine, I turn my face away.

"Awe, what's the matter, Landon? Is this too gay for you?"

I shove him off me. He doesn't go far, but it's enough that it puts some distance between us.

"This has nothing to do with you being gay, straight, or whatever the fuck you are," I seethe. "This has to do with me coming here to apologize to you and you being an asshole."

I shove him again. "I told you, I don't give a shit about your sexuality. But clearly *you* do." I start walking down the hall. "Put me in a position like that again and I'll report your ass to the coach."

I pause and bite back a smile. "By the way, your tutoring session is scheduled for tomorrow at 8am sharp at the campus library."

He narrows his eyes. "My first practice is at 8am."

"Did I say 8?" I give him a sardonic grin. "I meant *5am*. And I suggest you make sure you've read the English syllabus that Coach Crane gave you. I'd also make sure you read the first two chapters of *Romeo and Juliet* tonight because there will be a quiz."

I turn on my heels. I regret coming here. But hey, at least I tried to do the decent thing and apologize when I was wrong. Which is more than I can say about him.

I'm on my first step down the stairs when I hear him call out, "Landon."

I should keep walking and pretend I don't hear him. But it's the remorse in his voice that has me backtracking. "What?"

"I'm sorry. That was really fucked up of me."

"Yeah, it was." I shrug. "Look, I don't know the specifics of what happened to you in the past, but you're obviously still letting it dictate your future." I dig my hands in my pockets. "These people are going to eat you alive this year if you don't get your shit together, Asher. I just met you and even I can tell you're spinning out. People feed on that and they'll only try to bury you."

I gesture to the joint tucked behind his ear and the beer in his hand. "Word of advice? If the coach catches that shit in your system I can almost guarantee you'll be off the team. No matter how good your stats are. He's not one of those in it for the glory. He's the real deal. He cares about his players."

He nods and blows out a breath. "This is going to be awkward now, isn't it?"

That vulnerability's in his expression again and it makes me bend. "Yeah, probably. I mean, dude. You tried to *kiss* me out of nowhere. At least buy a man dinner first. Preferably a steak."

He pinches the bridge of his nose and laughs. "Fuck, I really am a special brand of asshole."

I turn and start walking down the hallway again. "Make it 6:30 am."

"Gee thanks, *nerd*."

I raise my middle finger in the air. "You're welcome, *jock*."

CHAPTER 13

BRESLIN

I take a deep breath and clutch the wooden bench I'm sitting on. It's funny what a memory can do to you. How it can bring back every single feeling and send all of your senses into overdrive.

Even when you think you're prepared for it. You never really are.

Wiping away tears, I close my eyes and root around my purse for my sunglasses, which I'm sure will make some people look at me funny seeing as it's drizzling outside, but I don't care.

It's better than letting these people see me cry.

"Breslin?"

For a moment, I think it's one of my classmates, no doubt wondering why I abruptly walked out of something as beautiful and epic as the Sistine chapel.

I'm relieved when Kit's small hand finds mine and she puts her head on my shoulder.

"How did you know I was here?"

I gave her a copy of my tour schedule but she's never tagged along on any of the tour stops. Since we've been here, all she does is spend her time with Becca and I've hardly seen her.

She shrugs. "Becca's still sleeping off last night at the hotel. I got bored and missed you. Figured I'd meet up with you today. But when I went inside, someone told me you walked out."

Before I can say a word, she reaches up, plucks my glasses off, and frowns at what I'm sure are my bloodshot eyes. "Him."

It's not a question, because we both know what *him* she's talking about.

"He let me paint the ceiling in his bedroom." I laugh through my tears and although Kit's brows furrow, she urges me to continue.

"I once told him that I wished I was talented enough to paint on someone's ceiling. That I wanted to paint something as beautiful as Michelangelo's Sistine Chapel one day."

I force myself to breathe. It's not the bad memories that hurt and keep me hanging on, it's all of the good ones that I can't seem to forget.

"The next day he surprised me by setting up paint supplies in his bedroom."

I hate myself for smiling, but there's no way I can't while recalling this memory. "Then he put me on his shoulders and I actually painted his ceiling." I bury my face in my hands, my smile growing wider. "God, it was awful and I kept freaking out thinking his mother was going to be pissed at me for ruining his ceiling, but he didn't care. He said he'd keep it up there forever and that when we bought our own house, he wanted me to paint on every ceiling in every single room."

The tears start falling again, much faster this time. "He made me so happy, Kit. But fuck, he hurt me *so* much. I just don't understand...I don't understand why I can't get over him." I point to my chest. "Why this stupid thing insists on hanging on to him and our memories."

She grips my hand. "Breslin."

"I want to get over him," I whisper. "I want him to stop haunting me. I want to be able to give Lan—" I stop, because I can't bring myself to say the words.

"But Asher won't let you, because he came first and there's no room for anyone else," she finishes for me, and my heart thanks her for saying what I can't.

"Landon is amazing," I say, stating the obvious. Those butterflies threaten to start swarming but I don't let them. "But I don't want to lead him on. I don't want to be with him until I'm sure I can give him all of me. It wouldn't be right."

"I get it." She stands up and pulls me to my feet. "However, you deserve more than this."

I shake my head but she presses her finger to my lips. "So, here's what we're going to do."

Before I can question her, she says, "We have a little over two weeks left on our trip. During the day, you're going to go on your tours and all that jazz. But at night, you're going to party with me."

When I open my mouth to object she shushes me. "You're going to sleep with hot European boys and dance on bars. You're gonna get drunk, flash your tits to some unsuspecting citizen on the street, and try some marijuana. You're going to live life like it's your last day on earth."

"How exactly is that supposed to get me over Asher?"

"It's not supposed to get you over him. It will be your way of getting *back* at him. Why should you spend the rest of your life miserable because of him?" She jabs a finger in my chest. "You're gonna party Asher out of your system. Consider it your personal fuck you to him...because he doesn't get to steal my best friend's sunshine anymore. It's been three years of letting him steal your happy, every damn day...it's time to take your life back."

I start to shake my head but she grabs me by the shoulders. "Do you want to keep dating Asher Holden? Because the reason you can't start a relationship with anyone else, including Landon, is because you're still in one with *him*. And I say this with love, Bre—it's time you put your big girl thong on and cut the cord. Because you're only going to end up hanging yourself with it...while he's off making his NFL millions and fucking everything that walks."

She flips her long blonde hair with now bright green tips and gives me a wink. "I'm making it my mission to make sure you have the time of your life every single night for the next." She pulls out her phone. "Two weeks and three days."

When I nod she squeaks and squeezes me. "I can't wait to turn you into a dirty little party whore. I've been waiting for this moment forever."

My expression must give away my thoughts regarding that statement because she starts laughing hysterically. "Just trust me."

"I do."

I take another breath. Maybe letting go for a few weeks and being reckless isn't such a bad thing after all. Because lord knows...I've tried everything else in my power to get over him.

I need to let go of everything that keeps me holding on to nothing. Because that's what Asher is to me now.

Nothing.

It's time I learn to accept it and move on. It's time to start chipping away at Asher so I can make room for the person who actually belongs there.

My chest squeezes when I feel my phone vibrating in my pocket. A big part of me can't help but hope it's Landon...but a bigger part of me hopes it's not.

Because I'm not sure just how long I'll be able to resist talking to him.

Because I really do miss him. So much it's starting to hurt.

Which is something I'm already used to.

CHAPTER 14

ASHER

His face is pensive as he scans over my quiz.

I look around the library and my stomach twists. He doesn't even have to tell me the bad news...I know I bombed it.

But then again, it's not like I actually tried *or* read the material. So there's that.

He makes a mark with a red pen on my paper and opens his mouth. He's cut off by the sound of his phone vibrating against the wood of the table.

I don't mistake the way his eyes light up or the slight smile he attempts to hide. In the mere four days I've known him, I've never seen him look like this.

My stomach twists for a different reason entirely then.

He's obviously seeing someone.

Not that I think I had a chance with him in the first place. And it's not like I'm looking for anything more than a few nights complete with a few blowjobs...but there's a disappointment now settling in my chest that I wasn't prepared for.

It mimics the disappointment on his face when he checks his phone, reads his text and frowns.

"Trouble in paradise?"

He slides his phone into his pocket. "Huh?"

I stretch my legs out on the table and cross my ankles, trying to remain unfazed.

If Landon doesn't know I want him in the sack by now, he needs a better prescription for those glasses of his. That said, it doesn't mean I'm going to keep hitting on him. He's already made it clear he's not interested and that his dick is as straight as an arrow.

But he seems like a cool guy, and whether or not he ever lets me fuck him shouldn't deter me from trying to be his friend.

Friend?

Christ, the term is so foreign to me. I haven't had an actual friend since...nope not going there.

"Your phone. It was your girl, no?" I waggle my eyebrows and fold my arms behind my head. "Or rather, it *wasn't* your girl and that's why you look so upset."

He bites his pen. Something I notice he does whenever he's uncomfortable. Which is a good 90% of the time around me. I hide my smirk, because I like Landon being uncomfortable around me. I take great pleasure in making my adorable nerd hot under the collar.

Shit. And now I have a fucking boner.

I quickly take my legs off the table and push my seat in, hiding the evidence.

When he doesn't respond, I decide to press. "What's her name?"

He snorts and glares at me. "Like I would ever tell *you*."

I place my hand over my heart, feigning offense. "Wow, that hurts. And here I thought we were friends."

He rolls his eyes and points to the back of the library. "The first time I met you, I caught you with not one, but *two* girls. There's no way in hell I'm telling you her name so you can work your voodoo on her when she gets back."

I lean in. "Afraid of a challenge?" I grin, purposely showcasing my dimples. "Don't worry, nerd. I'm most definitely not opposed to threesomes."

"Jesus." His jaw hardens. "Is that all you think about all the time? No wonder you keep bombing your quizzes."

He shoves a piece of paper in my face. I can't help but notice the mocking 49% circled in red.

"It's better than last time," I note and he pinches the bridge of his nose.

"It's still a big fat *F*. It's only higher this time because I threw you a bone and asked you what the two main characters' names were." He peers at me from underneath his black rimmed glasses. "Which is a given considering it's the name of the goddamn book."

I bite my lip, I'm digging this angry side of him.

However, he's not wrong about my poor performance during our tutoring sessions. I have no desire to read this book or do the assignments. It's boring as fuck.

"I don't understand why Mrs.—" I scratch my head, trying to remember the professor's name.

"Mrs. Sterling," he says through clenched teeth.

I snap my fingers. "Yeah, her. I mean no offense to you fuddy-duddies who enjoy this crap, but I remember reading this shit back in high school. Why the hell am I still doing it in my senior year of college?"

He closes his eyes, the vein in his neck all but bulging with restraint.

And fuck if that doesn't make my dick even harder.

Just when I'm about to excuse myself to go rub one out, he says, "You obviously weren't listening when I explained everything to you."

I lift a shoulder in a shrug. "It's not you. It's just...this shit is of no interest to me. Therefore, my brain automatically tunes it out."

"What kinds of things interest you?"

I lick my lips. "Football. Sex—" *You.* "I like games and challenges."

He thinks about this for a moment before he pulls some papers out of his backpack. "Okay, here's the breakdown. Mrs. Sterling loves the classics. Shakespeare is one of her favorites. It's why the first assignment is a paper along with a test on Romeo and Juliet."

He snaps his fingers. "You still with me? You're getting that faraway look in your eyes again and this is important."

I nod, trying my hardest to give him my undivided attention.

"Anyway, the first assignment and test is an easy one. And it counts for 20% of your entire grade, which is extremely generous of her. She knows you're all familiar with Romeo and Juliet already—it's basically her way of giving you all a curve. This way, when she moves on to the harder stuff like Poe, Austen, Brontë, and Aristotle...you can concentrate and actually get something out of it instead of figuring out how to pass a test. Understand?"

"Not exactly. You're basically saying that she's doing us a favor by adding on to our course load. How the hell does that help anyone?"

He lets out a frustrated sigh. "Because Romeo and Juliet is easy, Asher. It's an *easy* A which will help you maintain your grade for the semester. She's trying to help you. All you have to do is read the fucking book, do the assignment and take the test."

"It's boring," I argue. "Heck, it's probably why they ended up offing themselves in the end."

He cocks his head to the side. "So you did read it?"

"No, I saw the movie." I grab the edges of the table and shake it. "I'll never let go, Jack." I give him a wink. "Chick had a killer rack by the way."

"That's *Titanic*," he mumbles, looking even more frustrated now.

"Guess that explains why the old lady lived then." I glance at my watch, practice starts in 15 minutes. "I have to get going. See you tomorrow?"

He studies my face for a moment too long. "How's practice going?"

Shit. I guess I let my guard slip for a moment.

"Fine," I lie through my teeth.

The truth is the last two days have been hell on earth for me. In addition to failing every quiz Landon had given me, my new teammates hate me. Especially one in particular. One of the wide receivers named Theo O'Connor.

And because he's been on the team longer than I have and isn't part of a sex tape scandal involving another guy...everyone flocks to him and he does a good job of riling everyone up in the locker room.

For the most part, I've been ignoring it. But I can feel the thin thread inside me snapping like a rubber band, and I'm not sure how many plucks I have left until I snap completely.

"You planning on going to that party tonight?"

"Of course. Why wouldn't I?"

The sports team might not be big around here, but apparently the first party right before classes officially start is.

The campus is still half empty, but the students who moved in early, including everyone on the football team; get together at one of the fraternity houses.

I wasn't planning on going, but if I don't? It will put an even bigger target on my back.

He shrugs. "I don't know. Just asking."

He closes his eyes and reaches around for something in his pocket. I have no clue what happened in the last minute, but obviously something did because he looks out of sorts.

"Hey, man. You okay?"

He swipes his books off the table and into his backpack. "Fine. We're done here, right?"

Before I can answer him, he jumps to his feet and starts heading for the door.

I grab the guitar case that he left behind and run to catch up to him. "Landon."

When he turns around, he looks paler. He's also sweaty and squinting.

"Are you okay?" I ask again.

He snatches the guitar case from me. "I'm fine. I just have a headache and need to get home."

Before I can press any further, he runs off. For a moment, I debate calling Coach Crane and asking for his address since I know for a fact that he doesn't live on campus. But then I look at my watch and curse. Practice starts in 10 minutes and I'm not even in the locker room yet.

I give one last look in the direction of the parking lot and make a mental note to shoot him a text after practice ends.

CHAPTER 15

LANDON

"So he's doing well?" Coach Crane asks, looking up from his paperwork.

I shuffle my feet and look down. I respect this man and don't want to lie to him.

"Well, not exactly," I begin. "But I think if he tries hard and puts in the work he'll be okay."

"He needs to get a B or higher in all of his classes," he reminds me. "The Dean isn't budging on that."

I almost want to laugh, considering the Dean is his wife, but I nod instead. "I know."

He scrubs a hand down his face. "Okay. Thank you for coming down here."

"No problem."

I turn on my heels, walk down the long corridor, and past the locker room.

And that's when I hear it.

"So how much did you pay that guy to suck your dick, Asher?"

When there's no response, I hover by the locker room door that's partially open.

I know I shouldn't be doing this, but Asher's my student. Or rather, he's *Mrs. Sterling's* student...but I'm his tutor. Therefore, it's my job to report bullying on campus. Especially the kind that can hinder a student's performance.

Asher remains quiet and faces his locker, his expression unfazed. I see his shoulders rise on a deep breath when he pulls a t-shirt over his head.

Inwardly I smile. That's right, don't let these assholes get to you.

"Come on, *Asher Holden*. Tell us all about your little boyfriend," the guy continues.

"I bet if you let him suck you off he'd tell you all about it," another guy chimes in.

There's a round of laughter and my stomach drops. I want to burst in there and tell those fuckers off myself. But it would only make matters worse.

I can see him visibly straining to keep himself in check now and it's admirable. I don't know how he does it. I would have snapped by now.

"You know, I bet you're right," the guy continues. "I bet he wants nothing more than for us to line up for him so he can suck us all off." The guy cackles and slams his locker shut. "I bet you're just dying to suck my dick, *Faggot?* Aren't you?"

I take a step, anger pumping through my veins.

And that's when all hell breaks loose.

It all happens so fast, I barely have time to register what's going on.

There's a cracking sound, and then the asshole's on the floor and Asher's on top of him, throwing punches left and right.

The guy tries to deflect them. He even manages to get in one solid punch to Asher's eye. But Asher's got one thing on his side that the other guy doesn't.

Anger.

And right now, it's a perfect storm of bottled up rage swirling

COMPLICATED HEARTS   163

around in that locker room. The two guys who looked like they were about to jump in take a step back. Which is a good idea, considering the face of Asher's victim is a punch away from becoming ground meat.

The other guys stand around, looking both speechless and astonished. Guess they never expected Asher to fight back.

Asher yanks him up by his collar. "For your information, I only suck things I can see."

He spits on him and pulls his fist back once more, intending to send what I'm sure is one hell of a punch to his face.

However he's interrupted by the sound of a whistle blowing.

The guys all turn their heads when the assistant coach, Vincent Dragoni walks in.

"Alright, break it up."

He shoves Asher off the asshole and yanks the other guy to his feet. "Go get cleaned up, O'Connor." He looks around. "The rest of you get the hell out of here. *Now*."

The guys scatter, including Asher. That is until Dragoni barks, "Not you, Holden."

Asher pauses and mumbles a curse under his breath. I see a flash of fear in his eyes and he swallows hard.

My feet start moving, there's no way I'm going to let him get in trouble for defending himself. I'll go right to coach and tell him—

"I suggest you remember exactly why it is you're here," Dragoni barrels out. "And unless you want to see those ivy league brains of your brother's smashed against concrete before I do the same to you— you better get your shit together and stop fucking around. The Dragoni's don't take well to unsettled debts. We're doing you a favor for the next year. Understand?"

My stomach knots. Just what in the actual fuck is going on?

The muscles in Asher's neck tighten before he grinds out, "Yes, sir."

"You're dismissed," Dragoni says. "For now."

I move against the wall when I see Asher head for the door that I'm currently snooping through.

He's two steps down the hall when he stops abruptly and faces me. "Jesus you're really making a habit out of spying on me, aren't you?"

I ignore that comment. "What the fuck is going on? Why is Dragoni threatening you?"

His face screws up. "Tell me why you were spying on me."

"I wasn't spying on you. The coach asked me to come down to his office so we could talk about how you're doing."

He blows out a breath. "And?"

I avert my gaze. "And I told him the truth. You're going to need to put in the work and make an effort."

He starts walking. "Thanks a lot."

I run to catch up to him. "I refuse to lie to him for you." I reach for his arm. "Tell me what's going on with Dragoni. I saw what happened in that locker room and it was that asshole who deserved to be yelled at, not you." My shoulders tighten. "And where does he get off threatening you? He's a faculty member. He can't just—"

His expression hardens and he pushes me away. "You don't know what the fuck you're talking about, Landon. Forget whatever you heard and mind your own business."

"No," I argue. "He can't—"

"What happened to *you* today? Huh?"

I'm thrown off by his question. "I don't know what—"

"At the library, you left not only looking like shit but in a rush. Why?"

He cocks a brow, waiting for my answer.

My throat feels dry. "It's personal."

He hikes his gym bag on his shoulder and snorts. "Right."

"Asher," I call out. "I'm reporting him."

His entire body goes rigid. "You can't."

"Give me one good reason why—"

"You'll get me and my brother killed."

"**B**ut like how do policemen on bikes arrest people, Landon?" Brittany the girl I'm currently helping into bed, slurs. "I mean, like where do they put people on their bikes and stuff?"

I try not to laugh as I pull a blanket over her and set a glass of water beside her bed. I grab a garbage can and place it on the floor next to her as well. She's so trashed, she's going to need it.

I used to tutor Brittany last year and during one of our sessions I told her that if she was ever at a party and needed an escort home, to give me a call.

I never thought she'd take me up on the offer, not that I'm annoyed that she did. Even though she did rip me right out of a late-night music session.

When I met her at the frat house she was a step away from falling on her face. And when we passed one of the security guards in front of the building and he wanted to know what was going on, she broke out into a fit of giggles and asked him the same question she's evidently still pondering.

I quickly explained that she was coming home from a frat party off campus and that I was making sure she made it to her dorm safely.

"You know, you're really cute, Landon," she slurs. "I always wanted to tell you that but never had the courage." She springs up in bed suddenly and braces her arm against the wall. Then before I can stop her, she's undoing the string to her halter top. I try not to stare at her boobs which are now on display for me. "Do you have a girlfriend?"

Breslin. Her name wraps around my heart and squeezes. "I do. She's in Europe, but she'll be back in a couple of weeks."

It's not a complete lie. Just the part about her being my girlfriend.

Brittney pouts and trails a finger between her breasts. "I promise not to tell if you won't."

"No. Sorry, I—"

Thank fuck for the sound of the front door opening and her roommate walking in a moment later.

I lift my hands and back away. "She was just getting ready for bed. She's really drunk so make sure you keep an eye on her."

I ignore the look her roommate shoots me and close the door behind me.

I blow out a breath and start walking down the hall. Christ, if I don't stop being at the wrong place at the wrong time and ending up in these situations people are going to start to think I'm the campus peeping Tom.

I pull out my phone and check my messages. Surprise—there aren't any. At least none from her.

Tucking my tail between my legs for the umpteenth time, I press the call button, getting ready to leave yet another voice mail.

It's around 10 pm here which means it's early morning in Europe, so when I hear the click on the other line, I'm surprised.

I clear my throat. I've wanted nothing more than for her to pick up for the last week and change, and now that she has, I'm unsure of what I should say. "Hello?"

Music...the loud, electric dance kind greets me on the other line and I swallow down my annoyance.

Turns out Breslin didn't pick up the phone for me after all, she's too busy partying.

"Hello?" I say again for good measure before I hang up and fight the urge to throw my phone.

On the bright side, at least I know she's okay and that she arrived in Europe safe and sound.

I continue down the hall but slow my footsteps when I reach Asher's door.

I really should follow up with the bombshell he dropped on me today. I can't believe Dragoni is threatening him. There were rumors the guy was a little sketchy, but I didn't think he was a freaking hit-man.

I go to knock on Asher's door, but then I remember he told me he was going to the frat party tonight. With a sigh, I pad down the stairs and out the front doors of the dorm.

I'm passing a dumpster near a large oak tree when I hear it.

The unambiguous sound of grunting and skin slapping together.

I shake my head and continue walking. I've seen enough hookups this week and it only reminds my dick how lonely he is and how much he and I both miss Breslin.

"Yes, God yes," some girl moans. "Fuck me harder, Asher."

Curiosity holds my morals and brain hostage and I hate myself for turning around and ducking behind the large oak tree to get a better glimpse.

I can't exactly pinpoint what the driving force behind my nosiness is, and I don't have time to ponder it because I'm too focused on Asher's large form thrusting and pumping into her.

The blonde girl he's fucking scratches her manicured nails down his back and digs her heels into his ass. Asher growls in response and picks up his pace.

I never thought I'd ever find myself thinking this about another guy, but the way he takes her...

It's fucking hypnotizing.

He's like an animal in the wild. It's raw, primal and feral. There's no mistaking he's in complete control.

He directs the tempo of their fucking, and she moans in ecstasy every time her back hits the hard metal of the dumpster. My own dick stirs when he snatches the top of her dress down and buries his head between her tits. He plucks one of her nipples into his mouth and groans, lost in his own world of pleasure. Blondie tries to cant her hips and match his thrusts, but her rhythm is all wrong and wonky, she's no match for him.

Asher growls again, but not out of pleasure this time—out of frustration—before he takes her harder and faster against the dumpster, nearly splitting her in two.

The blonde loves it though and spurs him on with the heels of her feet, begging him not to stop.

And that's when he spins around...and his eyes connect with mine.

At first, sheer shock flashes in them and then they grow dark and heavy. Blondie screams that she's coming at the top of her lungs and he grips her hips, driving her over the edge with his frantic and brutal thrusts.

This is probably where I should walk away.

I realize how utterly bizarre this entire situation is. I take a step, intending to leave, but those crystal blue eyes of his hold my gaze, begging me to stay.

I'm not aroused by my current circumstance...but there's something oddly satisfying about knowing that I'm suddenly in control of this whole thing now.

His throat bobs and his face strains as he thrusts into her a final time, his eyes never leaving mine.

When he's finished, he puts the girl down and pulls up his jeans.

I go to leave again, but he nods in my direction...and that's when Blondie turns around and sees me.

"Oh my god," she screeches. "You were *watching* us?" She jabs a finger at Asher. "And you just *let* him?"

Asher lifts a shoulder in a shrug and disposes of the condom.

Thinking fast, I pull a small container of candy out of my pocket and walk toward them. "Not for nothing, but you were having sex in public." I toss the container into the dumpster. "I was just trying to be a good citizen and not litter."

Asher's lips quip and the blonde huffs out a breath before turning back to him. "I guess I should probably give you my number, huh?"

Before he can object, she starts rattling it off and I don't know whether to laugh or shake my head when I notice that he's only pretending to enter it in his phone.

She looks between us. "I—um. I'm gonna go up to my dorm." Her eyes blatantly roam over Asher and she bites her lip. "Give me a call. It was fun."

He gives her a salute in response and she starts walking away. I open my mouth but close it when he grins slyly and whispers, "Don't forget to tell your boyfriend I said hi." He looks at me. "She's O' Conner's girl. Or rather, she *was* before five minutes ago."

I can't help but grin myself now. "Guess it makes sense why you fucked her in public instead of walking the mere 30 feet and taking her to your dorm room."

"He started with me at the party. I didn't want to get into it with him again...so I found something else to take the edge off." He lifts a brow. "Question is...why are you here? I thought you lived off campus?"

"I do." I dig my hands into my pockets. "A former student of mine called me from the party. She was wasted so I escorted her home."

He wiggles his eyebrows. "Did you fuck her?"

I roll my eyes. "Of course not. Didn't you hear me? She was trashed."

He takes the joint tucked behind his ear and brings it to his lips. "I think I should do you a solid and tutor you when it comes to girls. When was the last time you got any?"

I rip the joint out of his mouth and stomp on it. "You just fucked a girl against a dumpster and you want to offer me dating advice?" I leer at him. "Besides I don't need your advice. I have a girlfriend."

He laughs. "No, what you have is a girl who's ignoring you and you can't take the hint."

"What—"

He pulls out another joint tucked behind his other ear. "Dude, you stare at your phone constantly and you walk around pissed off all the time." He gestures between us. "Not to mention, if you were hot and heavy with someone, I'd doubt you'd have time for these little *eye spy* extra-curricular activities you seem so fond of."

"She's in Europe," I say quietly. "Everything was great up until right before she left."

He lights his joint and takes a pull off it. "She's stringing you along, bro."

"She's not stringing me along," I argue. "Her ex hurt her and she's still not over it and I...I pushed her too far. I made the mistake of telling her I loved her too soon and in return she told me that she didn't want anything serious and to do my thing while she was gone. I never should have told her how I felt and scared her. I just thought she was finally ready—"

"Jesus Christ," he says. "Do you hear yourself? First of all— it's never a mistake to tell someone you love them if you feel it. Secondly —you're not even dating this girl seriously and she's got your balls in a vise like this?"

"Fuck you," I spew. "You have no clue how things are between us. She just needs some more time to work her shit out and get over her asshole ex. She'll come around—"

He inhales another cloud of smoke. "No, the only thing that's coming is her all over the dicks in Europe. While you're standing here like a love-sick puppy who can't buy a clue." He rolls his eyes and gestures for my phone. "Hand it over."

I back away. "No."

He advances toward me. "I'm doing you a favor, trust me. As soon as you stop calling her, she's going to start missing you. But you have to give her the chance to miss you first."

I slide my phone out of my pocket. "Fine."

He shakes his head. "Nope. I can't trust you to go through with it."

I hand it over. "Her contact name is 'B'."

"How original." He scrolls through my phone. "Damn, she

wouldn't even take a picture with you, would she?" When I don't answer, he whistles and presses the delete button. "You're welcome."

"What if something happens to her? What if—"

"Did she call you when she arrived in Europe?"

"Well no—"

"Did she call you when she saw the Eiffel Tower or the Leaning Tower of Pisa or any of that bullshit?"

"No, but—"

"Then if she calls you only when something bad happens to her...you're better off without her."

"She's studying abroad, Asher. She could just be busy."

Busy dancing in European clubs.

He sniffs and takes another drag off his joint. "Nah. An idiot, maybe. But not busy."

"She's not an idiot—"

He lifts his gaze to mine. "She is for not seeing what was right in front of her."

There's an awkward silence that fills the air between us and I shuffle my feet. "You never told me what was up with Dragoni."

He snuffs out his joint against the dumpster. "I gotta go. I'll see you tomorrow."

When he turns to leave, I reach for his arm. "Asher—"

The sky above me starts spinning and I close my eyes.

Fuck. Earlier at the library my sugar level was too high and I didn't have my insulin on me...and now I'm too low.

I try to think back to the last time I ate something, but thinking only seems to make me dizzier. Besides, it's not like it matters anymore because I'm dropping fast. I silently curse myself for throwing out the candy in my pocket.

I feel myself start to sway but then an arm is grabbing me and holding me upright. "Whoa. What the hell is the matter with you?"

"I need food. Sugar."

"You're a diabetic?"

When I nod, he sits me down by the tree and runs to the front door of the dorm building.

I see him fish in his pockets before he pounds on the glass beside the door. "Fuck, I forgot my key."

After pounding on the door a few more times, and screaming that the building was full of nothing but 'drunk assholes', he runs back over to me. "Give me the keys to your car."

I open my mouth to object but he screams, "I swear to God, I will fucking punch you. Hand them over or I will wrestle them from you."

I toss them to him and he hauls me upright with one hand and presses a button on my key chain with the other until he hears the horn beep.

When we're seated in the car and I'm a moment away from passing out, he looks at me. "Where's the nearest store?"

"My apartment is up the road from the college."

He slams on the gas and the tires screech in the distance as we take off.

CHAPTER 16

ASHER

I slide a glass of juice over the coffee table along with a sandwich. "This is the third glass of OJ you've given me. I'm fine."

I cross my arms and stare him down.

He rolls his eyes and reluctantly takes a sip.

I sweep my gaze around the room, taking it in. There's a couch, coffee table, and television—but there's also a queen-sized bed and a bookshelf located behind the couch.

"This place is pretty big for a studio apartment."

He takes a bite of his sandwich. "That's because it's a one bedroom."

I gesture to the couch that's at the foot of the bed and he laughs. "I use the room as my music studio instead of a bedroom."

I sit down next to him and pick up my own sandwich. "That explains why you don't dorm on campus."

"Yeah, I dormed my first year and it was horrible." He gives a shake of his head. "My roommate was an engineering major and hated any type of noise. He would hardly even speak, and whenever he did it was in hushed monotones." He points to his right ear. "I'm partially deaf in this ear so you can imagine how annoying it was for me."

I nod, surprised at how candid he's being with me now. "Guy sounds like a ball of fun."

"Yeah." His mouth tightens. "I've had diabetes since I was 12. I don't tell a lot of people about it."

"Why?"

He looks at the small pile of books on the coffee table. "I'll tell you what—Answer a few questions on Romeo and Juliet and I'll tell you everything you want to know about me."

"Seriously? It's Friday night. Only nerds study on the weekends."

He glares at me and picks up a book. "I'll start you off easy, asshole. What's Romeo's best friend's name?"

"Mercutio," I answer, suddenly thankful I read the first few chapters of the cliff notes.

He looks surprised. "Correct. Okay, shoot."

"What's your favorite instrument?"

"Although I love the guitar—the piano is my first love." He sits up straight and focuses on his book again. "Who's responsible for their deaths?"

"You're kidding me, right? They took their own lives; therefore, they are."

He slams his book shut. "Wrong. The correct answer is Friar Lawrence. I mean, sure Juliet and Romeo physically took their own lives, but it was the result of the actions; or rather in-actions of the Friar."

"How the hell do you figure that? Friar Lawrence was trying to do what was best for everyone."

"He dropped the ball, multiple times. Not only did he not deliver an important letter himself, he kept their secret. He should have told someone the truth."

"Maybe he couldn't," I yell and Landon makes a face. "Maybe he had a good reason for not telling someone...maybe he was being threatened by outside forces."

"What? Where the hell do you get that from? There's absolutely nothing to suggest that—"

I stand up. "Just because the book doesn't say it, it doesn't mean it's not a possibility."

His brows furrow. "Mrs. Sterling isn't going to like that answer. In fact, she's of the mindset that the Friar intentionally messed everything up after giving Juliet the potion so that they would die and both families would stop feuding."

"That's pretty fucked up."

He shrugs. "It is but it's the only motive that makes sense if you think about it."

"Okay, but how was he so certain it would work and they would kill themselves?"

"Easy—Love. I know you're not familiar with the concept, but love makes you crazy and irrational. Especially when you're a teenager."

I snort, the hollow ache in my chest almost becoming unbearable. "Trust me, I get it."

His eyes dart to mine. "You've been in love before?"

I close my eyes. "Unless they've invented a word that's deeper than love...yes."

He looks shocked. "Damn, I would have never guessed."

"High school sweetheart," I murmur. "Met her in 10th grade when I was new in town. It felt like someone clubbed me over the head with a bat made of steel...it was that intense." I draw in a deep breath. "Can't even say her name out loud without feeling like I'm suffocating."

"I guess that means you're not going to tell me what happened."

I glare at him. "What the fuck do you *think* happened?"

He swallows visibly. "She—shit. She couldn't accept you."

I run a hand through my hair. "Yeah, but that's only part of it. I fucked up...badly. I kept things from her that I should have told her about before they escalated."

"What kinds of things?"

"I—Only Preston knows the truth."

"Truth about what?"

"That video you watched? I didn't consent to it. What you saw was the tail end of me basically being molested while I was sleeping."

"Holy shit. Why didn't you press charges?"

A lump fills my throat. "To make a long story short, I was black-mailed. I haven't spoken to my father since the video went viral but he owns a popular football team and he's loaded. It's complicated, Landon. The guy basically threatened me with the video and a naked picture of my girlfriend. I had no choice but to play along and do whatever he wanted."

"That's fucking horrible." He runs a hand down his face. "So you're not—"

"I am. But I didn't come to that conclusion on my own.

"I'm confused—"

I snort. "Yeah me too. And so was he. I thought the blackmail was all about the money and control at first, even his sob story about his own dad that he told me, but it turns out it was more about his obsession with me. It's weird to explain...but I figured out that just because I didn't like the dick attached to the things he was doing...it didn't mean I didn't like the body part. Understand?"

"Sort of. I mean I'm not...I don't have those feelings, but I guess I can understand." He frowns. "But I'm guessing she didn't. Not even after you told her you were being blackmailed?"

"I never got to tell her that part. I decided to tell her the truth about the feelings I was having first—she didn't handle it too well." I stand up again, because I don't have the stomach or the heart to get into the rest of it with him. "I don't want to talk about her anymore. I can't."

I think about how much I fucked up with Breslin all the time. It eats at me day in and day out. I don't need to lay it all out for him just so he can tell me how much of an asshole I am.

I'm already well aware. The broken thing in my chest is my glaring reminder.

"I get it," he whispers. "We don't have to talk about her." He scans me intently. "Is the blackmail connected to your situation with Dragoni though? And what about Coach Crane? Does he know about this?"

"No, he doesn't and you can't tell him. And the former blackmail has nothing to do with this. The situation with Dragoni is all thanks to my brother Preston and his gambling problem."

His eyes look like they're about to pop out of his head. "Dragoni is a bookie?"

"Yup...well his family is. They're also connected to the mob."

His mouth falls open. "No shit."

"No shit."

He stands up and starts pacing. "But...how? Why?"

"I'll tell you on one condition."

"What?"

"Tell me about you."

He takes a breath and rubs his jaw. "I have a 10-year-old little sister. My parents are still married...sometimes happily, sometimes not. I—" Frustration fills his voice. "Education isn't what I want to do with my life, but my parents who are both teachers keep pushing for it." His eyes widen. "Not that I don't like teaching. I enjoy helping people...but—"

"Music is the love of your life."

His brown eyes practically twinkle. "Yeah...God it's—I've never felt more like me than when I'm in the studio making music or playing in front of a crowd."

More questions ping around the walls of my skull, but none of them seem to matter because there's only one thing I'm focused on now.

"Play something for me?"

One of his eyebrows go up slightly. "You mean like right now?"

"No time like the present."

He rocks back and forth on his heels before he waves a hand and gestures for me to follow him. "What's your poison?"

"Huh—" My words fall from my lips when I enter the room. I'm not really into music, although I do enjoy it on occasion, but you'd have to be blind not to appreciate the dedication that he clearly has for it.

There's a small, black baby grand piano in the middle of the room and various instruments either hung up or placed on shelves. There's also computers, speakers, and microphones all over. I can't even imagine how much time it took to put it all together.

I notice a bean bag chair in the far corner of the room and plop down. "Play me anything you want."

He rubs the back of his neck, I've never seen him look so nervous. "Well usually the first time I play for someone I ask them what their favorite band is so I can get a feel for what kind of music they like to hear."

"I usually listen to upbeat dance music while I workout—" Memories roll through me and I think back to the band I used to listen to in high school. "But my favorite band is Bush."

A grin curls the corners of his lips and my ears get hot. He looks so fucking sexy when he smiles at me like that.

"I think I might have misjudged you after all." He picks up a guitar and sits down on a stool. "You have really great taste in music... which tells me a hell of a lot about you."

Before I can come back with a smart ass reply, he starts strumming and I recognize the first few bars of *Comedown*. He closes his eyes, the former nervousness he once exhibited is long gone.

I sit back and relax, enjoying the performance.

Until he opens his mouth and sings...and I'm fucking gone.

The low and husky timbre of his voice sends shock waves through my system of the very best kind.

I can't help but notice the way his deft fingers strum with precision, the subtle tap of his foot keeping in time to the song, and the hypnotic energy coming off him in waves. The tiny hairs on the back of my neck stand up and my stomach somersaults, because the spell Landon's got me under is now airtight. There's absolutely nothing in this world that could break my focus from him.

When his eyes flit to mine, my heart speeds up.

He's utterly captivating and the weightiness of this moment catches me by the throat.

The song ends and a part of me aches at the loss. I point to the piano. "I need more."

I expect him to give me shit, but he doesn't. When he sits at the piano and his fingers graze those keys, I swear to God, the fucking organ in my rib cage beats like a jackhammer.

His muscles go slack and he closes his eyes, right before a feathery, yet deep, bell-like melody fills the room.

It's different from the guitar obviously, and he doesn't sing along to this tune, but it's no less mesmerizing.

He opens his eyes again, and this time they're trained on me. I can feel my Adam's apple bob against my throat and something inside my chest shifts. The air in the room becomes even more charged with every second that passes between us.

Landon has to know I'm into him, there's no way he can't at this point.

But that's not the cause of my current sweaty palms and racing heart...it's the fact that maybe...just maybe.

He might be into me too.

I open my eyes, look around, and grunt. I can't believe I fell asleep not only in his apartment, but in his music studio last night.

I glance down and laugh when I notice the blanket that's covering me.

Stifling a yawn, I get up and stretch before I pad back down the hallway that leads to his living room/ bedroom.

And I freeze.

Because white hot lust rushes into me like a damn tsunami as I take in a still sleeping and boxer clad Landon in his bed.

I figured he'd be on the lanky side...but I was wrong. Because even though he doesn't have an eight pack like me, his body is toned, cut, and defined.

But that's not what has my blood traveling south at warped speed.

It's the black ink taking up a majority of his back and upper arms.

Holy hell.

Not only are his tattoo's unexpected...they're sexy as fuck.

I study the large music staff and notes in the center of his back and the small print scrawled underneath that reads, *'Some pursue happiness, others create it.'* One of his arms is stuffed under a pillow so I can only see his right bicep which has a tattoo of a 3D guitar on it. However, I'd bet my next three paychecks from coach that his other arm has a piano keyboard on it.

He shifts slightly and I notice another music note, a much smaller one; behind his right ear. I quickly recall what he told me about his hearing impairment last night and my chest tightens.

Jesus...this guy.

This guy is going to be my downfall. Hell, this guy already *is* my downfall.

I haven't felt this way about another person since...

Terror clenches my heart and I force myself to breathe. I'm two seconds away from grabbing my shit and leaving, but then my eyes catch on something else when he shifts again.

I swallow hard as I stare at the smooth, pink tip of his morning wood that's currently peeking out of the waistband of his boxers.

My entire body stills, too afraid to make any sudden movements out of fear that what I'm looking at will disappear.

My heart pounds in my ears as I watch it grow bigger right before my very eyes. I silently pray to the God of bisexual men with crushes on their tutor's that his boxers slip a bit more so I can see all of him.

My own dick strains against my zipper, and I can't help but think about what would happen if I took the few short strides over to him and licked that glistening head of his that's taunting me.

Would he moan and urge me on? Would he groan my name and beg me to take him deeper?

I practically whimper when his hand wraps around his length and he gives his thick cock one long, agonizing, jerk through the fabric of his boxers.

I take a step closer to the bed but stop myself as reality comes crashing down all around me. A sharp pain infiltrates my chest, the impact knocking the air from my lungs.

Landon's not like me. He's made that perfectly clear already.

He shifts again and there's no way he's not going to wake up in the next minute and see me standing over him all but salivating at the sight of his dick.

I feel around my pockets for my phone and I high tail it the fuck out of there.

I do it just in time, because a moment after I close the door behind me, my phone rings.

"What's up, Preston?"

"Hey—" He pauses. "Sorry, didn't mean to interrupt your workout."

"I wasn't working out. I was—" I press the button for the elevator. "Never mind, it doesn't matter."

The depressing tilt of my voice must give me away because he says, "Like hell it doesn't, Asher. I called you to see how everything was going at Woodside and if you needed anything, but right now it doesn't sound like things are going too well. What's up?"

"Trust me, you don't want to know."

"Try me."

"I think I'm falling for my tutor."

"Is she hot like the last one?"

"Hotter...only she's a he."

"Huh?"

"It's a guy," I grind out as the elevator doors open.

I can hear his laughter on the other line before he says. "About damn time."

"What the fuck is that supposed to mean?"

"Look, brother. I've been by your side since the day you came out to me...but you've never really been out. You know what I mean?"

"Not really." I think about his statement. "I fuck plenty of guys."

He sighs. "Yeah, you fuck them. That's about it. You've never dated any of them."

"I—"

"I know," he interjects. "Kyle really fucked you up, Asher. I get it." He draws in a breath. "And if you like this guy, don't let him fuck this up for you too. You deserve to be happy."

Lead settles in my stomach. "There's only one problem with that."

"What?"

"He's not—" I step off the elevator and start the walk back to campus. "He's not into guys. At least I'm pretty sure he's not."

There's silence on the other line before he says, "*Pretty sure* isn't a guarantee. Do you get any vibes from him?"

"Not really. I mean...I didn't until last night."

"You could just come out and ask him. Maybe not ask him if he's into you outright, but ask him if he's ever hooked up with another guy and enjoyed it," he suggests and I inwardly groan.

"Why so it can make the rest of the year weird between us when he says no?"

"You won't know until you try, Asher. Make a move on him. Show your cards. What's the worst that can happen? It's no different from when you dated Breslin."

"I didn't have to try or wonder with Breslin, asshole," I growl, hating the fact that he brought her up. "I mean yeah, I had to work at keeping her once I had her, but us falling for one another was the easy part. The attraction and spark between us was instant for the both of us, no question."

I hear some crashing sound in the background before he yells, "Shit, I gotta go. My roommate and his girlfriend are arguing again."

"Jesus."

"Yeah." He sighs. "I can't wait until Becca gets back from her trip. This way, I can find us a place off campus and I don't have to deal with this crap anymore."

I stop walking. "What? You're seriously considering moving in with *her*? For Christ's sake, Preston, not only is she connected to the family who's threatening *your* family as collateral—her family is a bunch of bookies and mobsters. She's literally the *worst* girl for you to date."

"I get your reservations, but I told you I was serious about her." There's another crashing sound, louder this time. "Look, I have to go. We'll talk about this later," he says before the line goes dead.

I jog up the steps to the campus dorms, my head buzzing a mile a minute. I feel like my problems are piling up by the second since I've been here.

But maybe...Preston has a point. Maybe I should make a move on Landon.

Why so he can turn you down?— my mind taunts.

Fear skitters down my spine again. Making a move on Landon would be the stupidest thing I could do.

Not only do I not date— guys *or* girls for that matter. But it would ruin the friendship between us, in addition to making things awkward as hell once he declined. Because there's no doubt in my mind that he would.

I just need to find something to occupy my time so I can forget about the stupid crush I have on him, because that's exactly what it is. He's nothing more than an itch I want to scratch.

Or maybe you're just scared because of how things ended with the last person you fell for.

"Hey," a breathy voice behind me says, interrupting my thoughts.

I spin around and come face to face with the blonde from the night before. O'Connor's girlfriend. "Hey. Listen do you have a key for the building? I forgot mine upstairs and I need to get ahold of the RA."

"Sure. I think he's out of the building right now, but you're welcome to wait in my room." I don't miss the underlying meaning in her words.

I let my gaze roam over her tits and long legs. She wasn't a ten in the sack, but maybe she'll be better with her mouth. Either way, she's certainly one hell of a distraction.

My phone vibrates and Landon's name lights up the screen. I focus on the way her ass sways when she steps forward and opens the door.

Pressing ignore, I give the blonde a smile. "Lead the way."

CHAPTER 17

BRESLIN

I groan and bury my head in the pillow when there's a knock on the door.

"Breslin," Kit's voice calls from the other side. "It's me, open up."

I wave my hand in the direction of the door and silently shoo her away. I'm not in the mood to talk to her or anyone else.

Well, except for *him*. But he obviously has no desire to talk to me anymore.

Probably serves me right for ignoring him over the last week and a half.

Tears threaten to spill, but right when I'm about to give in, the door clicks open and I hear Kit's footsteps walking toward me.

I throw the blanket over my head for good measure and she taps her foot against the wooden floor. "One of your classmates told me you didn't show up for any of the tours today. What the hell is going on?"

"Hangover," I mumble, knowing that's the least of my issues at the moment.

The bed beside me dips. "I don't buy it, B. You've been in bed for over 24 hours."

When I don't respond, she releases a sigh. "Are you at least going to tell me what happened at the party the other night? You went upstairs with *Mr. Rico Suave* and came back down five minutes later in tears before you ran out the door."

When silence is my answer, she yanks the covers off my head. "After I kicked him in the balls and right before security threw me and Becca out, he swore nothing happened between you two, but if he did something to you we need—"

I squeeze my eyes shut. "He didn't hurt me. It was all me...I couldn't go through with it."

"Oh," she says before she frowns. "Why not? What happened—" She cocks her head to the side, her gaze scrutinizing. "Fucking Asher. I knew it. I knew he was—"

I sit up in bed and hug my knees to my chest. "No. It wasn't Asher I was thinking about."

"Then w—" Her words fall when I bring my hands to my face and burst into tears.

"Landon?" she questions.

I nod my head and sniff. "I fucked up, Kit. God, I fucked up so bad with him. I knew it the second I kissed that guy. It was like a bucket of ice water being dumped on my head. All I wanted was Landon."

"Well, shit," she says, her face breaking into a smile. "This is good. Great in fact." Her expression twists. "But I don't understand why you're so upset about it. Landon's crazy about you—"

My chest constricts and I reach for a tissue. "He blocked my number, Kit. He doesn't want to talk to me."

I stand up and start looking for my bags, adrenaline pumping through me. I have to go back home and make things right with him.

I never should have let Landon go in the first place. I know that now. Being with Landon made me happy—even through all of the pain over Asher—I somehow managed to find it again. Because

Landon loved me back to happy. And it took me so long to realize it, but now that I do, I can't let him go.

And even more than that? I'm sick of being miserable. I'm sick of being scared to ever let another person in.

And God knows, I'm *so* sick and tired of being heartbroken over Asher Holden. I'm done wasting my tears on someone who doesn't deserve them.

I've wasted *years*—some of the best years of my life—being broken over him, letting the sharp pieces' slice into me time and time again, allowing it to serve as a painful reminder of how much love can fuck a person up.

But not anymore. Not today.

Fuck that.

Fuck the past and the painful memories.

Fuck the happy ones, too.

Fuck Asher Holden. I'm sick of his brand of poison pumping through my veins.

It ends here. Because I finally realize that just because I wasn't meant to have a future with him, it doesn't mean I'm not permitted to have it with someone else. Someone who gives me butterflies and puts me on a pedestal, instead of making me feel like a flea who can't possibly compare or shine in his presence, like I'll never be good enough and that I'm not desirable or attractive. Someone who could go behind my back and cheat on me with my worst enemy. Someone who abused all the love I gave.

It's time to step out of Asher's shadow and into the light.

Into Landon's light. Because I know when I show up, hand *him* my heart, and tell him it's his for the taking if he wants it, he'll keep it protected and intact.

He won't let me fall with no intention of catching me. Landon will keep me safe, because he's already proven it.

I start tossing various things into my suitcase. "I have to fix things with Landon. I have to—"

"Breslin," Kit says sharply and I pause mid-packing.

"I say this with love," she says gently. "But I think you should give it a few more days before you make any rash decisions."

"No. I have—"

She exhales and rubs her forehead. "Breslin, unless you're 1,000 percent sure about this, you're only going to hurt him more and it wouldn't be right."

I turn to face her, appalled. "Excuse me? Who's friend are you?"

"Are you kidding me?" she screams. "You know I'm your friend. I'm just saying to give it a few days before you go marching back into his life and making declarations of love. If he blocked you, it's because you hurt him, Breslin, and he's had enough. And I know, it sucks to hear the truth, but that's what friends are for. If you still feel this way in another week I will personally go with you to the airport. Just give it more than five minutes to make sure you're not making a mistake that will hurt him even more."

"I—" Dread settles in my stomach. Kit's right. I was only thinking about myself, about my own self-preservation and my need for space. I never stopped to think about how much I was hurting Landon.

"Fuck, Kit. I don't deserve him, do I?"

She takes a step toward me. "No, that's not what I'm saying. You're amazing, B. Guarded, sure. But incredible. You're just gonna have to be ready to fight for him when you get back. But first, you need to make sure that *he's* what you really want and you're not just acting impulsively because he decided to ignore you now and it stings. Understand?"

I nod and take a deep breath, letting her words sink in. My eyes fall shut and my heart kick-starts, awareness surging through me.

I'll take the few days like Kit insists, but I don't need them.

Because my heart knows exactly what it wants and it's ready to fight like hell for it.

CHAPTER 18

ASHER

His mouth forms a straight line as he scans over my paper. It's hard to read his expression, mostly because he's been so distant and short with me during today's session.

It's been two days since I inadvertently stayed over his house, but today's the first time we've seen one another and it's been strange...almost like he's mad at me for something.

I drag in a low, slow breath when another minute goes by and he still hasn't said a word. I worked my ass off studying for this, I even cracked open the book instead of just scanning the cliff notes.

Finally, he looks up. "Much better." His tone is clipped, staccato. "See you tomorrow."

Before I can respond, he slams his own book shut, tosses it in his backpack, and stands up.

"Whoa," I all but growl, because I can't stand this passive aggressive bullshit any longer. "That's it? That's all you have to say?"

He opens his mouth to speak but then clamps it shut before he huffs and starts walking.

When I stand up and reach for his elbow, his entire body stiffens and his jaw flexes. "Did you block her number?"

His voice is low, almost deadly. It doesn't scare me, not by a long shot; but fuck if it doesn't turn me on.

When I don't answer, he faces me head on. "I tried calling her the other morning and I couldn't get through."

I swallow thickly. "When?"

He looks at me like I've sprouted another head. "What? Why does it matter? The morning after you slept over."

I feel like I'm being strangled with a live wire because two things become glaringly obvious at that moment.

One—using a special hidden app to block her number wasn't such a good idea after all because he's pissed—which means he still cares about her—which means that when she gets back, he'll be putty in her hands again.

And two—he called her *that* morning. The morning after I thought that maybe...something had happened between us. Or was *starting* to happen between us.

I'm a fucking idiot.

I snatch my bag off the table and charge for the doors.

"Really, Asher? *I'm* the one who has a right to be pissed off here, not you," he calls out after me.

I reach in my bag for my beanie and pull it over my head. It's not 100% effective in terms of not being recognized on campus, and its effect will wear down soon, but it helps some when I'm not in the mood to be noticed.

I can hear him trying to keep up behind me. "It's 90 degrees outside." He balks. "And I hate to break it to you, but that stupid hat isn't doing anything to hide who you are."

My hands clench into fists at my sides. "Go to hell."

"Asher." He grabs my shoulder and spins me around. I can feel everyone's eyes boring into us in the courtyard. "What I meant was— you don't have to hide who you are." He flicks a hand in the air. "Fuck these people."

"I installed a hidden app on your phone and blocked her

number," I whisper. "I was doing you a favor because I didn't think you'd be strong enough not to call her."

Confusion followed by anger flare in his eyes...and then he laughs. "Are we having two completely separate conversations at the same time?"

I can't help but laugh now too. "Shit, I guess we are."

I motion to a bench in the courtyard and sit. "I'm sorry." I look at him. "Actually, that's a lie. I'm not sorry. The way I see it is if you're not the very first stop when she gets back home, I did you a solid."

He thinks for a moment before speaking. "Yeah, I mean, it sucks...but maybe you have a point. It's just—" He breaks eye contact. "I care about her...a lot."

I exhale. "I know. I get it."

His hand grips the back of his neck and he looks around the courtyard. "I suppose I'll know for sure where she stands when she gets back."

I muster a smile that I hope hides my true feelings. "Yeah. Yeah, you will, man. I'm sure everything will end up turning out for the best."

He nods and I swallow down my pain as he hikes his bag on his shoulder. "Your beanie's not so bad by the way. You're kind of working that whole jock-hipster vibe."

When I cock an eyebrow, he grins. "See you tomorrow morning?"

I nod and watch him as he walks away, jealousy burning through me like a wildfire. This girl, whoever she is, must be something special.

Because he is.

He chews on his pen as he scans my quiz and I stifle a groan. Two more days have passed and this feeling has only intensified. Like a boulder rolling downhill and picking up speed. It's so bad, I have absolutely no desire to hook up with anyone else now—male or female.

Preston keeps telling me I need to make a move for my own sanity, but for someone so smart, that's dumb advice.

He looks up at me over the paper and his eyebrows crash together. "You okay? You're sweating."

"It's the end of the summer, of course I'm sweating." When he makes a face, I add, "I'm fine."

I'm the complete *opposite* of fine. I have a hard on the size of Texas and an insatiable appetite for him that I won't ever be able to indulge in. Sex won't cure it and ignoring it only seems to make it worse. Unrequited attraction with someone you're forced to interact with every day is one of the seven circles of hell, I'm sure of it.

I chew on my thumbnail and look around the library. I'm desperate to get out of here, desperate to get away from him. I'm actually looking forward to the grueling practice in this heatwave that's awaiting me after this.

"Dude, relax, you got an 80. You're almost there."

I stand up. "Great. Are we done?"

He stares at me open-mouthed and I adjust my gym bag so it covers the evidence of my attraction to him.

"Yeah. I mean, I guess." He taps his pen on the edge of the desk. "I um—do you have any plans this Saturday night?"

The hairs on my neck lift and my heart skyrockets. Is Landon asking me out?

I sit back down in my seat. "Nope."

"Do you want to watch me play? It's okay if you say no... it's just. I have this semi steady gig at an underground venue called The Black Spoon and—"

"The Black Spoon?" I interject and he nods, his knee shaking underneath the table.

"Yeah, but there's this band called *The Resistance,* and their lead guitarist is scheduled to have surgery on his hand over the Christmas break in a few months, and they need someone to fill in," he continues, not stopping for air.

Christ, I've never seen him so excited.

"They're like one of my favorite indie rock bands around, they're pretty popular too. And while I have no desire to be part of a band, this would be an awesome opportunity. Plus, the money is great and I would get to visit England for a week." He takes a breath. "Anyway, they'll be there Saturday night to watch me play. It's kind of like an audition and I...I could really use all the support I can get that night."

"I'll be there," I say and he smiles.

"Really? Fuck, that's awesome. I figured you'd think it was stupid and make fun of me for asking."

"Not at all." I lean back in my chair and grin. "Not that I want to gas your head up, but you're phenomenal, Landon. They'd be stupid not to hire you."

A cocky smile tugs at the corners of his mouth and he looks me in the eye. "Thank you."

Oh hell. It's no longer my erection twitching...it's my goddamn heart.

I need to get out of here. I stand up again but he halts me. "Do you want to hang out later?"

"Can't," I say quickly. "After practice I have to put all the equipment away and clean up the field.

"Really?"

"Yeah, it's...sort of my job. Coach pays me, so it's not like it's a hardship or anything. Helps me pay the bills since I won't have time for anything else besides football and classes once the semester starts."

"Do you want help?" He pushes his glasses up his nose. "I don't play football, but I'm pretty sure I can figure out where the equipment goes and clean up. Besides, it's hot as hell out today, you'll finish quicker if I help you."

"Yeah, sure," I say, despite my heart's protest. "Thanks."

He chews on the end of his pen and shrugs. "No need to thank me, man. What are friends for?"

Friends...right.

M y teammates laugh when O'Connor crushes his Gatorade bottle and throws it on the grass. "Have fun cleaning, fag."

I roll my shoulders back and take a step forward. I'm a second away from jumping on the motherfucker, but just then Coach Crane barks, "Pick that up, O' Conner or I'm benching you for the first game of the season. You treat the field and your fellow teammates with some goddamn respect."

He grumbles and sucks his teeth at me before he leans over, picks up his bottle, and tosses it in the trash.

When the guys are off the field, I remove my shoulder pads and helmet and place them on the bleachers.

"This is your team, Holden," Coach says behind me. "You have to whip them into shape or this is gonna get a helluva lot worse for you, son." He squeezes my shoulder before he walks off.

"O' Conner is a giant fuckwad," a familiar voice calls out. I look up and see Landon walking down the bleachers. Guess he watched what just happened.

I shrug and start stacking various equipment. "It is what it is."

"I don't know how you stand it." He begins searching the field for discarded bottles to throw out. "Guy needs to be knocked down a few pegs. O'Connor's not even that good."

I turn and look at him. "How would you know? Thought you hated football?"

"I do." He picks up a football off the ground. "But I'm willing to bet I'm much better than he is."

He launches it in the air and it misses me by more than a foot. "That's quite the execution you've got there."

He narrows his eyes. "Bite me. It wasn't like I was trying."

I pick up the football and toss it back to him. Thankfully his catching skills aren't like his throwing ones.

"Jesus," he grunts, flapping his hand around. "That was...*intense*."

I waggle my eyebrows and take a few steps back. "60 mph, baby. They didn't call me one of the best quarterbacks of our generation for no reason."

He rolls his eyes. "Nice to see you're so humble about it."

I wave him on. "Come on, nerd. I'm gonna teach you how to throw the right way."

He snorts. "I throw just fine."

"No. You throw like a pussy." I gesture between us. "We're friends, right?"

"Yeah."

"Well, my friends don't throw like pussies. Therefore, it's my duty to fix that disaster technique of yours."

"Christ, you sound like such an asshole jock right now."

I ignore that comment and set up the target we use for practice before walking across the field to him.

He looks confused. "I'm not throwing it to you?"

"You're not good enough to throw it to me, yet—" I stand behind him and point. "Keep your eyes on that target. Don't waver."

When he nods, I growl, "I said *don't* waver. Nodding your head is wavering, Landon."

"Are you always this much of a tyrant?"

"In my domain? Yes. Now pay attention." I tap his right leg. "Shift your weight and push off your back foot. That's where all your power comes from. The inside part of your back foot. Got it?" When he adjusts his stance and I see that his eyes are still focused, I say, "Now step your front foot toward your target."

I squeeze his bicep and ignore the way my cock jolts to life. I've never been aroused while on the field before, but I guess there's a first time for everything. "And now for the most important part—put your eyes where you want the ball to land. Pick a spot within your target. In this case, the small black dot—then let that motherfucker sail."

I can feel his sharp intake of breath before he pulls his arm back and launches the football in the air. My balls draw tight as I watch a bead of sweat trickle down his cheekbone before traveling down to the light stubble that lines his jaw.

"Holy shit—that was awesome. Did you see that?" he exclaims and I take a step back.

"Yeah, man." I clear my throat, trying to cover my fumble. "Not bad. Much better this time."

I start walking around the field, gathering equipment again.

"Fuck, I feel like I need to celebrate or something," Landon says and I bite back a laugh. "No wonder you love it. Hitting that target was a rush. I could only imagine the feeling when you throw the winning touchdown."

I don't have the heart to tell him I intentionally positioned the target much closer than the coach does for us. His happiness is intoxicating.

"Want to grab a beer with me when we're done here?"

"Sure," I say, even though what I should be saying is no.

"Yeah, Ma," he says. "I got the last package you sent me."
I hide my smile and look around the moderately crowded sports bar.

"No, Ma. I haven't forgotten to eat today. In fact, I'm currently eating a granola bar and some veggies now," he continues as he wipes his hands which are covered in chicken wing sauce and takes a sip of his beer.

"Yes, I've checked my level and I've taken my insulin." He lets out a sigh. "I have to go. I have a session with one of my students starting soon." He looks down. "I love you. Say hi to the little rug rat and Dad for me." He laughs at something on the other line. "Well, hi to you too, punk. How's that math class of yours going?"

There's mumbling on the other line and he laughs again. "Yeah, I know it sucks. But you'll get through it, kid." He plays with his straw. "Tell you what, email it to me and I'll give you some notes." There's more mumbling and what sounds like a squeal on the other line. "I love you, too. Hold down the fort and take care of the parental units for me," he says before he hangs up.

My chest squeezes and a smile pulls at my lips with the sincerity in both his tone and in his eyes.

I like that he has a great relationship with his younger sibling, reminds me of my relationship with Preston—even though unlike Landon and his little sister, Preston and I are close in age.

"Your family sounds pretty awesome," I say, ignoring the way my insides twist.

On the outside, my family looked like the poster board for the perfect family, but we were anything but. It's why me and Preston were always so close and I'd do anything in the world for him and vice versa. We were all each other had to confide in when shit got bad...which was *a lot*.

"Yeah—" He takes another swig of his beer. "Well, my mom in particular is kind of over protective ever since—" His voice drifts off and his face falls.

"Since what?"

For the last two hours, we've been disclosing random things about ourselves to one another. Mostly surface things like our favorite television show and favorite food, but I've been dying to know more about him. Like—what makes him tick? And all the things that make him who he is today.

His expression turns somber and I almost want to kick myself for prying. Just when I'm about to tell him to forget about it, he says, "I never really talk about this with anyone, but I lost my older brother when I was eight years old."

"Shit, man. I'm sorry to hear that." It's on the tip of my tongue to ask him what happened but I don't want to push him, so I stay silent, deciding to put the ball in his court.

"He died from complications with diabetes. He was only 12. My parents had no idea he had it because his doctor didn't check for it during his last checkup, despite it running in our family."

He shakes his head. "I was the one who found him in bed that morning. I thought he was playing around and faking because he didn't want to go to school. But when my mom came in and ran over to him—" He pauses to gather his composure. "She screamed for me to call 911, but it was already too late. He died in his sleep."

He takes a breath. "It was the worst day of my life. The second was the day my parents found out that I had diabetes."

I sit up in my seat. "They must have been scared out of their minds."

"Oh, they were petrified. They were already overprotective of me after Levi's death, but it brought it to a whole new level after that. I wasn't allowed to do anything or go anywhere other than school without either of them by my side. It was—it was hard to be a kid. Hard to make friends. They all knew something was wrong with me and that I was different. I got made fun of a lot and became somewhat of a social outcast, and in return; I internally resented both my parents and Levi for dying. I was miserable for so long. Miserable and *lonely*. Until the day I discovered up my first instrument—the piano—and taught myself how to play. Music saved my life, made me happy again. It was the one thing that was for me, you know?"

I nod, because I do. That's what football was for me.

I rest my forearms on the table, silently debating whether or not to tell him the truth about my upbringing now. "My dad," I say slowly and something inside me coils and it becomes harder to breathe.

"Hey," Landon whispers. "You don't have to tell me if you don't want to."

"My dad used to hit me." I look at him. "Beat me," I amend. "You'd never know it from the outside looking in though."

"Fuck, what an asshole." I can feel him eyeing the scar above my eyebrow. I almost want to pull my hat down further to cover it, but that would just let him know how much it still bothers me. "He did that to you?"

"Yeah." I lean back against my seat. "It was the first time I told him I didn't want to go to football practice and he didn't take it too well. It would have been worse, but Preston saved my ass that day. He also has a scar of his own to show for it."

"I guess that explains why you and your brother are so close," he says, studying my face. "And why you agreed to come here for him."

"Preston has some issues but...he's my brother. He's always been there for me and even though we're only two years apart, I've always tried to protect him the best I could. There's no way I wasn't coming here and doing this for him."

"What if you fail?" He blanches. "What will they do to you?"

"I don't know, but I don't intend to find out."

He nods. "I—uh. I'll make sure you keep your grades up." He looks around and rubs his neck. "I won't let you fail."

I give him a look, I'm not sure if he's saying what I think he's saying. But if he is? That only makes me feel worse.

Landon's not a cheater. He works his ass off to help those in need —it's part of what attracts me to him so much.

The fact that he's a good person. A person who cares more about others than he does himself. Him and Breslin both have that trait in common. Hell, maybe that's part of the pull for me, because it's a quality I've always lacked.

"I appreciate it," I say, picking at what's left of my food. "But I think for once...I'd like to really try."

I glance up at him and he smiles proudly. "I think you're going to do fine, Asher. You're already improving with every session. Hell, you may not even need me in another month."

Panic punches me in the gut. "Oh...um. Well, that sucks."

He makes a face. "Why?"

This is it. If there was ever an opening...it's right here. Staring me in the face with the softest brown eyes I've ever seen.

"I like hanging out with you. I—I like having you as a friend."

Jesus Christ, I just sacked myself.

"I do too," he says. "Me possibly not tutoring you anymore shouldn't stop us from being friends." He takes a sip of his drink and shrugs. "Not unless you want it to?"

"No." I start digging into my food again in order to hide my disappointment over my fuck up. "Now that we've got that out of the way, what else do you want to talk about? Euthanasia? Cancer? Perhaps the homeless youth epidemic?"

He laughs. "Yeah, I guess our conversation did take a turn there."

The waitress comes by then. After we order another round of appetizers he looks at me. "What's your biggest fear?"

It's my turn to laugh. "Let's see—I lost the love of my life. I've been blackmailed with a sex tape that went viral. And both me and my brother are currently being threatened by bookies and mobsters. I'm pretty sure I'm living it."

The color drains from his face and he coughs. "Yeah, I guess you have a point." He takes a bite out of his food. "Okay, it's your turn then. Ask me anything."

Opportunity rears its head again and I think back to Preston's advice.

I want to ask him...it's a question that's been marinating in my mind ever since Preston suggested it. But how the hell do you casually ask a guy if he's ever sucked another guy's dick and enjoyed it without it being awkward?

But then again...there may not be another opportunity like this. Hell, I can probably blame it on the beer if things get weird.

Resting my arm on the booth to appear nonchalant, I give him a cocky smile. "Ever hook up with a guy?"

There...it's out there in the universe. I did it. No going back now.

I'm so wrapped up in nerves, I almost don't hear him when he says, "No. Well—" There's a long pause that stops my heart. "Sort of, I guess. I don't know if you could really call it a hookup per se." He nibbles on a fry. "It's kind of a strange story."

I finish off the rest of my beer and reach for the pitcher, I have a feeling I'm going to need it. "I'm all ears. Strange stories are a guilty pleasure of mine."

The air around us seems to halt as I wait for him to speak again.

"There was this girl in high school," he begins. "Her name was Amber Alpine. Captain of the dance squad and the hottest girl in school. She was really—" He holds his hands out in front of his chest and winks. "Smart."

I laugh and gesture for him to continue.

"Anyway, I had the biggest crush on her. It was so bad I used to sneak anonymous mixed CD's in her locker." His fingers drum the sides of his glass. "I never thought I had a shot with her. You know, with me being a nerd and all." He shoots me a look. "But one glorious day, right before we graduated, I ended up losing my virginity to her and we kind of became an item briefly." He gives his head a slight shake. "I'm pretty sure it was only because she heard from her mother that guys with 4.0 GPAs made rich husbands—but I sure as shit wasn't going to question my good fortune."

"Can't say I blame you," I say, my thoughts going to Breslin. She could have had any guy she wanted. Why she chose me is anyone's guess, but I didn't question my good fortune either. I was thankful for it.

"Yeah," he continues. "Anyhow, her parents' were throwing her a huge graduation party and she asked me to be the entertainment."

When I raise an eyebrow, he says, "To play music."

"Gotcha."

"I was nervous as hell about it. Playing for my entire graduating class was scary shit at the time, considering I hardly ever played in front of anyone back then." He shrugs. "To make a long story short, mid-way through the night, one of her cousins who lived in their guesthouse offered me a little something to take the edge off. Said it would help me loosen up."

"Drugs?"

He nods. "I didn't realize it was ecstasy until after I was done and I was practically humping everyone and everything in sight."

"Oh, man," I say through laughter. "That must have made for an interesting night."

"It did," he muses. "God, everyone was blitzed out of their minds at that party. It would have been weird if I was sober." He shakes his head again and chuckles. "Anyway, Amber and I went upstairs to fool around and I must have passed out at some point between the third and fourth round because when I woke up—" He smiles into his hand. "Amber was laid out spread eagle next to me masturbating and the cousin who gave me the drugs had my dick in his mouth and was going to town."

"Holy shit."

He slaps the table. "Tell me about it. Apparently, they were the dirty version of kissing cousins, and it was a common occurrence."

"What did you do?"

He shrugs. "I closed my eyes and drifted off again. I was high out of my fucking mind. Amber and I ended things a few days after, though."

"Because of what happened?"

"Well, yeah."

My stomach drops and I focus on my food. "Makes sense. I know first-hand how much it can fuck you up when you wake up to find your dick in another guy's mouth."

His brows furrow. "That wasn't what upset me so much. I didn't give a shit about that. I mean everyone experiments in the 21st century, right? The thing I couldn't seem to get past was that she and her cousin had a steady *thing* going on. It just...I don't know. It wasn't even like they were step-cousins or hell, even third cousins. They were *first* cousins. The bloodline was strong. They even looked alike. Plus, she didn't think that fucking her cousin a few nights a week qualified as cheating on me since they were family." He reaches for his water and takes a sip. "On second thought, I think *that's* what really bothered me in the end."

"Wow."

"I know." He sets his water down. "I wish the girl well, but I wasn't exactly devastated over breaking up."

"You seem really laid-back when it comes to certain things...and people," I blurt out, wishing I could suck the words back in.

His eyes hold mine. "Probably because I grew up feeling different and an outcast. It made me sympathize with those who are different too. It also made me stronger. Levi's death taught me that life's too short to spend it not being happy and not being true to yourself. Life's all about evolving...changing. Discovering yourself and who you really are is pivotal. It's how you become comfortable in your own skin. So while I might just be an uptight geek to some people, it's fine. Because those people who are so busy making judgments about me, will never know who I really am, the other parts of me; therefore, they don't matter. I'd rather invest my energy on the things and people who are worth it. Know what I mean?"

"Yeah—no. It's something I'm still struggling with...not caring what other people think." I draw in a breath, my chest caving in. "I think it's because I lost the girl I loved when I told her the truth about me. I guess maybe I feel like I'll lose everything and everyone if I wear my sexuality like a badge of honor."

"Your sexuality doesn't define you, Asher," he says. "But that's something you have to figure out for yourself."

He stands up and throws some bills on the table. "It's getting late and I have an early morning tutoring session. Want a lift?"

"No, I'll walk. I could use the exercise."

He snorts. "See you tomorrow."

He pauses mid-stride, his back to me. "For what it's worth, it really was her loss."

Before I can respond, he walks out the door.

I thought finding out more about him would have dwindled my interest, but it only fueled it.

I pull out my phone and type out a text.

Asher: Make sure you check your sugar level and take your insulin when you get home or I'll kick your ass.

CHAPTER 19

LANDON

I look around the library and frown when I don't see him. Asher was supposed to meet me after football practice today and he's not usually late. At least not *this* late.

Annoyance flares deep in my gut—he's probably hooking up with his latest campus fling.

I freeze...wondering why the thought has me so on edge.

Because it shouldn't.

And yet...it *does*.

My phone rings and I'm relieved to see his name flash across the screen. "It's about time," I answer. "I only called you like 10 times in the last 30 minutes."

I expect him to make a joke about my phone issues, but he doesn't, instead he clears his throat and says, "Sorry. I—um. I don't think I'm gonna be able to make it today."

There's no laughter in his tone, no hint of a distraction either. If anything, he sounds panicked.

I stand up. "Why?"

"Something happened during practice." There's a sharp intake of breath. "I can't—"

There's muffling on the other line, almost like he's holding the phone away, before he grunts in pain.

My stomach recoils. "Where are you?"

"Still in the locker room. Haven't been able to make it out of here yet," he grinds out in agony. "But don't come here. I can handle this myself."

"Don't be stupid—" I start to protest but the line goes dead.

I roll my eyes and gather my things. Asher's talking crazy right now and it doesn't make a lick of sense. He's obviously in excruciating pain, why wouldn't he want anyone to help him?

I make my way across campus and into the locker room. Practice ended an hour ago so there's no one around when I push past the doors.

And that's where I find Asher sitting on a bench wearing a towel, hunched over in agony.

"I told you not to come," he says when he looks up.

I walk over to him. "You sounded like you were dying."

"Nope, not dying." His gaze is drawn inward and he scowls. "I'm pretty sure death would be sweeter."

I put my backpack down on the bench beside him. "You gonna tell me what happened here?"

His mouth tightens and he clutches his towel. "Nope."

"Fine. Can I at least take you to the hospital?"

He glares at me. "Hell no."

I pinch the bridge of my nose. Dealing with him right now is like dealing with a toddler. "Dude, you're in pain. You can't just sit here and do nothing."

He lifts his chin. "Sure I can."

When he winces in pain a moment later, I've had about all I can take.

I reach for the towel. "Let me see."

He pulls the towel back. "Trust me, you don't want to."

"Nothing I haven't seen before." I yank the towel harder. "We have the same equipment."

"Not right now we don't."

"Huh—" My words fall when he moves his towel down. "Holy—man, you have to get that checked out. Your testicle is the size of a planet right now."

He winces again and I ignore the heavy length of his cock hanging between his legs, because all I can focus on is the way his balls—or rather *ball*—looks like it's about to pop out of his body.

It's huge, inflamed. Way bigger than it should be... and it's *angry*. Hell, my own balls are screaming in protest and crying for him.

When I take out my phone, he looks like a deer in headlights. "Don't you dare take a picture of this, Landon."

"I'm not," I assure him. "I'm texting Coach."

When he opens his mouth to object, I say, "You need to see a doctor—a nurse. Someone, Asher. Unless you want it to fall off."

He grumbles and I take the opportunity to shoot a text to Coach Crane before I look around for a first aid kit.

I hand him an ice pack. "Lift your...yeah. And put it on the...you know."

The vein in his neck bulges, he lets out a slew of curses, and sweat runs down his well-defined abs as he maneuvers himself and places the ice pack over him.

"Do you know what caused this?"

I'm about to make a joke about his sex life to lighten the mood, but he clenches his hand into a fist. "Fucking, O' Conner."

"What?"

"His girlfriend tracked me down before practice today and told me she came clean to him." He shrugs. "I figured we'd brawl again...but no. The fucker did something much worse." He blanches. "I found a spider chilling in my protective cup when I was getting ready to hit the showers. O' Conner must have snuck into my locker before practice started and put it there. Didn't think much of it until pain like you can't even imagine fired through my balls and he flipped me the bird before he left."

It's my turn to wince. "Talk about hitting below the belt." I think about this for a moment. "I thought football players don't wear cups?"

"We don't," he says. "But apparently, some jerk tried suing the school last year because he took a ball to the groin during practice and now we're all forced to wear them." He tips his head back and blows out a breath. "I can't even fucking walk. And google—" He shudders. "Google is the fucking devil right now."

I give his shoulder a squeeze. "You're gonna be okay."

He nods and I look down again. Only it's not his over-sized testicle that snags my attention this time.

Because I'm watching his dick grow harder and firmer against his thigh.

He sucks in a breath and I hold mine. I'm not exactly sure why I'm staring at his cock right now. Sure, he's big...but hell, so am I. It's almost like the logic and reasoning switch has been turned off in my brain, forbidding me to think about the next possible action that might transcend in this moment between us.

I look at him and our gazes clash. Those dimples of his peek for a brief moment when he licks his lips and visibly swallows.

His cock jerks and a small shudder runs through his body. I take a step forward, unsure of why or what my intention is, because the only thing I can think about is what *he's* thinking about right now.

I want to know the reason for that heated look in his eyes and his throbbing erection.

"Landon," he rasps. His voice is strangled, almost pleading. And suddenly...I want to be the one to soothe the ache for him.

His chest rises and falls with quick, sharp breaths, and his lower abs constrict. He grunts in pain and I realize what I've done—that I've only made this situation worse for him.

I back up. "I um—sorry."

Just then the doors swing open and in walk the coach and two people wearing scrubs. One I recognize as the school nurse.

Asher quickly fixes his towel and adjusts the ice pack.

A few moments and a few obscenities later, they declare he'll be fine, but to elevate the area and keep a close eye on it for the next 48 hours in case it turns necrotic. That particular tidbit earned a scream out of Asher.

Coach Crane hangs back when they leave. "Christ, talk about dumb luck that a spider stuck his fangs into your balls." He rubs his forehead. "You're cleared from practice for the next 48 hours. Let me know if you need anything."

"It wasn't dumb luck. O'—" I start to say, but Asher gives me a look.

Coach crosses his arms over his chest. "Is there something I should know about?"

"Yes—"

"No," Asher grinds out, silencing me. "Everything is fine, Coach."

He nods. "Alright then." His eyes swivel to me. "Thanks for contacting me, Landon." He looks between the both of us and something passes in his gaze before he walks out.

I turn to Asher. "Why didn't you tell him about O' Conner?"

"Because," he says, attempting to stand up. "That would only make things worse. Besides, I have no proof. And last time I checked, placing a spider in a protective cup wasn't a crime."

"If the spider was poisonous it could have killed you," I say, anger flaring in my gut again. "Hell, as it stands now you might lose your balls over this." I hold up my hands. "But, hey. Not my problem."

He hobbles over to his locker and starts getting dressed. "I'll deal with O' Conner." He mutters a curse under his breath when he slides up his shorts. "Think you can give me a lift to the store so I can grab some things for this?"

"Sure."

He braces his arm against the locker. "Man, it's gonna suck trying to walk out of here."

I stand beside him and hold him upright. "I've got you."

It takes almost triple the time to walk out to the parking lot, but somehow, we finally manage to make it to my car.

Which just so happens to be parked next to O' Conner's car.

Asher's entire body goes rigid as we watch him make his way across the parking lot. "Well, isn't that cute," he drawls. "The fag and his little faggot."

"Yeah, a fag who fucked your girl better than you ever will," Asher growls.

He bares his teeth and lunges for him but O' Conner backs up. "I wouldn't do that if I were you." He points to the fading bruise on his cheek. "You see, I had a little discussion with the Dean, and she told me the next time you attack me, you and your scholarship are as good as gone." He takes a step towards us. "So go ahead, fudge-packer. Hit me."

Fucking hell—O' Conner's an even bigger homophobic asshole than I thought. It's clear this shit is only going to get worse and he's not going to stop provoking Asher until he gets him expelled.

Although under different circumstances entirely, I've faced assholes like this my whole life. And unfortunately, some people never grow out of the high school stage and can only be dealt with one way.

Violence doesn't solve problems...but sometimes it's all you have at your disposal. Sometimes it's the only way you can put someone in their place.

Asher lunges at him again but I take advantage of his injured state and shove him back.

Adrenaline and rage is burning through me like an inferno, and before I can stop myself, I cock my fist back and launch it into O' Conner's face.

And watch in sick fascination as he falls and passes out cold against the concrete.

"Jesus—Landon," Asher screams. "That was fucking awesome."

I ignore the throbbing in my hand and kneel down beside O' Conner. I breathe a sigh of relief that he has a pulse and then pull out my phone.

"Whoa, what are you doing? At least wait until we drive away to call an ambulance."

I shake my head. "Not calling an ambulance right now." I bring the phone to my ear and leave a voice mail. "Hey, Dean Crane. It's Landon Parker."

Asher's eyes practically bug out of his head and he tries taking the phone away from me.

'Please call me back at your earliest convenience. I was attacked in the parking lot today and I'd like to report a bias crime on campus," I finish before I hang up.

"What the actual fuck, dude?" Asher starts to say before I cut him off. "I need you to hit me."

He looks at me like I've lost my mind. "What? Why? No—"

"Because it's going to look really strange when I go into the Dean's office tomorrow and claim self-defense after pleading my case about him assaulting me because he thinks I'm gay." I gesture to O' Conner who's coming out of his haze. "This way, O' Conner gets expelled for good. Because he's going to keep pushing you until you either break or the Dean expels you. And you have to stay here in order to win the champi- onship, otherwise Dragoni and his goons will strike, and I can't let that happen." I point to my face. "So quit being a pussy and fucking hit me."

He stares at me. "You're fucking crazy, you know that?"

"Do it, before he wakes up and other people walk out and see us. Right now you're the only witness and I'd like to keep it that way."

"Motherfucker," I yell when his fist goes crashing into my cheekbone.

"You told me to hit you," Asher yells back.

I spit blood on the ground and glare at him. "You could have used a little more finesse."

He snorts. "Dude, I don't know how many fights you've been in... but there's no finesse in a punch."

I slide into the driver's seat and start the engine. "This was my first fight."

He gapes at me. "Seriously? Well, shit, Muhammad Ali. Not bad, considering you just managed to take out a 225 lb. wide-receiver with a single punch."

I peel out of the parking lot and shake my hand out. "Yeah, but my hand hurts like hell. I hope I'm able to play on Saturday."

He turns ashen. "Shit, I didn't even think about that. Fuck, Landon. You should have let me handle him."

"It's fine." I pull up to a pharmacy. "I'm gonna run in and grab some ice." I make a face. "And a pillow for your junk."

"A pillow?"

I step out of the car. "You can barely move right now, so you might as well stay at my place for the night. But I'm sure as shit not letting you rest your balls on my pillow."

He laughs, those deep dimples of his on display. "Duly noted."

"Thanks," Asher says, taking the plate from me.

He's currently sitting on the couch with both a pillow and an ice pack between his legs. It's only been a few hours, so the swelling hasn't gone down; but according to him the pain is a little better.

I sit down next to him and take a swig of my soda before I scarf down my third slice of pizza.

He eyes the glass in my hand for a second too long. He opens his mouth but quickly slams it shut, almost like he's waging a war within himself.

Finally, he speaks. "Are you sure you should be drinking that?"

I turn and face him, expecting to see the condescending judgment in his eyes, like most people; but to my surprise, I see something else entirely. Concern.

I open my mouth to answer but then he says, "I'm not trying to get on your case, it's just that everything I've read lately regarding diabetes says that you shouldn't."

"You read up about diabetes?"

Asher hates to read, it's part of the reason why I'm tutoring him.

He shrugs and takes a sip of his water. "Well, yeah. I mean, I wanted to see if there was anything I could do to help. Make sure you do what you're supposed to and shit."

He looks around the room. "Besides, I know a lot about diet and exercise. I could probably help make things simpler for you. Come up with meal plans and stuff. We can do it together so it's easier." He gestures to his phone. "I don't know your schedule but I can set alarms on my phone for when you should test yourself. I can shoot you a text to remind you. I know it's annoying, but maybe this way it won't be so bad."

To say I'm stunned would be an understatement. There are times when this guy is downright narcissistic and yet, he took the time to research my disease, intending to help me. "You—"

"Look," he bites out, cutting me off again. "I don't have many people in my life anymore. So I'd like to keep the ones that I do have around." He fidgets with the wrapper of his water bottle. "You need to start taking better care of yourself, man. I know it's a high mainte-nance disease, and I'm not gonna sit here and nag you. But if we're going to be friends, then I'm looking out for you. If that's an issue for you, I suggest you get over it, because there's no room for compromise about it."

He folds his arms across his chest, like he's waiting for me to argue with him.

And part of me wants to, but the other part of me is still floored that he cares. I've seen how he interacts with most people. I know he doesn't give a shit about much, only the things that concern him directly.

And while we're similar in some ways, we differ in that sense, because although I don't let the opinions of those who aren't close to me phase me; it doesn't stop me from going out of my way and being a good person to people anyway. Whether or not they deserve it.

Asher puts up walls, though. He acts like an asshole and pushes people away before they even have a chance to get to know him. Almost like he's testing people and intentionally getting under their skin...purposely seeing who cares enough to break through those walls of his. And while I don't agree with his method—I understand it. I know it's because everyone he's ever cared about has either used him or turned their backs on him.

I put my glass down on the table and push it away. "Okay."

I pull out my meter and insulin and take care of business. I don't miss the hint of a smile on his face before he takes a bite of his food.

My hand spasms and I lift the ice pack I have wrapped around it to assess the damage. It's sore, but I can move it, which means I'll be able to play in two more days.

Asher puts down his plate and looks at my hand. "Can't believe you punched him for me."

"O' Conner deserved it." I shrug. "I'm sure you would have done the same for me."

I chance a glance at him, purposely gauging his reaction, because the thing is— I'm *not* so sure that he would have done the same for me. But for some reason I can't pinpoint...I want to know that he would.

I want to know I'm not the only one who feels this shift between us.

"Yeah," he says, looking me in the eyes. "Yeah, I would have."

I pivot, facing him and his stare lands on the bruise coloring my cheekbone. "I got you good, huh?"

I roll my eyes. "I barely even feel it."

It's a lie, I do feel it. I'm pretty sure he even cracked a tooth. But it will be worth it when I sit down in a meeting with the Dean and get that asshole kicked out of school for good.

He lifts his hand, almost like he wanted to touch me, before he drops it.

And then before I can stop myself, I'm the one touching him. I lightly graze the scar above his eyebrow with my thumb. The scar he got from his asshole father. Little bolts of rage shoot through my veins and my chest tightens. I hate that scar on his otherwise flawless face. But even more than that—I hate that someone hurt him.

His shoulders rise and fall with a sharp intake of breath. He looks about as surprised as I feel over the contact, but we don't say a word as I continue running my thumb back and forth over his scar. It just hangs in the silence between us. The silence that seems to say more than words ever will.

Neither of us have talked about what happened earlier, which is something I'm thankful for because I'm still trying to make sense of it.

I've always identified myself as straight. I mean, I'm attracted to women...always have been. But today...for that brief moment in that locker room...lines got blurred and I'm not sure what to do about it.

Not to mention one very important factor—one that's like a record skipping inside my heart, preventing me from examining these potential feelings that are brewing for the person sitting across from me.

Breslin.

She's a loose end. Actually, that's wrong. She's so much more than a loose end...because I still want her. I'm angry as hell with her currently...but I still care about her. *I still love her.*

And just because you start developing feelings for someone

else...it doesn't mean they automatically disappear for the other party. That's not the way love works. It's not a 'here today, gone tomorrow' thing.

It's how I know Breslin *is* the real thing.

But I can't help but feel that Asher might be the real thing, too.

Therefore, I have a lot of stuff I need to figure out in regards to my feelings. And there's only one way to clear my head.

The studio.

I drop my hand and stand up. "I'm finally making some leeway on that song I've been working on, so I'm probably going to be in the studio for the rest of the night. Is that cool?"

He nods and reaches for the remote. "Sure."

He straightens himself and focuses on the television, completely detached. There's something going on behind those eyes of his, but I know better than to push him right now.

Plus, I need to get my own shit together and figure out exactly where I stand before I even think about navigating these murky and uncharted waters.

CHAPTER 20

LANDON

Dean Crane's eyes narrow into tiny slits and she purses her lips. I know this look, I've seen her give it to plenty of other students before.

She's trying to determine not only if my story is full of shit...but if there are any underlying aspects that would compel me to lie to her.

To most people, she's intimidating as hell. But this woman is someone I consider my mentor...therefore I'm calm and collected.

"So Theo O' Conner just picked a fight with you out of nowhere in the parking lot?" she questions, walking over to her desk.

"Yes, I was walking out of the library after a tutoring session and out to my car which was parked right next to his."

She presses her pointer fingers to her lips, appearing to think about this. "Theo says he never touched you and that you threw the first punch after he and his teammate Asher Holden had words."

I clear my throat, hiding my nervousness. I thought for sure this meeting would go a lot smoother.

I point to the bruise on my face. "He struck me first. And yes, I hit him back but it was self-defense. After he made derogatory statements."

"What kinds of statements? According to him, he's never even spoken to you before yesterday. In fact, he states that *no* words were exchanged between you two during yesterday's incident." She sits down at her desk. "He said there was an altercation between him and Mr. Holden—whom he's had previous issues with—and that *you* put yourself in the middle of it."

"That's not—"

"Look, I can only go by facts. And the fact is that you both are stating that Asher Holden was there—and both he and Mr. O' Conner have had prior incidents in the past...one that resulted in Mr. O' Conner being attacked. The other fact— is that according to Coach Crane you weren't at the library tutoring a student...you were in the locker room with Asher." She looks hurt. "I don't like being lied to, Landon."

I open my mouth but she holds up a hand, silencing me. "Now, I know that you are tutoring him. My husband informed me that he appears to be doing well academically under your guidance. That being said, if he's threatening you in some way and using—"

"Are you kidding!" I shout, much to the shock of the both of us. "I'm here reporting an assault that happened on your campus and you're trying to take the offender's side and twist this into something it's not?"

She rubs her temples. "That's not what's happening, Landon. If anything, I'm only trying to look out for you and get to the bottom of this." She holds up a file. "So, I'm going to level with you. Asher Holden has been known to cause trouble in the past. His record at his previous school speaks for itself."

She slams the file on her desk. "This file is full of reports from his previous University stating numerous incidents and issues that they've had with him—"

"You mean the file full of bullshit to cover their asses?" I scoff. "The one they put together after they just so happened to kick him out after a sex tape of him with another guy went viral. The University that dropped him on his ass and helped ruin his life when they should have been supporting him. The University that had *no* issues with him when he was on that field winning championships...until the day they found out that he liked to have sex with men and it was caught on tape for the world to see. The University that knew how much money Asher's family had and the potential lawsuits that would be awaiting them if he were ever attacked on campus for his sexuality, so instead they kicked him out so they didn't have to deal with it. That University?"

I stand up, disgusted. This is a woman I once held in such high regard. I feel like a kid discovering that Santa isn't real for the first time.

"I'll admit...I didn't like him at first either, Dean Crane. But then I got to know him...really got to know him. And I discovered things about him—things like why he needs that scholarship you've given him so badly."

When she gives me a look I say, "Because his own family turned their backs on him. And I can tell you personally that he's working his ass off, trying his hardest to put the work in even though classes haven't even started yet. Just ask your husband, he'll tell you."

My jaw hardens. "Or you can just take my word for it...because I'm telling you the truth. O'Connor is a homophobic bigot. And he's going to be an even bigger problem the longer you allow him to remain here. Asher Holden isn't perfect...not by a long shot. But he's trying."

She takes a deep breath. "Okay."

"Okay?"

She studies my face. "You're a good kid, Landon. One of the best students at this school. So if you think I misjudged Asher and the situation with O' Conner...perhaps you're right. I was originally going to suspend them both...but after careful consideration—I think it's in the school's best interest to expel Theo O' Conner. Now if you want to go to the police, I can go ahead and get the ball rolling for you."

Her face softens. "And for what it's worth, I'm sorry that you were attacked yesterday. I had no idea that you were gay." She pauses, as if catching herself. "Not that it matters...but rest assured that this University has a zero-tolerance policy when it comes to bullying and violence."

We both know she's covering her and the University's ass, but at least she's doing the right thing. I walk toward the door. "Thank you."

"One more thing, Landon," she calls out, halting me. When I turn around she says, "I have no problem with you tutoring Asher Holden. However, it's clear there is a personal relationship between the two of you. Now, the university has rules stating that TAs and students cannot date." Concern pulls on her features. "You've worked your butt off the last three years to be a TA this year, Landon. The hours, the studying, the doubling sometimes *tripling* up on classes. I'd hate to see all that hard work go to waste."

My stomach drops. "I— We're not dating."

She narrows her eyes, her gaze scrutinizing. "Well I thought—"

"No," I state quickly. "I'm not—it's not like that between us. We have a professional and platonic relationship, I assure you."

She thinks about this for a moment. "Well, then I guess we have nothing to worry about here."

"Great." I turn to the door but she stops me again.

"Word of advice? And I'm not saying this as the Dean—I'm saying this as a person who knows how quickly things can crumble if you're not careful. This is your last year. You're almost at the finish line. Please don't get caught up in things that might bring you down. Because I honestly think out of all the students who have passed through my doors...you're destined for greatness, Landon. Whatever road you choose to go down will be a great one. Don't let the wrong people take advantage of that."

"Thank you," I say again, closing the door behind me.

I dial Asher's number and bring the phone to my ear. When he picks up on the second ring, I say, "Hey, great news. O' Conner's being expelled."

"Oh," some deep voice that I don't recognize answers. "I'm sorry, this isn't Asher. He left his phone here earlier."

I swallow hard and grit my teeth, the impact of what he's saying slamming me in the chest.

"But hey, if you get a hold of him can you tell him he left it here?"

"Sure thing," I say before I slam the phone down.

CHAPTER 21

ASHER

"Let me get this straight," Preston says, pointing his beer bottle at me. "The guy that you're into not only showed interest in you, he beat up someone for you...and you in turn hooked up with someone else?" He pauses. "Or rather *two* people."

"Yes," I say over the music. "No—I mean—I couldn't do it. As soon as things started heating up between me, Gwen, and Tom...I ran out."

I also left my phone behind like an idiot. I glance at my watch. Landon should be coming on stage in the next few minutes.

"Yeah but he didn't know that," Preston says. "No wonder he's been avoiding you and hasn't spoken to you for the last two days." He takes a sip of his beer. "Now I don't know anything about being attracted to another guy, but I do know what it's like to feel like you got played."

"I know." I down the rest of my beer and order another. "I wasn't thinking...I just—"

"What?"

I look at my brother, hoping he can understand without me telling him.

But he doesn't...because no matter how close we are...he has no idea what it's like to be me.

"He's straight." I look down and frustration claws its way up my throat. "And his girlfriend will be coming back in a few days."

I take a big swill of my beer in order to wash down the bitterness rising in my throat. "And when she gets back...he's going to choose her. Because she's the easy choice. I'll just be a hookup that he'll either regret or chalk up to some college experiment." I shrug. "At least by pushing him away now—before anything might happen, I won't have to lose him as a friend."

He gives my shoulder a squeeze and frowns, until something behind me snags his attention. "Well don't despair, Cinderella. You've caught someone else's eye tonight at the ball. That guy can't keep his eyes off you."

"It's the tape," I grumble, not bothering to turn around. "Ever since it went viral I've had more opportunities from guys than I bargained for. It's like I'm wearing a neon sign on my chest that says, 'My dick is an equal opportunity employer. Try your luck.' "

Preston laughs. "For what it's worth he's not bad looking. I think he may even be a musician given the case he's holding. Might be just the thing to cheer you up."

I turn my head slightly to see who he's talking about. My eyes fall on some guy wearing leather pants—who just like Preston said—is eyeing me up and down. He smiles at me and looks like he's about to come over, but then a group of guys walk over to him and he starts talking to them instead.

My gaze catches on the guitar case he's holding...and that's when I realize.

I turn back to Preston. "It's the band Landon's auditioning for," I say, recalling the google search I did.

"Guess this night just got a whole lot more interesting then, because they're headed this way."

As if on cue, I feel someone's presence behind me. "Pardon me, love. But can I bother you for a fag?"

I spin around and come face to face with the guy wearing leather pants...who apparently has a very thick English accent.

The group of guys behind him laugh hysterically and one of them steps forward. "We keep telling him that's a very different thing in America, but he won't listen," he says, his accent as thick as his friends'.

"Stop trying to queer my pitch with the bloke," leather pants says, and my eyes go wide, which only causes them to laugh even harder.

"Don't worry," one of them says through laughter. "Charlie here is all mouth and no trousers."

"I don't smoke," I say and leather pants winks. "Didn't think so. But one can always hope, now can't they, love?"

"Oh, he likes guys," my brother chimes in, slapping my back. "And this here's the best piece of ass in 50 states."

I glare at him and he raises his hands. "I'm just trying to help."

The group of guys' laughter grows even louder. "You two are a riot," one of them says. "You must let us buy you a round."

My brother happily agrees and we all make the introductions.

"Do you come to this pub often?" leather pants, or rather, Charlie asks and I shake my head.

"It's my first time. My f—" I pause and subtly tap my brother's leg, hoping he catches on. "I heard there's an amazing musician scheduled to play tonight. Wanted to check him out."

"Yeah," my brother says loudly. "Landon's fucking awesome."

That gets everyone's attention. "Landon Parker?" one of them questions and I nod.

"We're here to watch him as well," Charlie says, sidling up beside me. "Bloke's wicked on those ivories, but he's just as good on the guitar." He scowls and points to his hand. "I have carpal tunnel and I'm scheduled to have surgery in a few months. Unfortunately, we have some gigs that can't be canceled in late December and I need someone to fill in for me."

I look at the stage. The guy up there now should be finishing any minute. "Sorry to hear that." I look around at his band members. "But you won't have to worry if you hire Landon. He's phenomenal. He can play anything."

Including the strings of my heart.

We all clap for the guy on stage before he walks off and Charlie leans in. "I take it you two are mates?"

I nod, silently wishing it was the American term and not the British one.

"We go to the same University. He's my tutor."

"Ah," Charlie says. "But you wish he was more."

I take another swig of my beer. "That obvious?"

"About as obvious as it was that I was chatting you up before." He stares at me. "Maybe this bloke isn't such a scholar after all. You're absolutely smashing."

I laugh. "He's straight. And he has a girl—" My words fall from my lips when Landon walks out on stage and the bar full of maybe 150 people go crazy.

I suck in a breath and my heart compresses against my chest. Charlie's saying something to me, but I don't hear a word...because I can't keep my eyes off him.

He gives the crowd of people a smile and waves, looking both relaxed and confident. He's wearing jeans and a simple black tank top that showcases his tattoos, and even with those adorable black-rimmed glasses that he has on, he looks every bit the part of a rock star up there. My blood rushes south and I can't tell if it's because of his sexy appearance, or the way he completely owns the stage.

He scans the crowd and his eyes land on mine. I see his bravado falter for split second, and I can't tell if he's surprised, thankful, or pissed that I'm here.

The lights in the bar dim and the small stage lights turn on, illuminating both him and the stage enough to let me see the way his jaw works as he walks over to the keyboard.

He's obviously ticked off that I'm here...but *he's* the one who asked me to come in the first place.

He tilts his head and speaks into the microphone. "Hey, everyone. I'm gonna play some original stuff for you in a little bit, but how about I play a rendition of one of my favorites to start you off?"

Everyone cheers and there's a hint of a smile on his face—one that falls when a haunting and addicting melody fills the room and his expression turns serious.

I faintly recall the song, but it isn't until he starts singing that I recognize it's *The Diary of Jane*, by Breaking Benjamin.

I'm glad I'm leaning against the bar because when the strong and fluid timbre of his voice permeates the air and he strikes those keys, my knees go weak. But it doesn't even compare to the way my heart hammers like a drum when he looks at me and sings.

He nails every part of the song, and even though he didn't write the lyrics or the music himself, he somehow manages to make it his own.

The utter despair and affliction in his voice makes all the tiny hairs on my body stand on end. Landon's not just giving us a performance right now, he's showing us part of his soul up there...and fuck, if I don't crave it like it's a drug.

When the song ends, I'm speechless and so are the people around me.

"Bloody hell," Charlie whispers beside me and his band mates nod.

Even Preston who always has something to say about everything is silent, looking floored.

I can't say I'm surprised, though. Landon's fucking magnetic and the energy that flows through him when he's up there is unlike anything I've ever witnessed before. It's downright palpable.

The only thing I can compare it to is when I'm on the field, right before a game and the adrenaline is pumping through my veins.

When he steps away from the keyboard, walks to the front of the stage, and picks up his guitar, a group of girls sigh so loud he laughs into the microphone.

"Any requests?" His tone is coy and flirtatious which causes a bolt of jealousy to shoot through me.

"I'll take my panties off if you play me *Glycerine!*" Some girl shouts in a drunken slur and everyone in the bar laughs.

My stomach squeezes in protest. It's my favorite song of all time...but there's no way that I can't think about Breslin while hearing it, seeing as it was playing during our first kiss.

It's too late, though, because Landon's already strumming those chords, causing a whirl of emotions to swirl inside me.

I tune him out and pull out my phone instead, concentrating as hard as I can on a stupid game...because the weight that's threatening to crush my chest when I think about *her* is too much.

I make the mistake of looking up when the song ends and his eyes turn hard. But there must be something in my expression that redeems me, because his eyebrows draw together and his face softens.

The cheering of the crowd brings him back and he takes a sip of water and clears his throat before he speaks into the microphone again, grinning. "So, you guys want to hear that new song I wrote this week?"

Every single person in the bar goes nuts, including the band standing beside me.

"This one is called Complicated Hearts," he says into the mic before he presses a button on the keyboard and piano music fills the room.

He starts strumming the guitar, and for a fraction of a second, I see Landon's mask slip and his nervousness shows.

I silently prompt him to look at me...because he's got this.

Hell, he was born for this.

I recognize the familiar light rhythm from the night he played this song for me in the studio. *It wasn't quite ready,* he told me then, but I loved it anyway.

I hold my breath and bite back a smile as the light melody continues filling the air...because I know any moment the beat is going to drop and he's going to bring the goddamn house down.

There's a sly smirk on his face when he does and goosebumps dance along my arms and the back of my neck. He's killing it up there.

When he opens his mouth and starts singing, I'm caught off guard. He told me this song was powerful on its own without lyrics and he was right. However, his raw voice, which is coated with so much emotion and depth...brings it to a whole other level.

I try to ignore the pang in my chest as he continues singing about a girl who's afraid to take the leap with him. It's got a soulful vibe to it, despite it being an alternative rock song; and his rasp laced with tangible longing about a girl who doesn't want him is enough to make me grit my teeth and turn my blood to lava.

I'm about to step outside because I don't know how much more torture I can take—but then there's a key change and he starts singing the next verse, and I realize there's no way I can be annoyed with this song, because my ornery feelings aside, it's fucking epic.

He leans back, strumming those talented fingers of his across his guitar, putting his whole entire body into his performance. The people in the bar eat up every morsel of it and he's feeding off their energy in the exchange—almost like he's siphoning it from them and using it to propel him forward.

Jesus—Landon on stage is like watching an asteroid explode into a thousand spellbinding fragments. He comes alive in a way I've never seen before.

He closes his eyes and taps his foot, getting lost in the music and bringing us all along for the journey with him.

When he opens his eyes again, they lock with mine. His stare is angry and all-consuming, commanding me to listen to him. The desire and craving in his raspy voice is even more intense now, penetrating me all the way down to my toes.

I focus on the lyrics again and my heart speeds up and my insides twist as I listen.

She captivates me.
Frustrates me.
And you, you fascinate me.
Complicate me.

My breath catches, his words soaking into my skin and rooting me to the spot—even after it ends and he takes a small bow and walks off stage.

"We have to hire him," one of the band mates says, zapping me back to the present.

The rest of the guys nod in agreement. Beside me, Charlie bristles and grunts out a, "Yeah."

It doesn't take a genius to figure out that a small part of him is threatened by Landon taking over for him in a few months.

I open my mouth, unsure of what to say, but then Landon comes up to me, or rather the band, and says hello.

"Damn," my brother tells me. "You weren't kidding when you said he was talented."

"I know," I say as I see the band members shake his hand in my peripheral vision.

One of them orders Landon a drink in celebration and he takes it, refusing to look at me.

I'll admit...it fucking hurts. He could have at least thanked me for coming. Or at least have the decency to tell me he doesn't want me here and to get the hell out.

"Hey," Charlie whispers into my ear. "Step outside with me for a second."

I give Landon one last look—a look that he doesn't exchange—before I follow Charlie's lead.

My brother looks like he's about to say something, but the look I shoot him causes him to stay silent.

There's no reason for Landon to be acting like such an asshole to me right now. I've done nothing wrong...he's made it perfectly clear since day one where he stands.

My heart pulls and I mutter a curse...because I realize that I'm a fucking idiot.

He's not pissed about another guy picking up my phone, he probably couldn't care less—he's pissed because he thinks I'm going to fuck up his chance with the band.

When we step outside and Charlie lights a cigarette, I decide to excuse myself.

"Sorry, I forgot my phone at the bar." I turn, intending to run back inside and grab Landon to explain things to him, but I can't, because I'm being shoved against a brick wall.

"What the fuck are you doing?" I snarl, getting ready to knock Charlie's lights out.

He leans in and whispers, "Helping you out," at the same time a familiar voice growls, "Jesus Christ, Asher. Is there anyone you won't try and stick your dick in?"

I shove Charlie off me. "This isn't what—"

Landon's gaze ping pongs between us before his eyes focus on me. His stare has so much disgust behind it, I reel back as if kicked in the nuts.

He scoffs, pulls his keys out of his pocket, and starts walking to his car. I start to follow him, but Charlie yanks me back. "You chase him now, you'll ruin your chance."

"Fuck you, asshole," I snap, shoving him away. "You just cost me a friendship with him."

My heart thumps painfully against my rib cage—*I lost another person I care about.*

I hear Charlie mumble something about it being clear that I want more than friendship, but I'm too busy throwing the door open and scanning the bar for my brother.

I'm so on edge, I all but snatch Preston's collar when I walk up to him. "I need you to drive me to Landon's. *Now.*"

The talk amongst the members of the band that he was chatting with comes to a halt and Preston nods without question.

The drive to Landon's apartment is taking too long and I close my eyes, fighting thoughts of Breslin the entire time.

Because it always comes back to her. *It always will.*

She fucked me up when she left me. More than that, she scarred me for life with her abandonment. And as much as I love her...a little part of me can't help but hate her for doing that to me.

I grab the door handle, anger coursing through my limbs. I'm like a bomb ready to detonate. Everything over the last few months, hell *years,* is rumbling in my chest, threatening to spill out.

My brother rambles on and on about his stupid girlfriend Becca and how he thinks he found a nice apartment for them to live it and I fucking lose it.

"Shut up!" I bark so loud the windows rattle. "It's not about you right now, Preston."

He looks at me like I've gone insane. "I was trying to distract you, you prick."

"What?"

"I was trying to keep your mind off *her* so you don't blow things with *him.*"

"I have no idea—"

He laughs to himself. "That's just it. You have *no* idea. You have no idea how you continue sabotaging your life over something that happened years ago."

"I'm not sabotaging anything," I say defensively. "And even if I was, it's only because Kyle—"

He pins me with a stare. "Forget the Kyle bullshit, Asher. You're stuck in the spin cycle of Breslin and you push everyone away and never let anyone in. It's not healthy, man."

"I—" My words fall when we pull up to the back of the apartment complex and I see Landon jog up the outside steps.

Lightning flashes through the sky, due to the heat in the air. I go to get out of the car but Preston grabs my arm. "Does he make you happy?"

When I nod he says, "Then don't let her get in the way. Because you deserve to be happy again, Asher."

If only it were that simple.

If only he wanted me the way I want him.

If only part of my heart didn't still belong to her.

CHAPTER 22

LANDON

I fish my keys out of my pocket just as lightning flashes across the sky. The humidity in the air is thick tonight and I can't wait for mother nature to just get it over with and rain already.

My mood is grim...no more than that. Right now, it's fucking black.

I don't know why he bothered showing up tonight. Sure, I invited him...but that was before...

Before what?—my mind taunts.

Stuffing down feelings that I don't want to acknowledge, I stick my key in the door.

And that's when I feel his presence behind me. Thunder booms in the sky above us...a mere second before the rain falls.

I stand under the awning of my door, refusing to turn around.

"I'm sorry," he says. "I didn't mean to mess up your chance with the band."

I shake my head, because yeah, it would be awesome to play with them; but that's not why I'm so upset.

It's because my life was mapped out and I thought I knew what direction I was heading in. I thought I knew myself inside out...

But now? Now I'm not so sure anymore. And it's all *his* fault.

"It's not the band," I grit through my teeth, finally turning around to face him.

It's the guy who answered your phone and the jealousy that burned like a firestorm inside me.

The rain is coming down in buckets, soaking his clothes so they're like a second skin on him. It's something I'm acutely aware of thanks to the way my heart starts beating faster in my chest, making it impossible to ignore or shut down.

Because I can't shut down these feelings for him anymore. Because they've always been there...drawing me to him.

I've been fascinated by Asher since the moment I met him. All those times I watched him and wanted to be around him. I chalked it up to admiration, maybe an affinity for him.

But now I know without a shadow of a doubt that it wasn't.

It's so much more.

He looks confused and my heart sinks. I want him to understand what I can't bring myself to say. I want him to do what I can't bring myself to do, because I've never been here before and I have no idea what the first step is.

My hands clench at my sides, I've never in my life wished for an instrument more than I do right now. I need to communicate these feelings out of me and to him before they eat me alive and swallow me whole. I'm like a pressure cooker ready to go off the longer he stands here.

But then again, maybe it's for the best that I don't. Because I don't want to explode when he won't be there to pick up my pieces...and it's clear Asher isn't the kind of guy to stick around for the aftermath.

It seems to be the type of people I attract.

He looks at me, confusion swirling in his eyes before he says, "Shit, I think I get it now."

I open my mouth but he lifts a hand. "I was trying to keep my distance these last few days because I was afraid that I made you uncomfortable. When what I should have done was found you and apologized for making shit weird between us."

"No. You didn't—"

He takes his beanie off and runs a hand through his hair. "But no, because that's what I do. I fuck shit up." He waves a hand in my direction. "You're amazing, Landon. And I'm...me." Remorse clogs his voice and something in my chest shifts as he continues, "I have an ex I can't get over, debts I have to settle... I'm a mess. And I hate that I brought you into all that. I'm sorry I invaded your life with my baggage and issues."

His expression fills with sorrow. "But not nearly as sorry as I am for having feelings for you. Because I know you don't feel the same. I mean, you've only made it a point to tell me almost every time we've hung out that you're not into guys." He takes a breath. "But if you give me a chance to fix this... I'll figure out a way to deal with it and keep my dick out of our friendship. Because I don't want to lose you." His voice cracks with emotion, he's so vulnerable right now I can feel him in my bones. "I *can't* lose you."

I take a step closer to him, my heart straining against my chest, all logic and reason thrown out the window, because none of that matters right now. "You're not."

When he lifts a brow in question, I close the divide between us— the only way I can.

By crashing my mouth against his.

CHAPTER 23

ASHER

This isn't happening—there's no way Landon's kissing me right now.

But when his tongue finds mine—tentatively, delicately, and my groin strains against my damp jeans...I know it's *definitely happening*.

Landon is fucking kissing me.

And hell if I'm going to do anything to stop it. I'm too much of a selfish bastard for that.

Instead my hand slides to the back of his neck and I deepen the kiss. He follows my lead, exploring my mouth with urgency and I walk him backward until his back meets his door.

He tries to come up for air, but I won't let him, because I know what's awaiting me with that breath of fresh air—clarity on his part—and I want to soak up this moment for as long as I can.

He fights for air and grips my shirt "Did you fuck that guy?"

I pull back and stare down at him. "What?"

His nostrils flare. "The guy who answered your phone. Did you *fuck* him?"

"No. I couldn't do it."

I don't mention that it was a guy *and* a girl, because that point is moot now. None of it matters if Landon wants me.

"Why?" His eyes drop down to my lips and I crush my pelvis against his. I bite back a groan when I feel that he's just as hard as I am.

I give him a cocky smile. "Why do you think, nerd?"

He's not amused. "Answer the fucking question."

I lick his bottom lip, "Because you're the only thing I see lately." I nip at his jaw. "And if you don't feel the same, you better tell me right now."

Our hips brush and arousal prickles my skin. "Does this feel like I don't want you, Asher?" His eyebrows draw together. "But—"

No, I don't want to hear what his *but* entails, because I know it will be about her.

Just like I also know I might not ever get this chance with him again, so I don't want to ruin it.

The rain outside is coming down in sheets, soaking everything including the ground around us, but I drop down to my knees anyway.

His throat bobs on a swallow and he looks like he wants to protest, but can't bring himself to, which only turns me on more.

The way I see it is...if I'm granted this one night before I turn back into a pumpkin. I'm going to spend it giving Landon the best damn blowjob he's ever received. One he won't be able to forget no matter how hard he tries.

I lift his shirt and the muscles of his stomach contract under my touch. He's trembling, no doubt equal parts scared and aroused, but when I motion for him to take off his shirt for me, he obliges.

I take my time with him, kissing and licking over the taut skin of his abdomen, letting him get used to the fact that it's stubble he feels and not the soft cheeks of a girl.

I'm usually the one on the receiving end of a blowjob...but I don't want to be tonight. Because this is about him and how much I fucking want him...whichever way I can have him.

I look up at him and his eyes are closed. I can't tell if it's in turmoil or pleasure, because he won't say a word. He's not frozen, but he's certainly not what I would call willing, either. And that's a deal breaker for me. I'm not expecting declarations or for him to bend over right now, but I am expecting him to show some kind of interest.

I stop kissing his stomach and stand up. His eyes pop open, sadness flashing in them.

"You don't want this," I say but he shakes his head. "It's not that."

My heart free falls, because if it's not *that*. It's *her*.

He feels like he's cheating on her. Even though they're not together. Even though she ended things with him and ignored him when she went out of the Country.

He feels like being with me is wronging *her* somehow.

I should respect that. Because even though I don't respect her for doing that to him...I should respect his feelings on the matter.

I *should*...but I don't.

Because fuck her.

She shouldn't have let him slip through her fingers for God only knows what reason.

Right now, he's *mine*. And as long as Landon still wants me...I'm going to fight like hell for him.

I rest both my arms on the wall on either side of his head and lean in, purposely ghosting my lips over his. "Who's in front of you right now?"

"What—"

"Who's here, right in front of you, Landon? Who's standing in front of you realizing everything you have to offer?"

He squeezes his eyes shut. "You are."

I lick his bottom lip and he groans, his mouth falling open. I take the opportunity to tease and lick the tip of his tongue, letting him know exactly how I plan to tease him below before the night is over.

When he moans, I incline my head and kiss his neck. Not one of those dainty kisses either, I suck his skin into my mouth, purposely marking him.

"Do you want me?" My voice comes out in a gruff rasp. I'm so fucking turned on right now I can barely see straight.

When he nods, I trail my lips along his throat, finally stopping just above his ear. "Then take out your cock so I can put it in my mouth."

His head hits the back of the door and his breath comes out in quick, sharp bursts. The sound of him undoing his belt and lowering his zipper is so loud it almost echoes as I drop to my knees before him again.

When I see that his cock is still contained in his boxers, I give him a look. He bites his lip in return and raises a brow as if to say, 'Take them off me yourself'.

I rise to the challenge and give him a smirk as I lower my mouth to him, purposely teasing his erection through the fabric of his boxers with both my lips and warm breath. I soon find the opening, and the second I graze his skin he curses and bucks his hips.

I dart my tongue out and dab the wet spot on his boxers. "Take them *off*," I growl, my need for him coming to a peak.

Less than a second later, he pulls them down and his cock springs out, heavy and thick for me.

My balls ache so bad, my own cock is begging to join the fun, but I don't focus on that right now.

Because I want to make Landon go crazy and scream my name loud enough to wake up the dead.

I grip the base of his erection and he stares down at me, lust and heat blazing in those brown eyes of his.

I silently smile to myself, he's probably expecting me to just get down to business, but that's not the way I operate. I'm not taking him in my mouth fully until I hear him *beg* for it.

His breath catches in surprise when I hold his dick in my hand and flick my tongue along the seam of his balls. I part my lips and pluck one into my mouth, watching in amusement when his nails dig into the door.

His mouth opens and he lets out a deep groan when I release him with a plop and lap at the bead of pre-come on his tip, tasting him. When I give it a kiss and pull back slightly—his eyes focus like lasers on the thin string of fluid between us and I hear his whoosh of breath.

"Fuck—" he starts to say before I lap at him again, savoring the salty liquid.

"I want more of that," I murmur against him, pressing my tongue into the slit of his dick.

"Then take it," he counters with a cocky grin. "Take it all. Right fucking now."

Fuck me—Landon telling me to take him is one of the hottest things I've ever heard in my life.

I pump him in my hand and run my thumb along the bulging vein on the underside of his shaft. I plan on running my tongue over it soon. But first—I stretch my lips over him and pull that broad bulbous head of his into my mouth.

Then I still myself and look up at him.

He swallows hard, his body going slack against the door in defeat. "Please," he finally chokes out a moment later. "I need your mouth."

I slide down as far as I can take him and he sputters a curse into the air.

I go slow, taking my time, enjoying the feel of him in my mouth, the way his thick vein throbs against my tongue as I take him deeper and deeper with every thrust.

"Asher," he rasps and I reward him by picking up my pace. He punches the wall and pushes his hips forward, fighting with himself.

I take one of his hands and place it on my head, letting him know it's okay. One of the perks of giving another guy a blow job is knowing first-hand what feels good.

He grips my hair and my jaw goes slack to make it easier for what he so badly wants to do. He pauses for a moment, still unsure. But then I suck him deeper and harder, purposely goading him into fucking my face.

His grip on my hair tightens and he releases a growl from deep within his chest as he grinds and pumps furiously. My balls clench, it's so fucking hot watching him lose control like this.

When he pauses in between thrusts, I take over and suction my mouth around him. I quicken my movements until I'm gagging, wanting to bring him over the edge.

"God, that feels so good," he says before a groan tears out of him and he screams, "Fuck, I'm gonna come."

His dick pulses and jerks. I take the opportunity to reach down and gently tug his balls as he fills my mouth and I greedily swallow every drop of him.

He grabs my hair again, this time pulling me up before he crushes his mouth against mine.

I figured he'd push me away, maybe tell me it was all a mistake, but he breaks the kiss and goes for my zipper.

"I need to return the favor." He swallows. "I mean, I've never done it before but I can try—"

I laugh and the tips of my fingers trace the stubble on his cheek. I'm not usually this affectionate with guys, or girls for that matter, especially after sex, but Landon somehow brings it out of me. "The only thing I want from you tonight are these lips on mine, okay?"

And it's the truth. I don't want to overwhelm him, no matter how much my dick hates me for it currently.

"Are you sure?"

I nod and he takes a step back, tucking himself into his jeans.

"I take it you're sleeping over tonight?" he questions as he opens the door.

"Only if you want me to."

He reaches for my hand and pulls me toward him, giving me his answer.

CHAPTER 24

BRESLIN

I zip up my last suitcase and check my flight reservation on my phone browser. Purchasing this ticket pretty much drains my savings account, but it's money well spent to fix one of the biggest mistakes in my life.

I check the time, hoping Kit's preoccupied with Becca...because there's no doubt in my mind that if she catches what I'm doing, she's going to try and stop me. Tell me to relax and enjoy my last four days here.

But I can't...because I've tried for the last week to tough it out and enjoy myself. It's a slow, agonizing torture I wouldn't wish on anyone.

All I see is *Landon*. The look on his face when I left him is burned into my memory. I *have* to make things right with him or I'm going to lose my shit entirely.

I need to apologize to him and make him understand that I was scared. I need to own up to my mistake and tell him that what I did wasn't right...but I'm ready now.

I'm ready for everything he wants.

I do one last check around my hotel room, making sure I have everything I need and walk toward the door.

Only to be stopped by the sound of it opening. I mutter a curse under my breath, remembering that Kit has a spare key to my room.

Her eyes widen when she walks in and sees that I'm all packed up and ready to go. "We have four more days here, B," she groans, blocking the door.

I lift my chin, preparing myself to plow right through her if need be. "I've already bought my ticket and drained my account. You can't stop me, Kit." The hand around my suitcase tightens. "I know you think I'm being hasty...or whatever. But I know what I want and I'm going after—

Her eyelids fall shut. "That's not why I want you to stay."

"Then why—"

She pulls a small jewelry box out of her pocket.

"Thanks, but I'm not really into jewelry."

She rolls her eyes and opens the box, showing me a very gorgeous and very *big* diamond ring. "It's not for you." She worries her bottom lip between her teeth. "It's for Becca."

My mouth hangs open. I knew Kit liked her and things were going well between them...but proposing? They've only been dating for a few months...she barely even knows the girl.

My expression must give away my thoughts because she looks down and says, "I know you think this is a mistake."

"No—" I clamp my mouth shut, because I don't want to lie to her. She's my best friend and we've always been honest with one another. "Maybe," I settle on, because it's the truth.

"I love her." She inhales deeply. "I know she's the one."

The determination in her eyes tells me she truly believes that. And even though there's something niggling in my gut that tells me something's off with Becca...the fact of the matter is she makes Kit happy.

My feelings don't count...because no matter what the future brings, I'm going to be there for Kit either way.

I nod, fighting back tears because I wish Kit would have told me her plans earlier, before I bought my new plane ticket.

She runs over and wraps her arms around me. "Does that mean I have your blessing?"

"Yes." I worry my bottom lip between my teeth and put my suit-case down. "I'm gonna call the airline and see if there's a way I can—"

She cups my face in her hands. "Don't you dare. And to be perfectly honest with you, I'm a little annoyed that you went behind my back and purchased the ticket yourself, you know I would have given you the money."

"It's my mess to fix, Kit. Not yours."

She drops her forehead to mine, pulling me close. "You finally know what you want?"

I smile, tears stinging my eyes again. "I do."

I want my future with Landon.

She shoots me a megawatt smile, tears running down her own face now. "Then go get him." She pulls back and winks. "I'll see you in a few days."

CHAPTER 25

ASHER

I watch him as he stirs in his sleep and my pulse jumps. I almost want to pinch myself, because I still can't believe this is happening.

But it *is*. I keep waiting for him to have that moment of doubt and tell me it's a mistake, but so far it hasn't happened yet. After we walked into his apartment we stayed up the whole night talking. He told me about what happened in his meeting with the Dean, and also warned me about how we have to be careful because technically he's not supposed to be messing around with students.

And although I hate being kept a secret...I completely understand it. Landon offered to set me up with another tutor and to come clean to Dean Crane, but I told him no. Because my attraction for him aside, he's one of the best tutors I've ever had, and I need him.

So, we both agreed that it was in my best interest to keep our personal relationship on the down low.

We didn't talk about the elephant in the room—but I know we're going to have to...and soon. Because the elephant will be back in a few more days.

He rolls over and gives me a sleepy smile. "I didn't know you went in the shower. You should have woken me."

Before I can answer, he hooks his finger into my towel and pulls me to him. I still can't get over how calm he is about this. Not only is he affectionate with me—he's relaxed around me.

He's handling this way better than I ever did.

"Are you sure you've never dated a guy before?"

When he lifts a brow in question I say, "What I mean is, aren't you freaked out about this? It's okay if you are, totally normal."

He sits up and leans against the headboard. I plop down beside him and prepare myself for a slew of questions. Because he *should* have questions and concerns.

He appears to be lost in deep thought before he speaks. "I think I'm more freaked out about how not freaked out I am about it. If that makes any sense."

It does...because I'm most definitely freaked out about how unruffled he is.

"Have you ever been attracted to guys before?"

He shakes his head. "Nope. You're the first."

My stomach starts to drop because that doesn't bode well for me, but then he says, "Well not exactly—" His face screws up. "I've never been physically attracted to guys in the past. But I've been emotionally and mentally attracted to all sorts of people. Women and men. Does that make sense?"

I shake my head, because it doesn't. I don't have a connection with many people...so my attraction has always been purely physical first and foremost. It's probably why I can separate sex and feelings so easily. Because I don't have them.

Well...with the exception of Breslin and Landon. It was the grand fucking trifecta with the both of them.

I wiggle my eyebrows. "Have you done the porn test?"

"Porn test?" he questions.

I run a hand along the back of my neck and shrug. "You know, jerked off to gay porn, see if it gets you all hot and bothered." I give him a side glance. "Unless nerds don't watch porn."

"No I haven't done the porn test, asshole." A flush breaks out across his face. "Besides, I'm pretty sure we did the porn test last night. You know, when you were sucking me off."

A lump fills my throat, because last night was only half the battle.

It's easy to let another person get you off. Hell, supposed straight guys have been lying to themselves for years, insisting that it doesn't make you gay just because you let a homo suck your dick.

I fold my arms across my chest, bitterness washing over me. Because I can see the end of us before we begin. I know exactly how everything's going to unfold. Last night was nothing more than research. An itch to be scratched before he crawls back to *her*.

I don't realize I've said that last part out loud until his eyes widen and his jaw ticks. "Is that what you think I did? That I used you last night?"

"No." I falter. "Did you?" Jealousy settles over me and wraps around my heart like a cloak. "What happens when she comes home?"

There's a long silence that makes my teeth clack, before he says, "I don't know."

He reaches for my hand and gives it a squeeze. "I don't want to lie to you, Asher." He frowns and looks at me. "I can't peer into my crystal ball and tell you what the future holds. The only thing I can do is promise you that I'll never lie to you about my feelings, and you'll always know where I stand."

I straighten my spine against the headboard. "Where do you stand right now?"

He shifts so he's sitting in front of me. "Where I stand is that I'm into you. Last night...wasn't an experiment. Gay, straight, or bi...the label doesn't matter—because I wanted *you*. And when I think about you doing it again—I still want it...I still want you." His eyebrows furrow and he points to his chest. "But someone was here first. And while most people would say that I don't owe her an explanation...my heart says that I do. I'm not going to lie to her about you, or my feelings for you...but I'm not going to sit here and lie to you about my feelings for *her*, either. Do you understand?"

I nod. "I understand, but you still didn't answer the question. What happens when she gets back? Who's your choice?"

His expression turns serious and he blows out a breath. "I can't make that decision right now." His face twists. "I don't think I'll ever be able to make that decision. All I can do is be honest with the two of you and let the chips fall where they may."

He leans in and slides his hand around my neck, pulling me close. "And right now, I'm really enjoying this chip in my bed." His teeth sink into his bottom lip. "God, that was cheesy."

I tilt my face forward. "It was, but you're hot as hell to wake up to so I'll let it slide."

His mouth curves into a grin and he licks his lips. "Is that so?"

I look down at my towel and gesture to the wood I'm sporting. "You tell me?"

He follows my gaze and swallows. I open my mouth to tell him that I wasn't insinuating that he needed to do something about it, but he kisses me.

And unlike last night's kiss...there's nothing tentative or delicate coming from his end. It's carnal and savage...virile. All teeth crashing together and tongues dueling, which only causes my balls to beg for gratification and my dick to swell.

When he presses his hand to my chest and starts working his way down my neck, I bite my bottom lip so hard I taste blood.

"Jesus," he whispers, his hand trailing along my abs. "I don't know whether to be jealous of your body or be grateful for it right now."

I lean back and rest my hands behind my head, giving him a wink. "I'm not opposed to either."

"Cocky asshole," he says, and then before I can stop him, he's opening my towel and sucking in a breath. "Even your dick is attractive. Pretty, even."

The object in question jerks against my thigh, as if to say, 'thank you, thank you very much.'

His tongue drags across his bottom lip and he slowly starts to lower himself. I'm lost in the battle of mind and body. My body wants what he's doing but my mind is screaming—*mayday*, if you let him do this and he doesn't like it, it's game over.

"Whoa," I tuck two fingers under his jaw and halt him. "Don't you think you should crawl before you walk?"

"Sucking your dick is walking?"

I give him a look. "What I mean is...don't you want to move slower? You know, make sure you really want this. Maybe try the porn thing first?"

"You were right before, I've never been one for porn." He looks down at my cock. "I much prefer the real thing."

Oh, hell. This guy's going to be the death of me.

He props himself up on his elbows, his face inches from my groin. "But I'll humor you. Where and how do you think I should start exploring you?"

My abs pull tight, because not only is Landon sexy as hell in bed...he apparently has a no holds barred attitude that both me and my cock find irresistible.

"Touch me," I say, my voice gravelly with desire. "Wrap your hand around my dick."

When he reaches out and gives my cock one long, languid stroke from root to tip...I almost come right then.

He swirls a drop of precum around the weeping head and I bunch the bed sheets in my fists, attempting to gather my composure.

Composure that goes right out the window when he switches out the hand on my dick for the other and brings his finger to his lips to taste me.

I thrust into his hand, desperately seeking more, and he winds his hand around my shaft. "How do you like to jerk yourself?"

I draw in a breath and release it in the form of a moan when he tightens his grip and pumps me harder.

"It doesn't matter," I grit. "Because you're gonna make me come in the next minute anyway." My body tenses and pressure tightens against my ribs. "You have no idea how much I want you."

His face perks up. "Ever think about me doing this to you?"

I look down at him. "Only all the time. Especially when you put the tip of your pen in your mouth during study sessions. Fucking drives me crazy—"

My sentence falls and a groan rips from my mouth when he licks the tip of my dick. "Like that?"

I nod, and despite the arousal coursing through me full speed ahead, there's also apprehension. Because I can't help but be nervous that once he crosses this line, he won't want to again.

"Tell me how you want it," he whispers, and for a split-second I see the worry in his own eyes.

I should tell him he doesn't have to do this...but the selfish part of me revels in gratitude when he licks my head again and sucks on it.

"All the way down. Until the tip hits your tonsils." I hold his gaze. "Play my dick like I'm one of your instruments and make me come, Landon."

I'm fully expecting him to protest, maybe stop altogether; but he doesn't. Instead his eyes turn hooded and he slides his mouth down my length as far as he can. He can't take all of me, but it doesn't matter because his warm mouth sliding up and down my shaft is fucking heaven. And what he lacks in experience, he makes up for with his eagerness.

He glides his mouth up and down my dick slowly, taking almost all of me into his mouth before pausing to pull back and swirl his tongue around my head. It's such a fucking turn on watching him not only doing this, but to see him explore my dick insatiably; like it's his own personal playground.

He looks up at me and places my hand on his head, just like I did to him last night. He's so eager to fucking please me, it kicks my desire up about ten notches.

I bite my lip and every muscle in my body clenches at once when I thrust into his mouth and I hear his deep groan mix with my own. My hands tangle in his hair, gripping the short strands for dear life as I pump my cock between his lips again. I let out a shiver when he gags and I watch saliva dribble out of his mouth, down his jaw, and onto my sac.

I'm so close to coming, both my cock and balls aching for release. "Landon, you might want to stop. I'm gonna come soon."

Ever the fucking stubborn and persistent one, he doesn't. He speeds up his movements until his name is tearing out of my mouth and my entire body is tightening and contracting as I shoot down his throat. I watch his Adam's apple bob, knowing he's swallowing it all and my dick spasms, causing another rope of cum to jet out of me. He consumes that just as willingly.

I fall back against the headboard. "Fuck, Landon."

He wipes his mouth with the back of his hand, a hint of a sly smile on his face. "I take it I passed the porn test?"

Yeah, with flying fucking colors. "You're full of surprises."

A cocky grin tugs at the corners of his mouth. The mouth that just gave me one hell of a blowjob. "You haven't seen anything yet."

I lean forward. "Why does that sound like a challenge, *nerd*?"

His gaze drops to my lips. "Maybe it is, *jock*."

I take his bottom lip between my teeth, then before he knows what hits him, I flip him so he's on his back. I hover above him. "Don't you know better than to challenge an athlete?"

He smirks. "Evidently not. Why don't you remind me?"

I reach inside the sweatpants he's wearing and give his cock a nice, long stroke before tugging them off and dropping to my knees by the side of the bed.

I ghost over his groin, purposely toying with him. "Tell me what you want, Landon."

"Start by licking my balls like you did last night," he says, his voice full of heat. "Felt fucking incredible."

I lower my head and swirl my tongue over his balls, gently lapping at each one before I pull them into my mouth. He groans and I inhale the masculine scent coming off him.

I pull the sheet he's lying on so that he's slightly off the bed, making it easier for my next move. The move that will have him seeing stars and begging for mercy.

I work my way up and down his cock with my hand, loving the way it throbs under my touch. "What else do you want?"

I hold my breath, knowing what his next words will be and craving to hear them. "I want your mouth—"

Before he can finish that sentence, I dive in, licking that sensitive part of his flesh between his asshole and his balls.

"Holy—" He jumps and twists. My grip on his dick tightens and the strokes of my tongue get deeper.

"Please don't stop," he pleads, nearly shredding the bed sheets that are balled up in his hands.

I continue lapping at his taint as he growls my name repeatedly, completely unhinged. He practically whimpers when I dip my head lower and lightly circle that puckered hole of his.

"Oh, fuck—" he starts to say but his words die on his lips when I push my finger in just a little, finding that perfect spot.

"Oh, God," he says, his voice throaty and breathless. He writhes around on the bed and bucks his hips into my finger. "What are you doing to me?"

"It's your prostate. Feels good, huh?"

"If you stop, I will bash your fucking face in," he rasps, before he clears his throat and says, "Seriously, please don't stop, Asher. I've never—it feels so fucking good. I'm so close to coming."

I keep up with my movements, stroking his dick with one hand and his prostate with my other as I lick at his taint. A moment later he shouts my name and his warm cum lands all over my hand and his lower abs.

I leisurely clean him up with my tongue while he fights to catch his breath.

"Learn your lesson about challenging me?" I muse and he smiles.

"Yeah, and it's a lesson I want to learn over and over again." He looks down at me. "Now get your ass up here so I can thank you properly."

I slowly make my way up his body, planting soft kisses over his torso.

"You make me happy," I murmur against his skin, my throat locking up because it's been so damn long since I could say that.

I lift my head to look at him, but freeze when I hear the sound of the front door opening.

CHAPTER 26
BRESLIN

I tow my luggage behind me, making the obvious decision to enter through the lobby and use the elevator.

I'm exhausted and jet lagged, but no less deterred. My heart is thumping so hard, I feel like I'm going to pass out.

The elevator up to my apartment seems to take forever, shifting the thumping in my chest into overdrive.

When the elevator doors open, I grip my rolling suitcase in my hand, hike my bag up my shoulder, and make my way down the hall.

I pause when I reach my destination, the ball of nerves lodging in my throat makes it hard to breathe.

I pace between my front door and Landon's, trying to steady my nerves. I don't know why I'm so nervous, because I still want this.

I'm just scared he won't still want me.

Maybe I should have called? Or rather, maybe I should have borrowed *Kit's* phone and called since he blocked my number.

He told me he loved me, I remind myself.

No matter how angry he is...love doesn't just go away in a mere three weeks.

A rush of emotion squeezes my heart—*I know that better than anyone.*

I take in a deep breath and let it out slowly. Then I drop my luggage and check my watch. It's late Sunday morning, which means he's probably either sleeping or in his music studio.

And if he's in his music studio...he's not going to hear me knock on the front door.

I look down at my keys in my hand and thumb over the one he gave me. The one he told me I could use whenever I wanted...including when Kit and Becca were going at it like wild animals when I was trying to get some sleep in between shifts this summer.

I close my eyes, perseverance pumping through me as I stick the key in the lock and push the door open.

And come face to face with the bluest pair of eyes I've ever seen.

Eyes that are seared into my soul.

Because Asher Holden is looking right at me.

And the school year hasn't even begun.
Things are going to get...complicated.

ABOUT THE AUTHOR

Want to be notified about my upcoming releases?
https://goo.gl/n5Azwv

Ashley Jade craves tackling different genres and tropes within romance. Her first loves are New Adult Romance and Romantic Suspense, but she also writes everything in between including: contemporary romance, erotica, and dark romance.

Her characters are flawed and complex, and chances are you will hate them before you fall head over heels in love with them.

She's a die-hard lover of oxford commas, em dashes, music, coffee, and anything thought provoking...except for math.

Books make her heart beat faster and writing makes her soul come alive. She's always read books growing up and scribbled stories in her journal, and after having a strange dream one night; she decided to just go for it and publish her first series.

It was the best decision she ever made.

If she's not paying off student loan debt, working, or writing a novel—you can usually find her listening to music, hanging out with her readers online, and pondering the meaning of life.

Check out her social media pages for future novels.

She recently became hip and joined Twitter, so you can find her there, too.

She loves connecting with her readers—they make her world go round'.

~Happy Reading~

Feel free to email her with any questions / comments: ashleyjadeauthor@gmail.com

For more news about what I'm working on next: Follow me on my Facebook page: https://www.facebook.com/pages/Ashley-Jade/788137781302982

Thanks for Reading!
Please follow me online for more.
<3 Ashley Jade

ALSO BY ASHLEY JADE

Royal Hearts Academy Series (Books 1-4)

Cruel Prince (Jace's Book)

Ruthless Knight (Cole's Book)

Wicked Princess (Bianca's Book)

Broken Kingdom

Hate Me - Standalone

The Devil's Playground Duet (Books 1 & 2)

Complicated Parts - Series (Books 1 - 3 Out Now)

Complicated Hearts - Duet (Books 1 & 2)

Blame It on the Shame - Trilogy (Parts 1-3)

Blame It on the Pain - Standalone

ACKNOWLEDGMENTS

Yup, this will be long. Because each and every one of you are so important to me and there will never be a good enough way to thank you for all the support and generosity you've shown me. A simple acknowledgment in a book doesn't do it justice, but I hope it matters all the same.

Complicated Hearts was and *is* a gamble. This duet isn't for everyone and a lot of people turn their noses up at this sort of story. They judge before they understand. Writing this duet was and is a journey...and it showed me the people in my corner no matter what.

I'm so incredibly humbled and grateful for each and every one of you. And truly, I thank you all from the bottom of my heart and the depths of my soul. I hope like hell I'm not leaving anyone out...and if by some horrible chance I did...just know that I'm sorry.

First off, I have to thank all of the amazing bloggers. You selfless, amazing people. I'm so incredibly thankful for you.

Tanya: I can't thank you enough for all that you do. From being my shoulder to cry on, making the very BEST covers and teasers, reading my MS 50,000 times, and letting me push that envelope of yours. I Love you...and I need to stop before I start singing *'Wind Beneath My Wings'* and get fined. You are hands down one of the best things that has *ever* happened to me. I. Love. You.

Jamie: Thank you for being there and listening to me and my idea. When I told you about CH, I expected you to talk me out of it; like some others before you had. But it was the opposite. You rooted for me and this story. You didn't even bat an eye. I do **not** have the words to thank you enough. You were and *are* pivotal for the Complicated Hearts duet and most importantly, *my life*.

Michelle: I don't think I can ever express my gratitude for all that you do. From the big things—to the small things that always add up to big things. You keep me organized. You keep me sane. You keep me *going* when I want to throw in the towel. Thank you, babe. So fucking much.

Pennie: Not every author is blessed to have a guardian angel in the book world. Thank you so very much for being mine. Thank you for supporting me and believing in me the way that you do.

K. Webster: You knew this was coming. :p EVERYONE needs to blame K Webster for Complicated Hearts being a duet and not a standalone. (j/k, guys- Don't blame her.) She's too fucking awesome and talented to ever yell at anyway. In all seriousness, while some others may not thank you for it, I do. Immensely. It was one of the best pieces of advice I've ever received and I'm so happy to call you not just my unicorn, but my friend and someone I look up to.

Erika: You know what you do and you do it so damn well. Thank you for pimping, believing, shouting from the rooftops, and throwing dandelions. I love your face.

Amy: You drive me crazy, baby. But I love you. Thank you so much for everything.

Tanaka: No one gets riled up about an Ashley Jade book quite like you do. You make me all warm and gooey inside. Thank you so damn much.

Shabby and Laura: Your support means the absolute world to me. Thank you so much for believing in me and for all that you do. #CornForever

Michelle R: Or as my husband would say, my 'New York' friend. Thank you for believing in me and this story. Thank you for giving us (both me and CH) a chance. <3

Avery: I had to sneak you in here right quick. Thank you, babe.

Nico: Thank you for all of your encouragement and kind words. You are such a sweetheart with such a gentle soul.

Michelle McGinty: Please forgive me for the senile science teacher. I love you long time, you sexy bitch!! (Who's crazy. :p)

My Bat Girls!!! OMG , MY BAT GIRLS!!!!: Jessica K, Belinda, Paula, Maria, Kim, Nik, Tammy, Di, Thai, Crystal, Jessica M, Danielle, Tijuana, Jadey, Melanie, Dee, Janie, Kim, Mari Ann, Hanan, Brandy, Janice, Nikki, Margie, Rose, Diane, and our other Bat Girl who gained her angel wings too soon- Heather Stanley.

I love you. I'm blessed to have the very *BEST* people in my corner. I will never, ever forget any of you. Because as far as I'm concerned- I don't shine without **you** all. Thank you for all that you do.

Ashley's Little Survivors Group: You babes' are my everything. Thank you from the very bottom of my heart for being one of the BEST groups in the whole world full of the very best readers out there!!!

The Complicated Hearts Arc group: Thank you for dealing with my crazy, and my teasers, and my 'Ahhh' moments. I hope it was worth the wait and it paid off. <3

Cassie- You were my very first 'fan'. Starting all the way back from the days of the 'Twisted Fate' series. I will never, ever forget that. Thank you so very much. You're my 'MVP' for life!!!

And last but not least...the person who makes my world go round'. My '**Hammie**'—My heart and soul. I couldn't do this without you, baby. My love for you knows no bounds...because we'd find a way to demolish anything standing in our way. You're my 'alpha', my strength, my weakness, but most importantly...my *everything*.

Made in the USA
Monee, IL
03 June 2023

35198010R00154